CRIMSON DEEP

A John Decker Novel

ANTHONY M.STRONG

WEST
STREET

ALSO BY ANTHONY M. STRONG

THE JOHN DECKER SUPERNATURAL THRILLER SERIES

Soul Catcher (prequel) • What Vengeance Comes • Cold Sanctuary

Crimson Deep • Grendel's Labyrinth • Whitechapel Rising

Black Tide • Ghost Canyon • Cryptic Quest • Last Resort

Dark Force • A Ghost of Christmas Past • Deadly Crossing

Final Destiny

THE REMNANTS SERIES

The Remnants of Yesterday • The Silence of Tomorrow

STANDALONE BOOKS

The Haunting of Willow House • Crow Song

AS A.M. STRONG WITH SONYA SARGENT

Patterson Blake FBI Mystery Series

Never Lie To Me • Sister Where Are You • Is She Really Gone

All The Dead Girls • Never Let Her Go • Dark Road From Sunset

CRIMSON
DEEP

West Street Publishing

Cover art and interior design by Bad Dog Media, LLC.

ISBN: 978-1-942207-10-8

For Sonya - who scares easily

PROLOGUE

THREE YEARS AGO

SOMEWHERE IN CENTRAL FLORIDA

LAURA WELLS HAD BEEN DRIVING for hours. Now as midnight came and one day slipped into another, she pulled off the interstate and followed the directions provided by the man she knew only as Mr. Smith. This was not his real name, she was sure. While there were many people in the world who bore that moniker, it was too obviously generic, even laughably so, given how often it cropped up in bad movies, to be genuine. This was to be expected. Which was fine. All she cared about was the twenty grand that waited a few miles ahead. But now, as she followed a back road deep into the central Florida woods, she started to have second thoughts.

Behind her, in the truck's bed, was a two by three-foot cage of the type commonly used to house large dogs. But her cargo today was anything but mundane. It still slept, thanks to the liberal dose of Carfentanil, a potent elephant tranquilizer, she had administered back at the lab. Even so, Laura was nervous. What if she'd given it too much and the animal was dead when she got to the rendezvous? It wasn't like she was trained in this kind of thing, being a lowly assistant who more often than not spent her days fetching coffee and cleaning out empty cages soiled with feces and urine. Still, she had watched the researchers and veterinarians go about their business and had, she believed, picked up a few tricks. Not least of which was how to subdue a snapping, angry animal that wanted nothing more than to take a chunk out of whoever was closest to its mouth.

And so here she was, miles from home in the middle of nowhere, racing to meet a man she knew nothing about except that he possessed a wad of cash. Enough money to save her hide, or rather, her husband's. The bills were piling up, and Jeff hadn't worked in six months. Not only that, but he didn't seem to have any inclination to change the situation. Which was the primary reason they had picked her, for sure. How they found her, she did not know. Likewise, how they knew the dire landscape of her finances. But none of that mattered. Another hour and all this would be over. The slumbering beast in the cargo bed would be gone, and Laura would be able to pay the mortgage company before they took her house.

The road had become a pair of narrow lanes surrounded by dense woodland. One in each direction with no buildings in sight. Laura started to think she'd misread the directions and taken a wrong turn. But then she saw a gate blocking the road ahead.

She approached the gate and stopped.

A chain link fence topped with razor wire led off in both directions through the woods. A sign on the gate told her this was the correct location.

PRIVATE PROPERTY.
No entry by order of
Sinclair Research Corporation.
Trespassers will be prosecuted.

Next to the gate was a keypad. A pole mounted camera watched as she entered the code Mr. Smith had provided. When the gate opened, she pulled forward and passed through.

A little further in, the woods thinned into an empty parking lot. A large four-story building sat on the other side across a shimmering, serene lake surrounded by manicured landscaping.

She came to a stop and waited, as she had been told to do. A feeling of unsettled nervousness nagged at the back of her mind, partly because she was so far off the beaten track, and also because she appeared to be alone.

Except she wasn't.

A pair of headlights snapped on across the parking lot, and Laura realized that an SUV was there, sitting in the darkness. Waiting.

The SUV moved now, driving toward her. After it stopped, a slender Asian man with graying hair got out. He stood and waited while she gathered the courage to move.

"You're late," he said as she exited her vehicle.

"It was a long drive." Laura realized she was shaking. She willed herself to calm down. "This place is really out in the boondocks."

"We value privacy." The man stepped closer. He glanced toward the crate in the bed of her truck, covered by a tarp. When he spoke, there was excitement in his voice. "Is that it?"

"Yes."

"Can I see?"

"What about my money?" Laura asked.

"I have it." The man chuckled. "You'll get it once I verify the package is genuine. Now, may I see?"

"It's real, I assure you." Laura went to the back of the truck and dropped the tailgate. She pulled the tarp aside. "There."

Mr. Smith came closer. He leaned forward, his eyes wide with anticipation. "Fabulous."

"I don't get it." Laura studied the creature, curled up in a fetal position on the crate floor as it slept off the sedative. It was three feet long with a thick scaly hide, muscular limbs, and a toothy snout. "Why pay so much for an alligator?"

"You think this is an alligator?" Mr. Smith laughed and peered into the crate, his face inches from the wire.

Laura shrugged. "Sure."

"Oh, my pretty. You're no alligator, are you?" he cooed the words, eyes roaming across the slumbering beast. "Oh no. You are much better."

"What's so special about this, anyway?" Laura found the creature repulsive. "It's ugly."

"That it is." Mr. Smith agreed. "But under that grotesque shell lies a work of art. Ancient genes, dormant for millennia, turned back on thanks to genetic engineering. Size, power, instincts, all reverted to an earlier, more primal stage. It's fascinating, and it's going to shave years off our research."

"Why bother to do the work yourself when you can just steal it?" Laura said, instantly regretting the words as Mr. Smith fixed her with a cold glare.

"You don't have much room for judgment, young lady. After all, you are the one who stole it for us," Mr. Smith said. "Speaking of which, you made sure it would not be missed?"

"Yes." Laura nodded. "These things are not terribly friendly, even to their own young. They tend to eat them."

"Survival of the fittest," Mr. Smith said. "A lot of animals eat their own offspring to thin out the litter. Remove the weak. The infirm. Nature is a cruel mistress."

"Well, whatever. I made it look like Mommy got hungry and chowed down on junior here. He won't be missed."

"Good. You did as we asked." Mr. Smith nodded toward the

crate. "Load him into my car, will you? And then you may take your money and be on your way."

"I'm not touching that monster again," Laura said. "Why don't we just drive it up to the building?"

"No." Mr. Smith shook his head. "Here will be fine."

"Don't trust me, huh?" Laura asked.

"Not one little bit. You proved yourself untrustworthy when you agreed to steal this beastie for us."

"Fair enough." Laura shrugged. "But I'm not moving this thing again. It was bad enough back at the lab. It's your turn."

"Very well." Mr. Smith sighed. He tugged the tarp clear and reached forward to pull the crate from the truck bed.

The creature opened an eye and observed him.

"It's awake," Laura said.

"I can see that." Mr. Smith withdrew his hand. "I don't suppose you have another dose of tranquilizer?"

"No. I gave it enough to knock out a horse for a week. It should still be in dreamland."

"Well, it's not." Mr. Smith rubbed his chin. "One of those genes they turned back on must have enhanced its metabolism. I can't wait to study this."

"Great, then get it out of my truck," Laura said. "I've had enough of this. I want to get my money and go home."

"Right-ho." Mr. Smith hesitated, clearly unsure about handling the cage while the creature was awake.

"There's a handle on top," Laura said. "Use that."

Mr. Smith nodded, yet he still seemed reluctant to move the cage, reaching out gingerly and flipping up the handle. He dragged the crate to the edge of the truck bed.

The creature stirred and let out an angry hiss, uncoiling and glaring at its captors.

"Hurry up." Laura eyed the creature, her apprehension growing. "Before the sedative wears off completely."

"Unless you would like to take over, I suggest you keep quiet," Mr. Smith snapped. He gripped the handle and lifted the crate from the bed, grunting at the weight, then turned to retreat back to his own vehicle.

The beast shifted position and watched him through the bars. Then it stood on its hind legs and jumped.

Laura shouted a warning. Too late.

The creature's snout pushed through the wire. Teeth closed on Mr. Smith's fingers. He yelped and let go. Blood trickled down his arm.

"Goddamned thing bit me!" He held his hand aloft to staunch the flow of blood and glared at Laura. "Get over here and pick this up."

But Laura wasn't paying attention. She was watching the crate and the creature inside. Because the cage door wasn't latched anymore. When the cage hit the ground, it had jolted open. With growing horror, she saw the beast take a step forward, then another.

"It'll get out!" She pointed at the crate. "Quick. Close the door."

Mr. Smith glanced downward, his eyes flying open with fear. He reached down but not fast enough. The beast was at the door now, pushing it wide with a nudge of its snout. And then it was outside in the clearing with them.

Mr. Smith let out a whimper. He kicked at the beast in an attempt to force it back into the crate, but the creature sidestepped his clumsy attack.

It stood between them on its hind legs, looking more like a dinosaur than a crocodile.

Then it hunched down, emitted an angry squeal, and leapt.

The creature caught Mr. Smith in the chest. He stumbled back, arms flailing, the beast's claws digging into his shirt. And then it clambered up toward his throat.

The stricken man pawed at the beast, attempting to rip it away, but it was no use. The creature was too strong. It reached his shoulders, darted in, clamped its jaws on his neck and tore a chunk of flesh away.

Laura screamed.

Blood was soaking Mr. Smith's shirt. He stumbled, his eyes meeting Laura's in a silent plea for help. Then he toppled backwards.

Laura found the will to flee.

She turned back to her truck, pulled at the driver's side door. She climbed in and fumbled to start the engine, but her hand was shaking so bad, she could not get the key into the ignition.

Outside, Mr. Smith lay where he fell, his upper torso a bloody, torn mess. He was clearly dead. But what really scared her was that the creature was nowhere to be seen.

She focused back on the task at hand, finally getting the key in, and turned it. The engine roared to life. But then, before she could move, something slammed into the truck. The passenger side window disintegrated. Glass exploded inward. And there was the beast, sitting on the seat, its snout dripping red.

She let out a terrified wail and pulled the driver's side door open, tumbling from the truck. The woods were twenty feet away. The building was too far to even consider.

Laura took off.

If she could reach the trees, she might live. It was a slim hope, but there was no other choice.

Except the beast was giving chase, racing after her faster than she could run. Then it leapt, hitting her square in the back.

Laura crashed to the ground. She rolled over, ignoring the throbbing pain from the fall, her scraped elbows and knees. She scrambled backwards, away from the creature.

It waited, head cocked to one side, beady eyes watching her. Then it moved again, advancing with slow, deliberate steps, and circling even as Laura staggered to her feet. She felt hot tears running down her cheeks, wishing she hadn't gotten involved with Mr. Smith and his money. But she didn't have long to rue that decision. The beast leapt again, and this time it started to bite.

Laura screamed.

She screamed when the beast ripped at the soft flesh of her stomach. She screamed when its snout pushed deep and found all the soft, tasty bits. But not for long. As the blood left her body, Laura slipped away until the pain became dull, then nothing at all.

A little while later, meal finished, the creature surveyed its new home. Then it went to the shimmering lake and slipped beneath the surface, happy to be free.

ONE

PRESENT DAY

JOHN DECKER STOOD on the hotel balcony and gazed over the thin line of sandy beach and the Gulf of Mexico's turquoise waters spreading to the horizon. He took a deep breath. The air smelled like surf and salt. The excited cries of beachgoers and the strains of a catchy tune drifted up from below. It reminded him of boyhood vacations to Pensacola, of the happy times before his mother died and his father went off the rails. He smiled and leaned on the balcony. For the first time in many months, he felt relaxed and free.

"Is the view as good as the desk clerk said it would be?" Nancy Cassidy asked, slipping through the half open French door.

"She didn't lie," Decker replied. "I think I can see all the way to Cancun."

"Are you sure that isn't just heat haze?" Nancy grinned and slipped an arm around his waist. "I'm pretty sure Florida is a long way from Mexico."

"Hey, don't break the illusion."

"Sorry." Nancy feigned a sympathetic look. "How do you feel?"

"Great." Decker leaned on the railing and watched a pair of motorcycles move along the beach road, engines throbbing, bikini clad girls on the back. "This was just what I needed."

"Me too." Her hand strayed up his back. She sighed. "It feels so weird, not having to worry about the diner."

"You did the right thing." Decker knew how hard selling the restaurant had been, not to mention the house. "That town was never going to let us alone."

"Even though you saved them all," Nancy said. There was a trace of bitterness in her voice.

"People have short memories. Plus, the idea that a werewolf was running around eating people is hard to swallow, even if the evidence is right there. Hell, I found it hard to believe myself."

"They still treated us like crap," Nancy replied. "That diner had been in my family for three generations. My grandfather opened it when he came back from World War Two."

"I didn't say it was fair."

"I know. It's not the same though, living so far away from Wolf Haven. I spent my whole life there."

Decker nodded. He knew how hard she'd found the last few months. They had rented a rambling old house across the Louisiana border close to Gulfport. It stood on stilts surrounded by flat marshes. The perfect place to retreat and plan a future neither one anticipated. He'd hoped this vacation to Florida's west coast would take her mind off all that. Now he realized that nothing would.

"Have you given any more thought to that job offer?" Nancy glanced sideways, her eyes meeting his. "The government one? We can't live off the restaurant money forever."

"Adam Hunt?" Decker had spoken to the government agent twice since leaving Alaska and told him the same thing both times. He didn't want to make a hasty decision. After that, he stopped answering the man's calls. "I don't know."

"Why?" Nancy pressed. "You love being a cop, and this might be the only opportunity you have left."

"But I won't be a cop." Decker shook his head. "I'll be some kind of government spook."

"Close enough."

"Is it?" Decker wasn't sure. A part of him wanted to say yes to Hunt, but another part, a more cautious part, wanted to stay away from whatever organization Hunt worked for. Yet he couldn't argue with Nancy's observation that he needed work, and it wasn't only the money. He felt helpless stripped of his badge, like he'd lost a part of his identity. He felt bare.

"Maybe you need to talk it over with someone." Nancy turned to face him. "Didn't you say there's a sheriff around here that you went to the academy with?"

Decker nodded. "Bill Gibson. We knew each other in New York. He moved down here for a slower life. A place called Leland. It's a ways inland."

"That's perfect," Nancy said. "He'll be a great sounding board."

"I don't know," Decker said. How many years had it been since he'd last seen Bill? After the academy, they remained fast friends, taking fishing trips together, swapping war stories over the phone. They still kept in contact once in a while, mainly by email, but even this had become sporadic in recent years.

"What have you got to lose?"

"I haven't spoken to him in over a year," Decker said. "Not since what happened in Wolf Haven."

"Just make the call," she said. "It'll give you some perspective. And you'll get to reconnect, hear a friendly voice. You need that."

"Fine." Decker knew when he was beaten. "I'll call Bill in the morning. Satisfied?"

"Yes," Nancy said, smiling. "Maybe then you can make a decision on this job and get back to enjoying your vacation."

TWO

PROFESSOR DANIEL HOWARD watched the bulky yellow crane inch forward on wide caterpillar tracks toward a circular expanse of dark blue spring water deep in the Florida woodlands. Hanging from the boom, held in place by two thick slings, sat LISA, the result of ten years grueling research. The bright orange submersible swayed when the crane bumped over a rocky outcrop, the sling shifting under its fragile cargo. Howard's breath caught in his throat, but soon the crane was over the hump and moving across even ground again.

Daniel gave a sigh and motioned toward Carlos, the crane operator. "Put her in. Easy as you can."

The crane swung outward over the pool and lowered the sub into the water a few feet from shore. A mosquito buzzed around Daniel's ear. He swatted it away, annoyed. They had only been in the Central Florida woods for a couple of days, breaking out the gear and setting up camp around the sinkhole, and he was already tired of the oppressive heat, stifling humidity, and the blood-sucking bugs.

"Are you sure about this?" Emily Bright, his research assistant, chewed her bottom lip, a stress indicator she had picked up during freshman year at college and hadn't quite ditched. From behind her right eye, the first dull throbs of a tension headache pulsed. There was a bottle of aspirin back in her tent on the other side of the clearing. It was only a short walk away, but she had no intention of missing such a momentous occasion. "We haven't tested LISA under such strenuous conditions before."

"This is what she was built for." Daniel glanced toward her and smiled. The gesture was meant to be reassuring, but even so, he worried that his own anxiety might show through. "Besides, if anything happens, we'll just send someone down to the hardware store for a new one. No big deal."

"Not funny." Emily eyed LISA, now bobbing upright in the water several feet from shore with a pair of divers working to release her from the crane's straps.

The three-foot-long unmanned submersible didn't look like much, but she was the result of many thousands of hours work by hundreds of engineers, computer programmers, mathematicians, and scientists. Her official name was the Deep Phreatic Autonomous Explorer; LISA was just a nickname her lead builder had come up with in honor of his wife. Onboard were instruments that could map entire submerged cave systems in three dimensions, take water samples, and even analyze those samples in real-time using an onboard microscope. Partially funded by NASA, a robotic explorer similar to this might one day find itself on Jupiter's ice moon, Europa, but for now, the Floridan Aquifer would be challenging enough.

Spanning five states and over 86,000 square miles, the aquifer formed when subsurface water ate away at a layer of underground limestone. Over many thousands of years, the water had carved channels and tunnels, creating a network of subsurface caves. It was these dark caverns, accessed by natural springs and sinkholes, which drew the researchers to this spot, one of the hundreds of such places dotted across the state.

"Come on." Daniel placed a hand on Emily's back. He steered her toward a tent pitched near the trees. "We'll go inside and watch on the monitors."

———

It was cooler inside the tent, thanks to the portable AC unit. A row of white folding tables held laptops, external hard drives, monitors, and a workstation equipped with an oversized joystick similar to those used in old video games. A mess of wiring snaked behind the tables to power strips, which were, in turn, connected to thick orange cables that weaved their way outside to a pair of throbbing 10,000-watt commercial generators nestled near the tree line.

A young man with shoulder length blonde hair sat in front of the joystick workstation. He wore a pair of torn stonewashed jeans and a red shirt emblazoned with the slogan *Girls prefer nerds*. When Daniel and Emily entered, he turned to them, a lopsided grin on his boyish face.

"How do we look, Alex?" Daniel asked.

"All systems check. We're ready to go where no man has gone before."

"Cute," Emily replied. "You know that LISA's a girl, right?"

Alex chuckled. "Actually, LISA's a forty-million-dollar submersible that can navigate on her own without the need for a pilot and adapt to the terrain in real time, all while relaying video, mapping the caves, and running a host of complex tests on her environment. She's so much better than a girl."

"Aw. I think he's in love." Emily feigned a pout. "And I thought you only had eyes for me."

"You know, LISA and I don't have an exclusive relationship. I could come by your tent later and make it up to you."

"Not a chance," Emily said, a grin on her face. "I don't share my men."

"Your loss."

"Focus, please, people. You can flirt on your own time." Daniel did his best to sound annoyed but didn't quite succeed. "Do we have a green light for go?"

"Sure do, boss." Alex scanned his monitor, double-checking the sub's settings and telemetry. "All systems operating within normal parameters." He tapped a few keystrokes on the keyboard. A view of the sinkhole, from the submersible's perspective, appeared on the monitors, including a 70-inch screen suspended above the workstations. The low angle view, with water lapping up to the lens, showed the shoreline and cluster of tents that made up base camp. "Check for video. Wireless stream is up and running at 2456 Kbps, but that quality will drop off as we go deeper. There's going to be a lot of rock between us and LISA."

"We're recording too?"

"Yep, preserved right here in fabulous HD." He patted a hard drive next to the laptop.

"Perfect. Shall we proceed?"

"Taking her in." Alex's hands flew over the keyboard, sending commands to the sub. A moment later, the viewscreen showed movement, the small vehicle nudging forward when its thrusters engaged. "Going under now."

The sub shifted and swayed as the thrusters tilted on their axis, pushing the nose of the machine down under the water. The calm view of the surface was replaced by racing bubbles that streaked across the camera lens as the sub plunged into the sinkhole.

"Systems nominal. We're heading down. Ten feet. Fifteen. Twenty." Alex checked off the depth as the sub descended, the camera's view growing dimmer as the machine dropped away from the surface. He stabbed at the keyboard. "Turning on floodlights."

"Wow," Emily said as the world around the sub came into

view under the bright spotlights. The vertical shaft at the opening of the sinkhole widened as they descended into a huge domed cavern that stretched away under the rock toward a dark opening at the far wall.

"Wow is right. It's a wonder more of the surface rock hasn't collapsed. This cave is enormous," Alex said. "Are we ready to go exploring?"

"Yes," Daniel said. "Give her a good shakedown, my boy."

The sub nudged forward, moving toward the opening in the chamber wall, and entered the tunnel.

"So far, so good." Alex checked his readings. "We have plenty of headroom, and LISA is performing flawlessly."

"We can take over if necessary, right?" Daniel asked.

"Sure. That's what we have this for." Alex motioned toward the joystick. "I doubt if we'll need it though; she's finding her way just fine. Not only that, we're getting plenty of real-time field data for NASA. This puppy will be on Europa before you know it."

The submersible moved deeper into the cave, slowing as the walls narrowed.

"Approaching Satan's Alley," Alex said. Satan's Alley was a narrow, dangerous tunnel, barely wide enough for the sub to navigate. On their previous dive this was where Daniel had decided to turn back.

"Keep going." Daniel wasn't making any such call this time. They had studied the topography data the sub collected on that dive, and the consensus was that Satan's Alley was worth the risk.

"Roger that." Alex tapped out instructions. The sub inched forward, moving slowly now as it mapped its new surroundings.

Emily realized she was holding her breath.

When the sub cleared the worst of the narrows, she released it with an audible gasp.

"We're through," she said with a grin.

"We are, indeed," Alex glanced toward her then back to the monitor.

The tunnel was widening now. Then, without warning, the cave floor fell away sharply, dropping off into blackness.

"This is new." Alex watched the sub get her bearings. She moved on toward the center of the chasm and hovered.

"Incredible," Emily said, still focused on the overhead screen. "We might be the first humans ever to see these caves."

"Incredible is right," Daniel said. "This chamber is even bigger than the entry point." He directed his attention toward Alex. "Can we keep going down?"

"Give it a second. LISA's scoping out her environment, mapping it. She'll be on the move again soon enough."

As if on cue, the little machine dipped its nose down and powered the thrusters.

"How deep does this go?" Daniel asked no one in particular.

Alex glanced up briefly before returning his attention to the readings on the monitor. "We've been descending steadily since we entered the first cave. Right now, we're at about four hundred feet below the surface and getting deeper."

All three fell quiet, watching the submersible swim further into the void.

"Look, we've reached the bottom," Emily said finally, breaking the silence. The sub had come to a halt above a rocky plateau that stretched beyond the scope of the twin halogen floodlights. Boulders of all shapes and sizes littered the sandy floor.

"We are level at five hundred feet." Alex kept his eyes glued to his monitor.

The sub repositioned itself, turning to map the cavern. More of the cave floor came into view.

"Can we move forward again?" Daniel asked.

"We will. LISA can detect the flow of water and follow it. Right now, she's creating a 3D topographic map."

"Wait." Emily pointed to the screen. "Did you see that?"

"See what?" Alex asked. "I didn't see anything."

"Something moved across the camera's field of view."

"Unlikely."

"I know what I saw. It was fast, but just for a second—"

"A small fish maybe, or an eel?" Alex shrugged.

"I don't think so; it looked too big." Emily shook her head. "Larger than an eel."

"Well, there's nothing there now. Besides, if—"

The sub tilted, the camera view slipping sideways. Alex worked on the keyboard. "Compensating."

"Rock fall?" Daniel asked.

"I don't think so. It could be a strong current. I'm going to take control, see if we can move out of the flow." Alex gripped the joystick. The sub lurched, first one way and then the other, before settling back upright in the water. A black shape streaked across the camera's field of view before being swallowed up by the darkness beyond the floodlight's twin beams.

"See?" Emily's voice rose in pitch. "I told you something is down there."

"Impossible," Daniel said, more to himself than the group. "What on Earth was that?"

"Beats me." Alex shook his head. "There shouldn't be anything bigger than a shrimp this far into the caves."

"Well, there's something in there," Emily said. "The camera doesn't lie."

"Okay, you were right." Alex leaned toward the monitor, as if that would gain him a better view. "That was definitely no eel."

"Indeed, it wasn't," the professor agreed.

"So, what was it?" There was a tremble in Emily's voice.

"No idea, but it's coming back for round two." Alex took hold of the joystick.

"And fast." Daniel pointed at the monitor and the speeding blur barreling toward the sub out of the inky blackness.

"Shit! No, no, no." Alex pulled back on the joystick, and

then... nothing. Alarms beeped. A message, *Signal Terminated*, flashed where the sub's telemetry had displayed moments ago. One last frozen image, caught on the monitors as the sub lost contact, showed a wide mouth and rows of sharp teeth.

THREE

FIFTEEN MILES from the research team and their stricken submersible, a lone truck with two occupants picked its way along a narrow road toward another spring, this one smaller and less remote.

In the driver's seat Carl Hawkins hunched over the steering wheel, his hands at ten and two. He had been looking forward to this trip for the better part of a month, but despite this, he could not shake the dim mood that had plagued him for days. He disliked his job at the best of times: pulling dents out of cars. The pay was lousy, and his boss was a jerk. But recently things had gotten untenable. The body shop was struggling. His boss had laid half the work force off. That meant Carl was pulling longer shifts for the same pay. Not only that, his boss had tried to cancel the vacation time he'd put in weeks ago. It was only one day, so that he could spend more time up at the spring, but even so... There had been an argument. Carl threatened to quit. He'd kept the vacation day, but he feared that it came at a price. The next time cuts had to be made, Carl knew who would be on the shortlist for getting laid off.

He did his best to push the dark thoughts away. This was

supposed to be a fun weekend, and he didn't want it ruined by his jackass of an employer.

His eyes scanned the landscape ahead, looking for the trail that led to the swimming hole. After a few minutes he spotted it and turned onto a dirt track that wove deeper into the woods. He did his best to avoid the deep troughs left in the mud from the frequent afternoon thunderstorms that rolled through the region during the humid summer months, but still his front left tire caught a rut and bumped down hard, jarring the occupants of the truck.

Carl swore.

His passenger ignored the profanity. Instead, he fiddled with the radio, twisting the tuner between stations, pushing the selector buttons in and out, jabbing at them with a bony finger.

They were close now. Carl recognized the faded sign that marked the entrance to the waterhole. The lettering was cracked and peeling, barely visible but still legible.

Area Closed.
Danger - No Trespassing.
BY ORDER OF FLORIDA PARKS AND WILDLIFE.

They passed beyond the sign, ignoring it. Neither of the men in the truck had any clue what danger the sign might refer to, but they paid it no heed. The waterhole would be as safe today as it had been on the four or five other times they had ventured up here. Carl wondered if the park rangers even remembered why they had closed the area in the first place, it had been so long.

Bureaucracy.

He snorted and shook his head, turning his attention back to the road ahead. That was the real danger. The final part of the trail was treacherous, with a series of switchbacks that could result in a nasty encounter with a tree if you weren't careful.

"We're almost there," Carl said, glancing sideways at his

younger brother, Ray, before turning his attention back to the road ahead.

"Huh?" Ray was still distracted.

"I said, we're almost there," Carl repeated, swatting at Ray's hand. "For pity's sake, would you quit it?"

"What?"

"Fiddling with that damned radio."

"What's your problem?" Ray flipped the radio off and pushed his hands deep into his pockets.

"It's annoying, that's my problem," Carl grumbled.

"Can't you get a decent radio in this thing? You don't even have a CD player, let alone MP3 or Bluetooth," replied Ray. "Even my truck has a CD player, and I've had that thing for years."

"It is what it is."

"Satellite radio would be nice," Ray added.

"Yeah, well, if you're so damned unhappy riding with me, why didn't you drive?"

"Because I drove last time," Ray replied. "Besides, these trails kill my tires."

"And they don't ruin mine?" Carl eased up on the gas. They were coming to the narrowest part of the road where it thinned to barely the width of the vehicle. This was the hardest part of the trail, and if they were going to run into a problem, this was where it would be. The dirt road made a sudden left turn and sloped dramatically. Carl took a deep breath. Twice before they had gotten this far and found the mud too slick, and he really hated it when they were forced to turn back. Today though, the truck handled the incline with ease. From here on in, it was plain sailing.

"Weather service said there could be heavy rain tonight. We should camp on high ground. We don't want to get washed out."

"We'll pitch the tent on the bluff like last time." Carl said as the trail made a final turn to the right before opening up into the clearing. They had been coming up to the waterhole for years. A tradition started by their father when they were boys. Now, as usual, the view as they came around that last bend made Carl's heart leap. The black mood eased.

Trees crowded the edge of the space, their branches reaching into the small oasis of sunlight like arms stretching toward the sun. On the left side of the open space, the ground was considerably higher. An old fire pit, still partially visible even after four months, marked the spot where the two had camped the last time they visited. In the center of the clearing, surrounded on one side by a rocky outcrop and on the other by a gently sloping shelf of sand, was a perfectly round hole in the ground filled with crystal clear spring water.

Carl brought the truck to a stop. A tingle of excitement coursed up his spine. "Looks good."

"Yeah. Water level looks high too." Ray flipped off his seat belt. "That's good."

"Want to get a dive in before we pitch the tents?"

"Hell, yeah," Carl said. "We've still got a few hours of daylight left; might as well use them." For the first time since they had left Tampa, Carl forgot about his boss and his worries of unemployment. All that mattered today was the water and the caves that waited to be explored within.

FOUR

THIS IS BULLSHIT, thought Frank Denning as he sat outside the Sixth National Savings and Loan, his foot on the brake pedal of the stolen Mustang with Kansas plates, holding it against the idling engine. Only six months into his parole, and here he was, angling for a one-way ticket right back to the big house.

His problem, he surmised, was being too willing to help out. He couldn't say no, never had been able to. That was what had landed him in prison the first time and would, most likely, be what earned him a fast pass right back into a ten by eight cell. Still, this was the last time, he told himself. If they got away, he was going clean. The money from this gig would be enough to start the landscaping business. Prison had been good for one thing. It had taught him a trade, and now he intended to put that hard-earned education to use.

He stared out through the rain streaked windshield, watching a city bus trundle down the street and pull up to the curb twenty feet distant. The doors opened, and a gaggle of riders stepped off. One of them went around to the front. Moments later he emerged, wheeling a bicycle. Two more passengers waited to retrieve their bikes from the nose-mounted rack while a mother pushing a stroller hesitated at the side of the road, looking for a break in the traffic.

The bus showed no sign of moving any time soon.

Great. The last thing he wanted was to get stuck behind the damned thing. It was stuff like this that drove Frank mad — the crap you couldn't control. One piece of bad luck and that was it; game over.

He drummed his fingers against the steering wheel and glanced sideways toward the bank.

This was taking too long.

For a moment he contemplated slipping the car into gear and driving away. It would be easy, and nobody would know he was ever here. The car was parked in the one blind spot not covered by the bank's external surveillance cameras. Except that the bank doors were opening now, flying wide, and through them, wielding their shortened shotguns and carrying a stuffed duffel bag, came three figures. They raced toward him; features disguised by black full-faced ski masks. It wouldn't take long for startled pedestrians to realize what was going on, but it didn't matter. By now the bank's silent alarms had surely alerted the police, which meant there was less than thirty seconds to make their escape.

Frank reached down and hit the trunk release, watching the lid lift as the closest of the three reached the vehicle and threw the cash-stuffed bag inside. Moments later the robbers piled into the car, slamming the doors.

"Go, go, go!" The figure in the front passenger seat, Louie Walker, pulled his mask off, shouting the words as he did so, slapping the dash with his free hand for emphasis.

Frank threw the car into gear and slammed the accelerator to the floor, twisting the wheel even as the vehicle lurched forward. He barely cleared the SUV parked in front, briefly afraid that he had underestimated the Mustang's power and would clip the other vehicle, but then he was clear and speeding down the road.

At least until the bus pulled out.

Frank slammed his foot on the brake pedal, a curse escaping his lips.

The Mustang came to a shuddering halt, the back fishtailing to the right. For one gut wrenching moment, Frank thought they were done, but then he wrestled the car back under control.

A new voice rose from the back seat. "Jesus, Frank!" It was Jerry Biggs, Frank's old cell mate at Georgia State Prison, a man he was not supposed to fraternize with given their parole status. "Don't stop. Go around it. For chrissakes, go around."

"What do you think I'm trying to do?" Frank snapped, his temper flaring.

"Get us caught," Jerry said. "I think you are trying to get us all caught."

"Go to hell." Frank pulled on the wheel, inching the car around the bus. As he did so, he glanced up and caught sight of the driver looking down at them, a shocked expression on his face. Behind the driver, craning their necks for a better view, wide-eyed passengers looked on, their attention drawn by the abrupt squeal of tires. One of the riders, a kid no older than fifteen, lifted his cell phone and held it there, tracking the car.

Great, Frank thought, the little shit was recording them. It would be hard to claim he was at home in bed, sleeping off a bender, when the cops had a video of his face behind the wheel of the getaway car. There went his alibi. Visions of a bleak future flashed across Frank's mind, a future in which he was back in jail, sharing another dingy cell with Jerry. The landscaping business felt further away than ever. If he went to prison again, it would be for good this time.

Three strikes and you're out.

The words echoed in his head as he coaxed the car around the stalled bus and revved the engine.

"Goddammit, Frank, you drive like a girl," Jerry said.

"My grandmother drives faster than this," Louie chipped in.

"You want to drive?" Frank shot back. He pressed down on the accelerator, zigzagging around a pedestrian caught in the middle of the road, frozen in place with a look of terror upon her face.

"Maybe. I couldn't do any worse." Louie shook his head.

"How about I just stop right here, and we can change places." He swerved to avoid a delivery truck and slammed the wheel to the left.

"How about we stop and leave you on the side of the road?" Louie countered.

"Go to hell."

"You first." Louie lifted the sawed-off shotgun, pointing it toward Frank.

"Cut it out," a female voice said from the back of the car. A hand came between the seats and batted the gun down. "That's enough."

"He points that friggin' gun at me again, I'll break his neck." Frank glanced in the rear-view mirror. Liz Marshall was the reason he was behind the wheel. He'd met her years before when she dated his best friend, Darren. Hard as nails, she fit easily into the life despite her petite frame and long hair that made her look more like a runway model than a criminal. That had all changed the year Darren died, knifed behind a downtown bar. She cut her hair short and got the first of many tattoos. Already careening off course, she derailed completely. Frank still harbored guilt for not being there to save his friend, and by extension, Liz. When she asked him to drive, one last job, he could not say no.

"He points the gun at you again, and I'll do the job myself," Liz replied, living up to her reputation. "Now, let's all play nice, shall we?"

"Fine." Louie wedged the gun between his legs into the seat well, out of sight. "As soon as I get my cut, I'm out of here."

"Good riddance." Frank steered the car left, down a side street, and eased up on the gas. A few moments later they pulled up behind a dark blue panel van. Unlike the Mustang, this vehicle was not stolen. It belonged to Jerry's cousin Alan, who ran a plumbing business, at least on the days when he was sober enough. The promise of a ten percent cut had been all it took for him to hand over the spare keys. A few days from now he would report the van stolen to cover his ass, but right now it was a clean vehicle.

"Not so fast, boys," Liz said. "We keep to the plan, take the van to the cabin and sit this out for a while, let things settle down, then you can all have your cuts."

"We got away clean as a whistle. I know we did," Louie said. "Why bother waiting? I say we split the money now and be done with it."

"No," Frank replied. "Liz is right. We need to be careful, make sure we weren't identified. We created a bit too much of a stir back there, drew a heap of attention. I can't afford to wind up back in the slammer."

"Me either." Jerry was pulling his door open. "Can we please load up the van already? I don't want to be here when the cops find this car."

"Louie, grab the money from the trunk and put it in the van," Liz ordered. She was already half out of the car. "Frank, take a look around and make sure there's nothing in the car that can tie us to it."

"Sure, boss." Frank gave the car a quick once over and climbed out, wiping down the steering wheel even though he was wearing gloves. There was no such thing as *too* careful, not in this game. As he closed the door and turned toward the van, Louie appeared, carrying the bag, a large blue stain spreading across the fabric.

"Look at this." Louie threw the bag to the ground and glared at it.

"What's wrong now?" Liz sighed, her eyes dropping to the ruined bag. "Dammit. There was a dye pack in there. It must have exploded when we were driving away."

"No way. It would have gone off the moment we left the bank."

"Not necessarily," Frank countered. "Just depends what range it was set to. Lose the radio signal, and splat."

"Shit." Louie slammed a fist into the side of the car. "Shit, shit, shit."

"Now what do we do?" Jerry asked.

"We open it up and see how bad the damage is," Liz said, her voice calm despite the angry look on her face.

Louie bent down and unzipped the bag. He tipped the contents out. Bundles of bank notes spilled onto the hardtop. He threw the bag to the curb and looked down at the stained cash. "Ruined."

"Not all of it." Liz pointed. "There are some stacks that hardly have any dye on them."

"All that work. I'm not going to jail for a few thousand measly bucks. This is so messed up."

"Well, who filled the bag?" Liz glared it him. "I told you to watch for dye packs. You only had one job, one thing to do, and look how that turned out."

"Maybe you should have checked the bag yourself." Louie leaned against the car, a cloud over his face.

"Good idea, genius. I'll just put my gun down and do your job for you. And then we can all get shot."

"It's not my fault." Louie's voice was rising in pitch. He sounded like a whining kid. "I did what you told me to."

"Guys. Cool it." Frank placed himself between his arguing companions. Then a thought occurred to him, and not a pleasant one. "Don't they put GPS trackers in those dye packs?"

"Crap. He's right." Liz glanced around, nervous. "We can't stay here."

"What about the cash?" Louie said.

"We'll take whatever we can and leave the rest here." Liz bent down and scooped up several stacks. "Only take the notes without too much dye on them. And hurry it up. I don't want to be around when the cops show up."

"Me either." Frank grabbed a few more stacks, kicking the

worst of the ruined bills out of the way, and headed toward the van. When he looked back, Louie was still leaning against the car, looking at the destroyed loot, his face dark and glowering. "You coming, or what?"

"Yeah." Louie cast one last wistful look at the cash, and then stomped toward the van. "Seems a shame to leave so much money behind."

"Better to leave it behind than get twenty to life for armed robbery." Frank was at the van now. He pulled the door open and jumped behind the wheel, even as a wail of sirens rose through the rain-soaked air.

FIVE

THE AQUIFER SHIMMERED in the afternoon sun, a deep blue circle in a sea of green foliage.

Ray lingered a while at the water's edge, taking in the tranquil scene, and then stepped off the rocks and into the water, reeling off a guideline as he went. Without this thin sliver of nylon rope, they might not find their way back to the surface. Cave diving was dangerous. One wrong turn down an unexplored shaft, with no way to break the water's surface for air, could lead to death.

He adjusted his tanks, strapped one on each side for easier maneuverability rather than the usual back mounted configuration, and checked his gas mix. Satisfied that the equipment was in order, Ray swam lower to allow his brother to enter the water. Light from their dive lamps played off the shaft walls, dancing over smooth rocks and jutting outcrops in shifting patterns. Giving Carl a quick thumbs up, Ray flipped over and swam down into the darkness, approaching the spring's sandy bottom and waiting for his brother to catch up.

The floor was littered with debris, decades of trash that had found its way into the spring. Brown and green beer bottles glinted under their lamps, thrown in by generations of teenagers and miscreants with no thought for the consequence of their actions. Other trash, plastic bags, disintegrating food wrappers, a single shoe with laces bobbing in the current, poked out of the sand like unwanted prizes. It wasn't always junk though. Carl had found a half dollar once, sticking out of the sand as if it was placed there just for him. Later, back on dry land, they cleaned away years of crusted silt and uncovered a Walking Liberty from 1929.

"This is silver, baby. One hundred percent," Carl had exclaimed, pocketing the coin with obvious glee. From that day on, the half accompanied him on every dive, a good luck talisman tucked into a pouch on his utility belt.

Ray shook his head and swam on, sad that such a beautiful place had been desecrated. He was happy to leave it behind and move further into the caves, to places untouched by the hand of man.

It only took a few minutes to reach the first cavern, a large domed room that fell away, twenty feet deep, thirty wide, and as long as a football field before tapering into a narrow tunnel that led to a much more impressive space, which they had dubbed the Cathedral. Here, ages old stalactites thrust down from the roof, evidence that this particular cave had once been above water.

They crossed the cavern without pause. They had been here several times before, and with only limited dive time, they would rather discover new wonders than linger over old ones. When they reached another tunnel, Ray, the more experienced diver, took the lead, swimming a few feet ahead, his guide rope spinning out behind him.

Deeper down, the visibility dropped. Sediment had settled on the bottom, which now billowed up around the divers as they made their way along the passageway, hindering their ability to see. They swam around a jutting outcrop, the rocks sharp and eager to rip their wetsuits, or worse, an air hose. They pushed on for another few minutes before the tunnel opened up, the floor dropping away to reveal a circular cave that resembled a hub of sorts. Six tunnels led away from this chamber. Beyond these more caves wound for thousands of miles, linking freshwater springs, large and small lakes formed by sinkholes, and small rocky openings like the one they had entered through. It was this vast system of caves, the aquifer, which provided drinking water for millions of people on the Florida peninsula.

Ray checked his watch, and then aimed downward with a twist and a flip of his legs. He moved toward the base of the cavern and a space they had partially explored on their last dive. Their time in the caves was limited, and they would need to preserve at least two thirds of their gas for the trip back, which meant the ingress and exploration phases of the dive were short by necessity. Safety came first, and neither man wanted to join the unfortunate divers whose wetsuit clad corpses could still be seen if one knew where to look.

They pushed through into the smaller chamber and swam on toward a point where the chamber split into two dark, murky tubes of rock.

Ray paused, waiting for Carl to catch up, and motioned toward the twin tunnels, signaling for him to choose, left or right. This was as far as they had ever gone, and he was eager to explore one of the shafts before their air dipped below the safety threshold and they were forced to turn back.

Carl indicated left with a wave of his hand and kicked off, swimming toward the tunnel. He paused near the entrance to take the silver half dollar from his pocket, as he often did when entering a new space. It was good luck, he said, despite claiming not to be superstitious. Then he gripped the tunnel's rim and pushed forward into the shaft.

Ray waited, treading water at the cave entrance. Once Carl was far enough in, he would follow behind. Except that his brother wasn't moving forward. Instead, he had come to a halt.

Ray waited, impatient.

Precious time ticked away.

Ray peered into the shaft, his flashlight beam illuminating Carl's legs and torso.

Something was wrong.

Ray felt a tickle of fear.

And then Carl was moving again, only in the wrong direction now. He wriggled back toward the opening, legs flailing as he attempted to exit the tight space.

Ray reacted on instinct, attempted to grip his brother's legs and guide him out, but he couldn't get a hold. Carl was moving too fast, propelled backwards out of the opening like a cork from a bottle. His tanks smacked against the tunnel walls, dislodging chips of limestone that floated down toward the cave floor. A dark, heavy mist followed Carl out of the cave, shrouding his upper body.

Ray froze momentarily, too stunned to react.

Carl's momentum slowed. His arms hung limp in the water, his body drifting backwards on the current, trailing a widening crimson ribbon.

For a moment, Ray didn't know what he was looking at, but then, in an instant, he understood.

Carl's head was gone, his neck a circle of bloody, raw flesh.

Ray forgot where he was.

He opened his mouth to scream. His mouthpiece fell away, releasing a stream of precious gas into the water. He struggled to grasp the floating regulator, clamping his mouth shut to avoid gulping in the blood-filled water until he could get the apparatus back into his mouth.

Carl's body was descending now, sinking toward the cavern floor, arms flapping in the current like he was waving a grotesque goodbye. He hit the bottom and bounced twice before coming to rest. Carl's good luck talisman fell from his lifeless hand. Ray watched the silver coin turn end over end in the water, dropping down into the sediment, where it settled and was lost.

Ray froze, unsure what to do.

And then he came to a new realization.

He was not alone in the cavern. Something was inside the tunnel, watching him. He saw it from the corner of his eye, nothing more than a shift of the darkness inside the shaft, beyond the beam of his lights. But it was there, daring him to make the next move, waiting.

A stab of fear clenched Ray's stomach.

He couldn't stay here. Whatever had killed his brother would come for him next.

The sudden realization spurred Ray into action. He pushed off, following the thin nylon line hand over hand, retracing his way back toward the surface. He moved through the caverns, each chamber bringing him closer to safety. When he reached the entrance cave, he felt a surge of relief. Welcoming sunlight filtered down from the surface. He was going to make it.

Except that he was ascending too fast, ignoring the stage tanks on a decompression line they had lowered into the water before entering the spring.

That presented a new danger.

The bends. Nitrogen bubbles that formed in the blood due to a rapid decrease in water pressure.

Already he could feel his joints starting to ache. His vision was closing in at the edges. But it was either that or stay below with whatever had attacked his brother. Ray weighed his options, taking only a moment to decide. Better to risk the bends than to tangle with whatever was in the caves. He kicked upward, the surface a tantalizingly short distance away.

He'd only risen a few feet when it found him, barreling out of the depths, delivering an agonizing blow that knocked the wind out of him. Ray tumbled through the water, disorientated. By the time he regained control, the beast was lost again in the black water.

Ray hung in the water, too dazed to move. It felt like he'd been hit by a freight train. His facemask was painfully askew. A sharp throb told him his nose was probably broken.

He glanced upward toward the pale circle of light that signaled the cave's entrance. What had appeared so close mere seconds ago now felt like an impossible distance.

Worse, it was coming back. Ray sensed, rather than saw, the beast shoot from the darkness.

Powerful jaws clamped down, pulling him deeper into the cave.

He struggled, lashing out in a blind panic, but he could not break free.

This is it, he thought. *I'm dead.*

Only he didn't feel any new pain.

His mind struggled to comprehend this latest development, but then he understood. The creature must have latched onto one of his scuba tanks. He reached down and found the latch that held his tanks on and released it. He took a deep breath, filling his lungs with as much gas as possible, and then shrugged the tanks off, wriggling free.

And then he swam, striving for the surface.

His lungs screamed for air. He fought the urge to open his mouth. He shouldn't be holding his breath, he knew. There was real danger that as he ascended and the pressure changed, he would rupture his lungs. A nasty way to die.

Higher up, near the cave's entrance, were the oxygen bottles on the decompression line. He kicked upward and located the guide rope — more by luck than anything else — then pulled himself along. Red and yellow spots danced before his eyes as his lungs used up the last of their reserves.

He felt light-headed. But then, not a moment too soon, the oxygen bottles appeared, bobbing in the current. He breathed in a couple of quick gulps and waited for clarity to return.

Under normal circumstance he would linger here for at least forty-five minutes, waiting for the nitrogen in his bloodstream to dissipate, but there was no time.

Light filtered from above.

Wonderful, life-saving sunshine that sparkled through the

spring's entrance. If only he could make it there, he would be safe, so long as the rapid decompression didn't kill him.

It was a risk he had to take.

Ray swam on, leaving the oxygen bottles behind.

He was nearing the surface now, but the danger wasn't over. The creature might finish its tussle with the dive tanks at any moment and come racing up, jaws wide.

But it didn't. By some miracle, he reached the surface, breaking through the water's plane and gulping in cool evening air.

But he wasn't out of danger yet.

The creature was still below, and worse, he didn't feel good. His stomach churned, and his muscles were on fire. His lungs felt like they were being pricked by a thousand needles. His muscles were stiffening already, making it hard to move.

Despite this, Ray heaved himself from the water and flopped down on the cool flat rocks at the edge of the pool.

Ray pulled his facemask off. The glass was cracked, and blood had pooled on the inside. His nose hurt like hell, and his leg throbbed from a deep gash.

He needed urgent medical attention, or he would die.

If the blood pumping from his damaged leg didn't do the job, his body's elevated nitrogen levels surely would.

The bends. Every diver's worst nightmare.

If he had access to a hyperbaric chamber, he might survive. But where was he going to find one of those in the middle of the woods? Ray's only chance was to reach the hospital back in town, and they probably didn't have one. It wasn't exactly a common item, even for a medical facility.

Ray forced himself up, fighting a crippling wave of nausea, and focused his thoughts on the truck parked fifteen feet away near the edge of the clearing.

He staggered forward, one foot in front of the other, forcing his screaming muscles to continue.

He reached the truck and yanked on the driver's door, frantic, flopping into the seat.

And then he came to an awful realization.

The keys were back near the water's edge, where the two divers had suited up, tucked into Carl's pants pocket. He let out a strangled cry. Hot tears of frustration streamed down his face. He wasn't sure he had enough fight left to go retrieve them.

Not that it mattered, because something was pulling itself out of the water, something large and monstrous, with the devil's eyes and glistening sharp teeth. He'd thought he was safe here, but impossible as it was, their attacker could come onto land.

In that moment Ray knew, with absolute certainty, that he was never leaving this place — at least, not alive.

SIX

EMILY WATCHED Alex fuss over the controls that should have brought LISA, the small metal submersible, back to the surface already. It had been two hours, and in that time, he had gone from confident, through hopeful, to despair.

"This is no good. Dammit!" Alex pushed the joystick away, flopped back in his chair. He scrunched his eyes closed and rubbed them with his knuckles. "Nothing's working. LISA's gone."

"Are you sure?" Emily asked, even though she was fighting the same heavy cloud of despair.

"I don't know what else to try. I've sent reset commands, tried to reboot her. She's dead in the water."

"We should send the divers down. Maybe they can fix her."

"Not going to happen." Professor Howard's voice drifted through the open tent flap. After pacing the room while Alex fussed and cursed, he'd given up and went outside to smoke a cigarette, something he only did when he was under pressure. Now his frame filled the entrance, silhouetted against the early evening sun. "Too dangerous. Whatever attacked our sub might still be down there."

"There shouldn't be anything down there," Alex said,

rubbing his forehead. "At least, nothing big enough to mess with LISA."

"Well, something sure thought she looked like dinner." Howard pushed his hands deep into his pockets. "NASA is going to be pissed."

"Not to mention the university," Emily added. "They have a pretty hefty pile of cash tied up in this project. What are we going to tell them?"

"The truth." Alex glanced up at the monitors, at the frightening image still frozen upon them. The last thing LISA relayed before she went offline. "A monster ate our submersible."

"What do you think it is?" Emily couldn't help but shudder when she looked up at the screen, at the gaping mouth and razor-sharp teeth. "An alligator?"

"In the aquifer?" Professor Howard scratched his head. "Not likely."

"Then what?"

"A giant eel?" Alex swiveled around in his chair. "I've read about Conger eels growing to twenty feet or longer."

"We're not dealing with a Conger, not in the aquifer. Not in fresh water." Howard shook his head. "Besides, there wouldn't be enough food down there to sustain anything even a quarter that large, even if it was coming up to feed at the springs."

"Some kind of a fish?" Emily asked.

"Not that deep." Howard said. "Most of the life should be concentrated near ground level, in the springs. That far down it should be pretty much lifeless."

"Well, Doc," Alex said, "my video feed would beg to differ."

"Something's down there," Emily agreed. "Something big."

"Yes, that would appear to be the case."

"We need to get LISA back, see if she recorded anything else after the feed was cut," Alex said, a new excitement in his voice. "We might have discovered something entirely new and unknown to science."

"And just how do you propose to do that?" Howard asked. "The sub isn't responding, and I've already said we're not going to risk the divers on such a foolhardy errand. Even if whatever attacked the submersible is gone, we don't have the equipment to mount a dive that deep."

"Come on—"

"He's right." Emily reached out, took Alex's arm. "A dive like that, we'd need guide ropes, halogen floodlights, not to mention that we don't have the right mix in the canisters."

"Why don't we have all that stuff?" Alex asked. "You knew how deep we were sending LISA. Isn't that what the divers are here for?"

"Yes, it is." Professor Howard wiped a bead of sweat from his forehead. "But we're on a tight budget. All that extra equipment costs money. The divers are fine for shallow dives and surface support tasks. Might I remind you that LISA is designed to operate under extreme conditions? We've spent years working on her, making sure she can handle these environments."

"We should have been prepared for this."

"For what, my dear boy?" the professor asked. "For something to attack our sub?"

"No, for an unexpected failure."

"I made a decision not to purchase expensive equipment we probably wouldn't need to better preserve our funds." The professor drew a long breath. "It was a gamble, I admit."

"Then we just abandon LISA?"

"I never said that," Howard replied. "We'll keep trying to get her back online remotely. If all else fails, I'll call the university, get some help down here, but that is a last resort. I'd rather not draw attention to this hiccup unless I have to."

"Hiccup?" Alex said. "We're way past a hiccup here."

"I agree, which is why you will keep trying to make contact with our submersible."

"Obviously," Alex said. He fell silent for a moment, and then spoke again. "I still think we should send the divers down though."

"I've already said no." The professor narrowed his eyes. "Too dangerous."

"I don't believe what I'm hearing." Alex looked away in disgust.

"Why are you fighting me on this?" the professor asked. "I'm in charge here, not you."

"I know," Alex said, much of the fight leaving his voice. "But I hate leaving LISA down there."

"And I hate the idea of getting someone killed over a foolhardy excursion to save a bunch of metal and wires. This was a test of the sub. We learn more from failure than we do from success. If this had occurred on Europa, there would be no divers available to save the day."

"I still don't like it."

"You don't have to," Howard said. "I've made my decision. It's final." He turned and walked away, pulling out another cigarette as he went. "I suggest you both get an early night. Tomorrow may prove to be a very long day."

SEVEN

DECKER AND NANCY walked along the seafront, their footfalls leaving perfect impressions in the wet sand. It was a humid night, the air heavy with the remains of the daytime heat. The only relief was a stiff ocean breeze gusting between periods of relative calm. Low on the horizon a full moon glowed with silvery light that made it easy to see despite the late hour.

Decker let his gaze wander out across the water. He watched the waves begin far out to sea, the surf tops rising until they crashed against the shore before receding again. Further along the beach, half a mile distant, was their hotel, lights aglow. It was late, past eleven o'clock, but he was glad that Nancy had suggested they walk back. It topped off a perfect evening.

First came a meal of blackened redfish, freshly caught and artfully cooked. The restaurant had a deck overlooking the water, the sun slipping below the horizon as they ate, the sky turning a thousand shades of yellow and red. Afterward, they lingered at the bar and sipped local brews to the accompaniment of a live musician. It was relaxing. Romantic. And even if the troubles of the past year still lingered at the back of his mind, Decker could tell this was just what Nancy needed. Now, as they strolled along the beach, she chatted happily.

"I talked to Taylor this afternoon," Nancy said. "She said to tell you hello."

"How is Taylor?" Decker asked. She was starting college in two months and had already relocated to Boston and found an apartment.

"She's doing great; settling in and making new friends."

"Good." Decker put his arm around Nancy. "Taylor's a trooper, that's for sure."

"Always has been." Nancy nestled into him, her body soft and warm.

"Like her mother," Decker said. "The pair of you are so much alike."

"I don't know about that." Nancy met Decker's gaze. "I worry about her being alone."

"She's hardly on her own. You said it yourself, she's making new friends."

"I know, it's just that—"

"Stop worrying. You're supposed to be on vacation. Besides, if Taylor needs you, she'll call."

"You're right." Nancy nodded.

"Then relax," Decker said. "Getting on with life is the best thing for Taylor, and for you."

"That's why I love you," Nancy said. "You always know how to put my mind at ease."

"I do my best." Decker pulled Nancy close. He slipped his arms around her waist and looked into her eyes.

"I really do love you, John Decker." Nancy's voice was soft and light. She leaned in close, her lips finding his.

"I love you too," Decker said, and then he kissed her again as the waves lapped at the shore and the moon slipped behind the scudding clouds. This was, he thought, the perfect end to a perfect evening.

EIGHT

AT A QUARTER past ten that night, Frank Denning steered the plumber's van off the interstate and down a winding forest road that soon turned to hard-packed dirt. They had been driving for hours, taking a circuitous route from Atlanta along I-16 to Savannah then turning south toward the Florida border and Jacksonville. From there, Frank turned inland and took back roads the rest of the way. Now it was dark, and they were nearing their destination, a ramshackle summer cabin deep in the woods, the perfect place to lay low and wait for the heat to die down.

It was a moonless evening. The canopy of trees blocked what little illumination filtered through the clouds. Frank almost missed the trail leading to the cabin, but at the last moment he saw it and swung the wheel hard to the left.

"Who needs GPS?" he muttered, pleased with himself, as the van pulled up in a wide clearing ringed by towering pines.

"Good job." Liz waited for the van to come to a stop before opening her door. "Boys, say hello to your home for the next month."

"Where's the beach?" Jerry asked. "When you said we were

going to Florida, I assumed you meant sun, sand, and margaritas. This is the middle of nowhere."

"There will be plenty of time for margaritas once the cops have gotten bored of looking for us," Liz said.

"How did you find this place anyway?" Louie asked. "You subscribe to the World's Worst Lodgings Monthly or something?"

"My grandfather and a few of his friends got together and bought the place years ago to use as a hunting cabin," Liz said. "They'd come down here in the summers and spend weekends hunting deer. He brought me along a few times."

"If this belongs to your family, why are we here?" Jerry asked. "It won't take long for the cops to come looking for us."

"It's not in my grandfather's name. When he died, it went to the only remaining member of the original group of hunters. That was the agreement; whoever lived longest got sole ownership. When the last of the group passed away, his oldest daughter inherited the cabin. She has no interest in hunting. It's been empty ever since."

"I wonder why she didn't sell it?" Frank mused. "The land must be worth a few bucks."

"Sentiment maybe, or just laziness," Liz said. "Either way, who cares? It's not on anyone's radar, and we won't be disturbed."

"Lucky us," Louie said. "Is there even a bed in the place?"

"Not sure." Liz unbuckled her seat belt, slid from the passenger seat and stretched. "I was fourteen the last time I spent any time here."

"Seriously?"

"Don't throw a fit. We have everything we need in the back of the van. There are air mattresses, bottled water, and enough coolers of food to keep us going for weeks. And lanterns too, since the generator probably doesn't work. If it's even still here."

"No electricity either." Louie punched the back of the

passenger seat with a clenched fist. "This just keeps on getting better and better."

———

The cabin was no better on the inside than it was on the outside. An old sofa stood against one wall. There were a couple of chairs, one missing an arm, the seat fabric stained and torn. On the right side was a kitchenette with a propane stove. A gap at the end of the counter must have held a refrigerator but it was long gone. Frank wondered if the stove worked and decided it probably didn't. Even if it did, the likelihood that there was still a useable propane tank around was remote.

Frank brushed a cobweb away from his face and dropped his backpack on the floor. "I've stayed in worse."

"Damned right." Liz reached out and flipped a light switch. Nothing happened. "And if we can get the electricity on, it might even feel like home."

"Where's the generator?" Frank asked.

"Out back," Liz said. "There's a lean-to with a tin roof. It should be in there."

"Perfect." Frank turned to Jerry. "You with me?"

"You bet." Jerry nodded.

"There's no way you're going to get it working," Louie said. "Even if there's still gas back there, it will be stale."

"That's why we brought our own," Frank said. He turned to Jerry. "Let's get this done."

"Lead on," Jerry said, waiting for Frank to step past him into the night before following along behind.

"You want me to come too?" Louie called after them.

"I think we can handle it." Frank was fairly sure Louie didn't really want to come along. Even so, he quickened his step just to make sure.

There were twelve red five-gallon gas cans in the van, which meant they had a total of sixty gallons. If they were frugal, it

ANTHONY M. STRONG

would last several nights. After that, they would need to refill, which would be risky, but they could worry about that later. First, they needed to get the generator running. Frank grabbed a couple of cans and waited while Jerry took two more.

The lean-to was little more than a five-foot square shed made up of rusted tin panels nailed to a sagging frame of two-by-fours. Debris and leaves had accumulated on the sloped roof, and a broken tree limb lay blocking the entrance. Frank heaved it out of the way with a grunt and tugged at the door. At first it refused to budge, but then the hinges popped free and he was able to wrestle it open wide enough to peer inside. A dark form, probably a rat, scurried out from the darkness.

Frank jumped back in surprise, bumping into Jerry.

"Watch it, man." Jerry grumbled, stepping back.

"Sorry," Frank said. He stepped around the door and aimed a flashlight into the hut. "Dang it."

"What?"

"It's gone." Frank played the flashlight over a cracked and empty concrete slab. "No generator. Looks like we're using the lanterns."

"Meh." Jerry peered at the patch of broken concrete where the generator had once sat. "Even if it was still here, it would probably be all seized up by now anyway."

"Yeah. Probably." Frank dropped the gas cans. "Won't be needing these anymore."

He turned to leave.

Jerry caught his arm. "Hold up a minute."

"What?"

"Louie." Jerry rubbed his chin. He glanced around, made sure they were alone. "I don't trust him."

"Me either," Frank admitted. "He's too jumpy."

"You and me, we did time together. We understand each other. Liz… she's solid, a pro. I don't know squat about Louie."

"I agree," Frank admitted. "He just might do something stupid and get us all nabbed."

48

"Between you and me, I don't understand why Liz brought him in on this. He's a liability."

"She had no choice." Frank slapped at a mosquito. "He's the nephew of some big shot in New York. A lieutenant on some syndicate. He wanted Louie to learn the ropes, and Liz owed him a favor."

"She could have said no. A job like this, you gotta have trust."

"Yeah." Frank grimaced. "Louie's uncle, he's not the kind of guy you say no to, if you catch my drift."

"I still don't like it."

"Look, I've known Liz a long time," Frank said, leading them back toward the front of the cabin. He paused at the door and turned to Jerry. "She'll keep him in line."

"I hope you're right." Jerry pulled the cabin door open.

When they stepped inside, the front room was empty.

From further inside the cabin, Frank heard voices. He crossed to a door on the far wall, beyond which was a narrow corridor, and three more rooms at the rear. On the left was the master bedroom. To the right was a smaller bedroom and a bathroom. The sink, cracked, and black with filth, had fallen through the rotten floor and now sat on the dirt beneath.

They would be taking their toilet breaks in the woods.

He grimaced and glanced around. Liz and Louie were in the large room inflating an air mattress with a manual pump by the light of a second lantern.

"Generator's gone." Frank stepped into the room. "Looks like we'll be roughing it."

"That's a shame," Liz said. "Still, I expected as much."

"Is this where we're bedding down?" Frank asked, noticing as he spoke that there was only one mattress in the room.

"It's where I'm bedding down." Liz nodded toward the smaller room across the corridor. "You boys can sleep in the other room, or out in the main area. Your choice."

"Nice," Jerry said. "How come you get the penthouse suite?"

"Because I'm the woman," Liz said. "And also because I'm the boss."

"A floor's a floor as far as I'm concerned," Frank said. "I'll make up my bed in the front room. Someone should cover the door anyway, just in case. It's hardly Fort Knox around here, and I don't want any nasty surprises, like the cops barging in unannounced."

"No one is going to find us here," Liz said. "But I agree. Best to cover every eventuality, no matter how unlikely."

"I guess I'll take the other bedroom with Louie," Jerry said.

"Why can't I sleep in the front room instead of Frank?" Louie didn't look happy. "I don't want to sleep with Jerry. He snores. He slept for half the trip down here. You should have been in the back of the van. I could barely think straight it was so loud."

"You'll bed down with Jerry," Liz said. "That's the end of it. I want Frank out front."

"This is bullshit," Louie grumbled. He glared at Frank, then Jerry, before stomping away.

"This is going to be so much fun." Jerry watched Louie go.

"Liz," Frank said, rubbing his chin. "Next job you set up, do me a favor and leave Louie out of it. I'm tired of that man already." He cast a knowing look toward Jerry, making sure they were on the same page about watching Louie.

"I thought this was it for you," Liz said. "One last job as a favor to me."

"It is."

"Doesn't sound like it." Liz chuckled. "Face it, Frank. You're a crook, and always will be."

"Yeah. Whatever." Frank yawned and turned back toward the front room. "It's late. I'm beat. See you in the morning."

NINE

EMILY BRIGHT WOKE WITH A START. Her eyes snapped open, but still it took a moment before the tent's roof swam into view against the inky blackness. She wondered what had roused her from sleep. Nothing seemed wrong, out of the ordinary.

And then it hit her. There was one thing different.

The air should be thick with the sound of cicadas and tree frogs — a chorus of chirping and deep throated croaks that had kept her up for hours the first night they were here.

Only it wasn't.

The air was still and quiet.

She felt a tingle of apprehension.

Where were all the bugs? It was inconceivable that they had unanimously decided to go mute at the exact same time.

She held her breath and listened, ignoring the nagging fear that flitted at the edges of her mind. The silence stretched on, a maddening void that confounded her senses.

And then she heard it — a faint footfall, followed by another in quick succession.

Her heart thudded against her ribcage.

Someone, or something, was outside the tent.

She opened her mouth to call out, but then she thought better of the notion, realizing that she might not wish to let whatever was prowling outside know she was there. She glanced at her phone. It was 3 AM, too early for the divers to be up and about preparing their gear for the day. Besides, there was nothing to prepare. LISA was still lost somewhere down in the murky depths of the aquifer.

It was probably a wild animal. There were plenty of those out here for sure. Just two evenings ago one of the divers claimed he saw a bobcat watching him from the brush. Carlos, the crane operator, swore a black bear had sauntered through the camp one night, looking for scraps of food. There were white tail deer and raccoons too. This was the reason they double bagged their food waste and stored it in airtight plastic crates until the trash could be driven out of the woods for disposal. Still, that didn't mean they hadn't drawn the attention of a hungry scavenger.

She strained to listen, but there was nothing now. Maybe it had moved back into the woods.

She thought about settling back down, but she wouldn't be able to relax knowing there was nothing but a thin piece of canvas between her and a hungry prowling animal. She wouldn't fall back to sleep. Of that she was sure.

That left two options. She could hide here in the tent and wait until sunrise, or she could leave the relative safety of the tent and satisfy herself that the clearing was secure.

Neither option sounded great, but at least out in the open she would be able to see if there was a predator in their midst, and if there was, she could raise the alarm and bring the rest of the team running. But alone, in the flimsy tent, she was blind and vulnerable with no way to defend herself.

That settled it.

Emily scooted from her sleeping bag, dressed quickly, then unzipped the tent flap and crawled through the opening.

The clearing appeared to be empty.

To her left and right were five more tents just like hers.

Beyond these, near the woods, a stark black outline reared fifteen feet into the air. The track crane used to lift LISA in and out of the water. It looked out of place in the woodland — a metal anachronism against a backdrop of towering trees and dense primordial undergrowth. This far into the woods she could not even hear the rumble of traffic on the interstate to their west. It was a weird and unsettling feeling.

Emily pushed the thought from her mind. A gentle breeze ruffled her hair, and she brushed an errant strand from her face before turning to examine the rest of the clearing. During the evening hours, when everyone was up and about, two sodium arc lamps erected on tall poles cast pools of garish white light across the space, illuminating the camp. At night they were turned off, partly to save fuel, and also because the lamp's brightness and generator noise would keep everyone awake.

Now she wished they were still on.

The thought that a creature might be out there, swathed in darkness, watching from the woods, sent a shiver along her spine. She felt no safer out here than she had before. Why had she ever thought this was a good idea?

Emily turned to retreat back inside her tent.

A twig snapped, off to her left.

She froze and peered into the night, but saw nothing out of the ordinary. It was probably just a racoon mooching around in the bushes. She started to relax... but then, rising on the breeze, she heard a low rumbling cough.

Emily swallowed her urge to scream. She could feel the blood rushing in her ears. A whimper escaped her lips. She backed up toward the tent, her breath coming in short ragged gasps, much too loud.

There was movement from the shadows, a shape that detached from the gloom.

Emily felt the scream welling in her throat.

And then a voice drifted on the wind. "Emily?"

Giddy relief washed over her. This was no bear. It was her boss.

"Professor Howard," she said.

"What in blazes is going on?" The professor's familiar figure emerged from the shadows.

"I heard a noise," she replied. "I thought there was a wild animal in the camp."

"Oh dear." Professor Howard looked apologetic. "I didn't mean to frighten you."

"What are you doing out here at such a late hour?" Emily asked.

"Call of nature." He looked sheepish. "I didn't think anyone would be awake, so I found a tree."

"I guess I'm a light sleeper." Now it was Emily's turn to look sheepish. "I didn't mean to disturb you."

"All taken care of." Howard waved a hand, dismissive. "Now if you don't mind, I'm going back to bed. Morning will be here before we know it, and I'm a grouch if I don't get my full eight hours."

"Sure." Emily smiled. "Goodnight, Professor."

"Sweet dreams." Howard shuffled back toward his tent.

Emily watched him go, and then turned in the direction of her own accommodation. As she did so something caught her eye, a gliding disturbance at the periphery of her vision. A barely perceptible shifting of the darkness near the shoreline, followed by a gentle splash.

Her eyes roamed the landscape, searching for whatever had caused the movement, but there was nothing to see. The only sign that anything had been there at all were a few shimmering ripples on the water's glassy surface.

And then she noticed something else. The cicadas and tree frogs had started their nightly chorus once more, filling the air with the rhythmic soundtrack of the woodlands.

TEN

JOHN DECKER ROSE as the first rays of morning sun inched through the blinds. Nancy was still in bed. Back when she owned the diner it would have been inconceivable for her to sleep past six, but now she had nothing to wake up for.

He made a cup of coffee, crossed to the glass doors leading onto the balcony, and went out.

The beach below was empty. It was too early for the tourists. Another few hours and the sandy strip would be packed with sun worshippers, the green tinted waters filled with pleasure boats, jet skis, and the multi-colored chutes of parasailers. Decker preferred the beach the way it was right now. It was more intimate, like the sand and sea were there for him alone.

It was at times like this, when he was alone with his thoughts, that the events of the past twelve months pushed their way back into his mind. Annie Doucet and her crazy killing spree. The aftermath that cost him his job. Worse, Nancy had been forced to sell the diner or go bankrupt, since no one in town would go there anymore. Then there was Taylor, who was forever changed, despite the brave face she put on. Even her choice of college, which seemed innocuous enough, suggested that she wanted to put as much distance between herself and

Wolf Haven as possible. At first, she had toyed with the idea of attending school in Mississippi, but after her brush with death and the loss of her boyfriend, she back peddled on that idea and ended up in Boston. She rarely spoke about her ordeal, and the beast that had stalked her through darkened corridors, but he knew it was her frequent companion, hiding at the edges of her mind, because he could feel it too. None of them would ever be the same after that stormy, dangerous night.

He turned back to the room. When he stepped inside, Nancy murmured in her sleep, rolling over with the sheets tangled around her legs.

He dropped the empty coffee cup into the trash and picked up his cell phone.

"What time is it?" Nancy looked up with sleepy eyes.

"Early. A little after six." He scrolled through his contact list until he came to a particular name. Bill Gibson. "I didn't mean to wake you."

"You didn't," Nancy said. "Come back to bed."

"Nah. I'm awake already."

"Climb on in anyway. Keep me company," Nancy said. "It's too early to be up. We're on vacation."

"I was about to call Bill," Decker said. "See when he's available to meet up."

"I can't imagine he'd appreciate that at this time of the morning."

"He's a cop. He'll be awake and on his way to the station already."

"The call can wait an hour." She reached out and took his hand. "Please?"

"All right." He put the phone down. "Just for a while."

Nancy waited while he climbed in next to her. She pulled him close and laid her head on his chest. "See, that wasn't so bad."

"No, not so bad." He cradled her in his arms.

"I wish you could put that job out of your mind."

"I know."

"You will take it, or you won't." Her voice was soft and soothing. "Either way it will be the right choice. Life has a way of working itself out."

"I know."

"But right now, maybe I can help you relax." Her hand brushed across his chest. "You know, since you can't sleep." She lifted her head. Her hair spilled down. Her lips brushed his.

"If you insist."

"I do," she said in her most seductive voice. "And afterward, you can buy me breakfast."

ELEVEN

EMILY BRIGHT CLAMBERED out of her tent and suppressed a yawn. She looked around the clearing. Her eyes settled on the round pool of deep water in the middle. It seemed so peaceful, serene. She had a feeling that under the surface it was neither of those things.

Her mind returned to the night before and the movement she thought she saw out of the corner of her eye. At first, she'd tried to tell herself that it was nothing, just her mind playing tricks, but the more she thought about it, the more convinced she became that it was no such thing. That raised another question. Had she crossed paths with whatever had attacked their sub? It didn't seem possible, but then again, neither did the prospect of a large predator living in the aquifer.

She shuddered and hurried across the clearing toward the control tent.

Alex was already there with Professor Howard. They were hunched over the monitors, talking in hushed voices.

"Any luck?" Emily asked, trying to keep her voice steady despite the twinge of unease that gnawed at her.

"What do you think?" Alex sounded morose. "LISA's still unresponsive."

Professor Howard scratched his head. "We've tried resetting the comm links, ordering a reboot, initiating a self-diagnostic. Nothing works."

"Either the sub is too damaged to respond, or she got carried out of range by the current."

"How can the sub be out of range?" Emily asked. "Isn't she built to operate over vast distances?"

"Yes, but the communications equipment has limitations, especially under so much rock. The gear that will be used on Europa will be way more sophisticated. Hell, NASA hasn't even invented some of the stuff they'll need yet. Besides, LISA was designed to work autonomously, without constant monitoring."

Professor Howard straightened up. "The distances we're working with here should be no problem for her though."

"Plus, if it was merely a comms issue, she would have returned to the spring last night under her own steam," Alex said. "Whatever attacked the sub must have done some real damage. I don't get it. There shouldn't be anything down there bigger than a minnow."

"The evidence would beg to differ," Howard said.

Emily shuddered when she recalled the last image the sub sent back before she went offline — a large gaping mouth and row after row of wicked teeth. "Any idea what could be down there?"

"Whatever it is, the damn thing killed LISA." Alex swiveled his chair away from the monitor and rubbed sleep from his eyes.

"It's probably an alligator," Howard said. "It must have thought LISA was a turtle or some such thing."

"An alligator?" Alex asked, incredulous. "Down there? You know as well as I do that alligators don't live in the aquifer."

"Have you got a better idea?"

"Not really," Alex admitted.

"I think the professor is right," Emily said. "There could be an alligator in the aquifer."

"What makes you say that?" Howard turned to her, his eyes narrowing.

"Last night, after we talked, I thought I saw something. It was only a fleeting glimpse, but whatever it was went into the spring."

"You're sure about this?" There was an edge of excitement in Howard's voice.

"Pretty much," Emily said. "I don't know what I saw, but something sure disturbed the water. It was big too."

"This complicates things." Howard looked worried. "If there's a hungry animal out there, one that can come onto land, we could all be in danger." He paused, letting the words hang in the air before speaking again. "I think maybe we should pack up and leave, at least until we know what we're dealing with."

"No way!" Alex jumped up. "I'm not abandoning LISA. Besides, if there is a large predator down in the aquifer, we should find out what it is, not run away."

"We're not zoologists, my boy."

"But we are scientists. Come on, Prof. A few days," Alex pleaded. "We don't even know if this thing is dangerous."

"No, we don't. Likewise, we don't know that it is not dangerous." The professor glanced at the screen. "And our first encounter would hardly class as benign."

"We'll never get another grant if we abandon LISA."

"Perhaps not."

"If we can get her working again, we can record this animal, find out what it is, alligator or otherwise. We'll be giving LISA a true test. Think about that."

"What do you say, Emily?" Howard turned to her.

"I'm scared," Emily admitted. "But I also recognize a great opportunity when I see one. We know that alligators don't live in the aquifer, like Alex said. As far as we know, nothing close to the size of whatever attacked our sub does. This could be a new species, or at the very least, a new behavior of a known species."

"Or it could be a confused gator," said Howard. "A fluke."

"But what if it's not?" Emily wondered what she was doing. Did she really want to stick around after her scare the night before? Not really. But the scientist in her was curious as hell. "It would be a waste to walk away now. This could be a gift."

"Two days," the professor said, his face stoic. "You have two days to get the sub back and figure out what is going on."

"Thank you." A wide grin spread across Alex's face.

The professor ignored him. "In the meantime, I am going to email the recording of the sub's demise to the university." He glanced at the monitor. "Maybe someone there can tell us what we're dealing with."

"Whoa. Let's not be too hasty." Alex shook his head. "The university will know we lost the sub if you do that."

"No, they won't," replied Howard. "And if anyone asks, I'll tell then the sub returned to the surface a little battered but in one piece."

"Let's hope they don't ask too many questions then," Alex said, a look of concern on his face. "Lying to the university about losing a multi-million-dollar piece of tech could get us all fired."

"Agreed. Which means you'd better find a way to get LISA back," Howard said. "Unless you have a desire to join the unemployment line."

TWELVE

CHARLIE COGAN AWOKE WITH A START.

For a while his brain refused to click back to reality, and he was overcome with a sudden panic. He was back in the Gulf. Flak was going off all around him, and he was cowering in a makeshift shelter. Then he remembered where he was, and with that came the realization that the flak was really just branches moved by the breeze, tapping on the old car hood that formed his roof.

He sat up and looked around, confused.

Usually the mixture of muggy heat and cheap alcohol meant that he had slept right through the afternoon hours, passed out in an inebriated slumber, but not today.

So what had roused him?

Through the openings in the sides of the shelter, he could see at least three other impromptu dwellings, and further away, nestled among the trees, a couple of ragged and dirty tents. Inside some of these, he knew, were other homeless people. Residents of the small ghetto that had sprung up in the woods, and which would, when the residents of the fancy houses nearby got frustrated enough, be moved on by the local sheriff's department.

He scooted forward, his head aching with the sudden movement. He paused, wincing, and waited for the throbbing to pass. This was what happened when he sobered up. Usually he would reach for the booze and self-medicate, but first he wanted to find out what had disturbed him. If it was the police, then he was in trouble. If it was another bum trying to steal his meagre possessions, he would be forced to put up a fight.

Charlie moved forward, parting the shelter's front flap. At first everything seemed normal, the space in front of his hut empty as usual. Maybe it was just a raccoon or possum skulking around.

That must be it.

Charlie felt the tension drain from his body. He glanced toward the six-pack of beer he'd purchased earlier in the day with spare change scrounged from motorists. There were only two left now, but one was all he'd need to numb his senses enough to fall asleep again.

From outside, another noise, faint and low. Charlie tensed. He forgot about the beer can and turned back toward the narrow slit in the canvas.

The noise grew louder. Something moving through the underbrush. Something big.

He reached for the old baseball bat that stayed by his side whenever he was in the hut. With a growing sense of unease, he pulled back the canvas flap.

"Who's there?" he shouted. Then, for good measure he added, "I'm armed, just so you know."

No answer.

Charlie gripped the baseball bat tight enough that his knuckles turned white.

The sounds were getting closer. He could feel the ground vibrate with each footfall.

"I have a gun," he lied, hoping a show of bravado would be sufficient to ward off whoever was outside. "I'm not afraid to fight."

In truth he disliked fighting and was not good at it, despite having gotten violent on occasion, mostly when he was intoxicated. Usually though, it did not take much to put him on the floor. A well placed punch to the belly or even a quick jab at his face. The ever-present alcohol did not help, the liquor in his bloodstream keeping him in constant danger of stumbling even when he was not engaged in a confrontation.

Two more thuds.

Charlie realized he was still holding the canvas open with his free hand, yet he hadn't actually raised the courage to stick his head out.

He gulped, steeled his nerves, and inched forward, parting the flap wider.

The first thing he noticed was the smell. Pungent, a carrion stench like rotting meat. He'd seen a couple of corpses over the years, vagrants who had passed away and laid there for a while, and this was the same odor.

He wrinkled his nose and fought back the urge to gag.

But it wasn't the smell that made Charlie's blood run cold. It was the monstrous visage that blocked his view of the woods, a demon from hell with sulfurous eyes, a wide gaping mouth and sharp, wicked teeth.

Charlie let out a strangled gasp and scuttled backwards. The canvas flap fell closed, cutting off the view. He scrunched his eyes closed, as if doing so would render the creature outside the hut harmless. When he opened them again, the canvas flap was moving.

A long, scaly snout pushed through, nostrils flaring.

Charlie scrabbled to the rear of his den, heart pounding against his ribcage. A frightened whimper escaped his lips.

The beast thrust forward.

The hut shuddered and creaked under the sudden assault. The makeshift car hood roof shifted sideways. Sunlight streamed through the widening gap.

Charlie had gone as far as he could. His back hit the rear

wall. The roof shifted further and slid off entirely, hitting the ground with a thump.

Charlie swung the bat as the creature advanced. It didn't seem to notice. Instead, it opened those terrible jaws again.

A blast of fetid air hit Charlie, the sickly smell of decomposing meat.

He turned away in disgust, an involuntary reaction to the stench.

When he looked back, the beast was pushing closer. It was so close now that he felt certain those teeth would find him in short order.

And then the rest of the makeshift dwelling began to lift sideways under the unusual assault. It groaned and swayed before losing its battle with gravity. For a split-second time froze, and then the air was filled with debris.

Charlie cowered, the hut flying apart around him. The back wall collapsed, and he fell through, shielding his face from the crumbling remains of his hut.

A timber crashed down, barely missing him.

Another cracked and splintered.

He scrambled out of its way.

The creature gave a frustrated hiss and rose on its muscular hind legs, swatting at the remnants of the hut. But Charlie was already running, fleeing in terror. Putting as much distance as he could between himself and the nightmare that had torn his home apart.

THIRTEEN

LOUIE WAS STILL mad when he woke up. His dark mood had kicked in the evening before after Liz made him bed down with Jerry. It didn't help that the cabin was a dump. At some point rats had found their way in and nested, leaving droppings everywhere. The smell of their piss had kept him up half the night, the stench burning his nostrils as he lay on the cheap air mattress and stared at the ceiling.

Not to mention Jerry's snoring. Christ, that guy could snore. The worst of it was that he wasn't even consistent. He would rumble along for a while, then simmer down to a quiet wheeze. But just when you were falling asleep, off he would go again, like some demented freight train. By the time dawn broke Louie had gotten two hours sleep, if he was lucky, and was feeling far from cheery.

So now he paced back and forth between the cabin's cramped kitchen and the living room, unable to settle and ignoring the silent glares from Liz, who had spent much of the day obsessively streaming the Atlanta news stations on her phone, which somehow still had enough service to connect to the internet.

"I think we're in the clear, boys," she had announced at one point. "Cops don't have a clue; they even got the number of robbers wrong—said there were two gunmen, not three. Morons."

That only made Louie even madder. The cops didn't even know it was them, yet Liz wanted to hide out here for weeks in this crap hole. It didn't make sense. Not that he said that to her, because he knew it would do no good. So instead he paced, the loose board near the fireplace creaking every time he stepped on it.

Frank, sitting in the corner on the threadbare sofa, looked up from his book, a scowl on his face. "Holy crap, Louie. Can't you sit down or something?"

"You pass the time your way, I'll pass it mine," he replied, his eyes falling to the book. "What are you reading, anyway?"

"Dickens," Frank said. "*Bleak House*."

"Never heard of it," Louie said. "Why are you reading that anyway?"

"If you must know, I worked in the prison library when I was doing time in Georgia State. They didn't have the latest bestsellers, so I made do with the classics. Developed a taste for them."

"Classics. Pure torture, more like," Louie said. "Isn't Dickens that dude who wrote *Wuthering Heights*? They made me read that book in school. Awful stuff. It was reading crap like that made me think school was a waste of time."

"And it shows." Frank snorted and went back to his book.

"What's that supposed to mean?" Louie could feel Jerry and Liz watching him. "You think I'm not as smart as you?"

"I know it." Frank placed the open book on his lap. "For a start, *Wuthering Heights* was written by Emily Bronte not Charles Dickens, which you would know if you had half a brain. And second, the very fact that you thought you were wasting your time reading is a significant indicator of your lack of intellectual prowess. Yeah, I'm smarter than you."

"Just because I don't use fancy words and read boring books, that don't make me stupid."

"No, but it doesn't make you Einstein either." Frank lifted his book, breaking eye contact with Louie. "Now stop with the chitter chatter. I'm trying to read."

From the other side of the room, where he was sprawled out on Frank's air mattress, Jerry snickered.

"Shut it." Louie turned to Jerry.

"Leave him alone," Frank warned without looking up.

"You know what, Frank, screw you." Louie could feel the anger bubbling up inside. What kind of person read Dickens while they were hiding out from the cops, for Pete's sake? No one did, except high and mighty Frank — Mr. know-it-all. Louie clenched his fists, choking back the rage that threatened to overpower him.

Frank glanced up and then looked down again without uttering a word. If Louie's demeanor worried him, Frank did not show it.

"This is bull." Louie turned and stomped toward the front door.

"Where do you think you're going?" Liz asked.

"Outside." Louie was at the door. "I need some fresh air."

"You need to go have a sulk, more like," Jerry said.

"Funny." Louie pulled the door open.

"Stay close to the cabin, and make sure no one sees you." Liz's words followed him out, but he didn't respond.

———

Louie let the door swing shut behind him and made his way along the small covered porch to the far edge of the cabin. It was no cooler outside than within the cabin, which surprised him, and if anything, it was more humid. There were also hordes of insects that swarmed around, biting and sucking on every inch of exposed skin. Even so, he felt calmer out here away from the others. They weren't like him. Frank was pompous, with an inflated sense of self-worth, like his shit didn't stink. Plus, he and Liz knew each other from way back. Frank knew Jerry too, having spent time in a cell together. That made Louie an immediate outsider.

He took out his cell phone, leaned on the porch railing, and dialed a number. What was good enough for Liz was good enough for him.

It took three rings before the call was answered. A female voice said, "Louie, is that you?"

He opened his mouth to reply, feeling better already.

The next thing, the phone was flying from his hand, landing with a thud and skittering across the deck floorboards. It bounced twice and came to rest near a rotten rocking chair.

Louie's ear throbbed.

"What the hell?" He turned, confused and angry.

Frank stood a few feet away, his face emotionless. He took a quick step forward, his foot coming down on the phone. There was a sharp crack. Frank twisted his heel to finish the job. When he lifted his boot, the device was in pieces, crushed and useless.

"Damn it, Frank!" Louie fumed. He looked down at the shattered phone. A cold rage simmered in his gut. "What did you have to go and do that for?"

"Are you insane?" Frank kept his voice low. "I thought we agreed, no cell phones."

"Right." Louie glanced toward the cabin. "I guess those rules don't apply to all of us."

"What are you talking about?"

"Liz." Louie stuck his chin out. "How come it's all right for her to spend all day browsing the web on her phone, but I can't make a quick call to my girlfriend?"

"You really are a dumbass." Frank shook his head. "She's using a burn phone you moron. It's one of those pay as you go jobs. Untraceable. She's keeping tabs on the news, making sure we're in the clear. Is your phone untraceable, Louie?"

"Well…"

"Exactly. For all you know, the cops are at your girl's house right now, waiting for you to call so they can figure out where we are. Hell, even if the phone's in sleep mode, they can still access the GPS, turn it on remotely and find us. Please, for the love of god, tell me you didn't have that thing powered on the whole time."

"Of course not." Louie felt a warm flush spread across his face. He felt stupid and hated Frank for belittling him. "Besides, it was one little phone call; how bad could it be?"

"Ask me again after the cops show up," Frank said. "I'm not going back to the joint because of a stupid little toad like you."

"Watch it now, Frank." Louie said, taking a step forward, his fists clenched.

"Or what?" Frank met Louie's gaze. "You're going to take a pop at me? Bring it on."

"I'm just saying leave me alone is all."

"You're pathetic." Frank turned away, the disgust in his voice evident. Then he swiveled, a quick hand shooting out and catching Louie by the shirt. He shoved the smaller man against the wall. Louie's head snapped back and cracked against the timbers. The breath whooshed out of him. Frank leaned in close, inches from Louie's face. "A word of advice, pal. If you're going to make threats, be sure you're man enough to follow through."

"Let go of me." Louie squirmed, his anger turning to fear.

"From now on, you are going to do as you're told, stop all the useless moaning, and ride this out along with the rest of us. Then, when the heat is off, you can take your split and go blow it however you see fit, and we'll never have to cross paths again. Understand?"

"Sure thing. Whatever you say. Now lay off me." Louie twisted free and scurried to a safe distance. "I suppose you feel like a big man now, huh?"

His words went unanswered. Frank was already walking back inside the cabin, leaving Louie alone again. He looked down at his phone, the screen a spider web of broken glass, and in that moment, Louie made up his mind.

FOURTEEN

CHARLIE COGAN STUMBLED through the woods. He wiped his face with the palm of his hand, clearing the sweat from his eyes, and risked a backward glance. Nothing was following him so far as he could tell, and that was good. Maybe it had gotten caught up in the remains of his shelter, or maybe it found something better to eat. Someone in another tent. Either way, he was happy the creature was not pursuing him. Not that he had any intention of letting up his frantic pace. Still, his mind kept returning to the same question: just what had attacked him?

An alligator.

That was the first thought that came to mind. It must have been a big old hungry gator roaming around looking for an easy meal. But that made no sense. For a start, he'd never heard of an alligator making such a violent preemptive attack, especially so far from water. He'd lived in the woods for a long time and come across gators more than once around retention ponds and waterholes. He gave them a wide berth, and they reciprocated. None had ever chased him. It was only folk who fed the animals or got too close that ran into trouble. Besides, the creature that had torn his home apart had reared up on its hind legs. Gators did not do that as far as Charlie knew. It looked more like a dinosaur. But that was impossible. Charlie might not have much of an education, but he knew that dinosaurs were long extinct. But what other explanation could there be? Regardless, he was relieved to be alive, and the further he went, the more likely it appeared that he would stay that way.

Charlie slowed up. His lungs burned, and his muscles ached. It had been a long time since he had put his body through this much physical exertion, and he wasn't sure how much longer he could keep going. Which was why he was relieved when the trees thinned out and a ribbon of black smooth asphalt came into view.

The road.

He would have cried with relief except that he was too winded. There was only enough left in him to stagger forward, puffing and panting.

He emerged from the trees and scrambled through the drainage ditch before taking stock of his surroundings.

A big old pickup truck was cruising toward him at a clip.

Charlie put his arms up and waved. The driver slowed but did not stop. Instead, he steered into the other lane to avoid the crazy homeless man. And then the truck was speeding up again.

Charlie stepped further out into the road to make avoidance that much harder. If only someone would stop, they could give him a ride into town or at least take him far enough that he didn't have to worry about the dinosaur finding him again.

Another car appeared, this one coming the other way. Just like before, the driver slowed, surprised to see a pedestrian on such a lonely stretch of highway. They beeped at Charlie, waved for him to move aside, and then swerved when he didn't. Once clear, the car accelerated until all he could see were a pair of dim red taillights, and then it was gone completely.

Charlie wondered what to do next. He was used to people giving him a wide berth, but this was a life or death situation.

Where was their humanity?

He knew the answer to that. It didn't extend to vagrants.

Regular folk were scared of him. They didn't like to face the harsh reality of homelessness. They also assumed that he must be crazy, violent, or both. There would be no help from any of the motorists he encountered. That much was clear. He would have to keep moving on foot, but at least the road made it easier. He had no intention of going back into the woods. Out here, in the open, it would be harder for that creature to ambush him. The question was, should he go toward town or away from it to the industrial estates and farms that dotted the road further along? He was a loner, preferring his own company to that of others, especially the local townsfolk, but right now having other people around sounded great. There was safety in numbers.

His decision made, Charlie started along the road toward Leland.

But he didn't get far.

No sooner had Charlie started to walk than a whooping siren sounded behind him. Charlie stopped and turned. One of the motorists he'd tried to flag down must have called the cops, because there, in the road behind him, was a state police cruiser.

FIFTEEN

FRESHLY SHOWERED, dressed in a pair of navy shorts and a white polo shirt, Decker left Nancy sitting on the balcony and made his way to the rental car parked in the hotel's side lot.

Exiting the parking lot, he turned onto the beach road and followed the shoreline for a couple of miles before heading inland.

It was noon. The GPS told him it would take sixty minutes to get to Leland, the small town nestled in the heart of Central Florida that Bill Gibson called home.

While he drove, Decker's mind wandered. It had been several years since he'd last seen Bill. He wondered how much his friend knew of the events in Wolf Haven. Bill was aware that he was jobless and looking for advice. Decker had said as much over the phone. But did Bill know about why Decker had been dismissed, the internal investigation?

He was still musing on this when his phone rang.

Decker used the car's Bluetooth to answer. Nancy's voice filled the cabin.

"I thought I'd give you a call, see how you are doing."

"I'm coming into town now," Decker said.

"I hope Bill can help you make a decision," Nancy said.

"Me too." Decker could hear the sounds of the beach in the background.

"Give me a call when you're done with Bill?"

"Of course," Decker said. "I'll be back soon."

"Take your time," Nancy replied. "I love you."

"Love you too," Decker said and hung up just as the town of Leland came into view.

SIXTEEN

PARK RANGER ANDREW WILSON was on his third doughnut of the day when he turned off the main road and onto the unpaved trail leading to the waterhole. Next to him, on the truck's passenger seat, sat a small plastic bottle in a zip lock bag and a pair of disposable latex gloves.

This was the fourth time Wilson had been up to the spring this year. He had lost count of the visits he'd made over the past half-decade since a pair of teenagers looking for somewhere secluded to fool around had discovered a bright green film floating on the surface of the water. Thankfully, they had the good sense to report the odd greenish blue slime instead of ignoring it and going for a dip anyway; otherwise, they might have been in for an unpleasant couple of days. It had been many years since the toxic algae last made an appearance, but even so the swimming hole remained officially closed, and so he made the bimonthly trek with his sampling kit. Maybe one day his bosses, in their wisdom, would heed his reports that the water was clean and reopen the area, but until then he did his job.

Not that he minded these excursions. In fact, he relished the chance to be alone, away from the hikers and tourists who stumbled around during the summer months, getting themselves lost, leaving their trash in the woods, and generally causing mischief. Sometimes he felt that his job was more babysitter than park ranger.

Up ahead the trail narrowed and entered a series of sharp bends before opening into a wide clearing around the waterhole. Park Ranger Wilson tapped his brakes and gripped the steering wheel with both hands. The trail was bumpy, marred with potholes and ruts left by summer monsoons, and jarring ridges where expanding tree roots had pushed the ground up. He cursed when one of his wheels dropped into a particularly large depression, fought to keep the truck steady, and then he was past the rough terrain and entering the clearing.

Sunlight streamed down through the circular break in the canopy above, spattering the ground with dapple points of light that painted the ground in hues of white and yellow. In the center of the space, ringed on one side by a ledge of smooth rock covered in lichen and undergrowth, and on the other by a gentle slope of sandy earth was the waterhole. It sparkled in the sun, a sapphire green fading to deep blue in the center. This darker color denoted a change in depth where the bottom fell away into a fathomless jagged hole, an entrance into the underworld created when the ceiling of a subterranean cavern collapsed, creating an entrance to the caves below.

Wilson brought the truck to a halt and reached over to collect his sample kit. It was only then that he noticed the other truck, parked in the shade under the trees fifty feet away. He stopped, his hand resting on the sample bottle, and scanned the clearing, searching for any sign of the vehicle's occupants, but he saw no one.

He muttered under his breath.

This was all he needed — some darn fools coming up here and messing around. Couldn't they see the signs? The swimming hole might not pose a danger, but the untended trails leading from the clearing certainly did. Not to mention that if some idiot went and got themselves lost, the park rangers would have no idea where to look for them, because no one was supposed to be here in the first place. He heaved his door open and stepped down, making a mental note to suggest putting a gate at the trailhead. That way people would not be able to waltz on up here. Not that he would get very far. There was barely enough budget to pay wages, let alone make much needed improvements to the woodland roads and trails.

Wilson slammed his door and jogged across the clearing, approaching the unauthorized vehicle. With any luck, he would find a clue regarding the whereabouts of the owner, and then he would give them an earful. But when he was a few feet away, he slowed, a feeling of dread settling over him.

Something was wrong.

Now that he was closer, he saw the condition of the truck. There were large dents creasing the driver's side door. The window was shattered, a spray of glass coating the ground. Someone had really done a number on the vehicle.

He stopped and took stock of the situation.

Was the truck stolen? It wouldn't be the first time that kids had jacked a car, gone for a joy ride, and left it battered and abandoned in some lonely place. He glanced around, suddenly nervous. In all likelihood, the perpetrators were long gone, making their escape in another vehicle.

Except when he inspected the ground, he didn't see a second set of tire tracks. It had rained on and off for most of the previous week, and the ground was still wet, which meant the truck had dug up the still soft earth when it entered the clearing. If another vehicle had been here, it would have done the same thing, but there was only one set of tread marks, ending at the truck.

Now he saw something else.

Two piles of clothes were sitting at the edge of the swimming hole. Shirts, jeans, shoes. There was also a discarded diving mask, cracked and broken.

Wilson's heart fell.

Divers.

He'd seen this before. Stupid people who thought it could never happen to them until it did. Chances were, they went into the water, got stuck and couldn't get back out. Two more corpses that wouldn't see the light of day again.

Except for the discarded mask.

That didn't feel right at all.

Wilson took a step toward the stricken vehicle, glass crunching underfoot, and peered in. The cab was wrecked, seats torn, dash crumpled. The truck's headliner was stained crimson, as if someone had thrown paint up there. But it was what he saw in the front seat that made Wilson's eyes fly wide.

A corpse in a diving suit. Torn and mangled, a mass of entrails and ripped tissue, the man's left side gone completely.

Wilson shrieked and staggered backwards. Vomit forced its way up his throat. He reached for the radio on his belt and pulled it free. Then, before he could use it, his breakfast made a sudden, unwelcome encore.

SEVENTEEN

DECKER TURNED ONTO MAIN STREET, looking for the Grounds and Grains Coffee Shop, where Bill had suggested they meet on his lunch hour. The town was small, less than half the size of Wolf Haven, with only one traffic light that flashed yellow despite the time of day. As he drove, Decker observed the businesses that flanked the street. There was a bar, a laundromat, a grocery store and a hardware store. Many units were empty, with lease signs hanging in their windows. Some of the buildings looked like they had been vacant for years. The town was clearly in decline.

Up ahead, past the shops, he saw a squat red brick building with a sign hanging out front that read *Coffee Shop*. This was surely his destination. He pulled into a parking space in front, threw a handful of quarters into the meter, and made his way inside.

"Can I help you?" asked a slender woman in her mid-thirties. She leaned on the counter and smiled.

"Coffee would be nice," Decker replied, noticing her unusual dusty grey eyes. She reminded him of a slightly younger Nancy with her pear-shaped face and silky black hair tied back tight to her head.

"Regular?"

"Sure." Decker spied a glass case with pastries inside. "Give me a Danish, too."

"Absolutely." She took a carafe from the back counter and poured Decker's coffee. "Haven't seen you before. You new in town?"

"Vacationing on the coast," Decker said. "Meeting an old friend. The town sheriff."

"Bill Gibson?"

"That's him."

"Well, any friend of Bill's is a friend of mine. I'm Sharon."

"John." Decker shook her hand and watched while she slipped a Danish onto a paper plate. "Nice town you have here."

"I like it." Sharon handed him the pastry. "But then, I'm a small town kinda girl; always have been."

"I hear that," Decker replied, glancing over his shoulder as a bell above the front door jingled.

"John. Good to see you, man." Bill Gibson strode into the café and grinned when he saw his old friend. "How long's it been?"

"Too long," Decker said. "Last time we saw each other was that fishing trip to South Carolina."

"Man, we had a blast. Must be eight years ago at least." Bill approached the counter. "I hope you weren't waiting too long."

"No. Just arrived a few minutes ago. Haven't even had my coffee yet," said Decker. "It was good of you to see me at all on such short notice."

"I always have time for old buddies, especially when they need my ear," Bill said. He turned to Sharon. "That said, I'll take my coffee to go. Lunch hour just got canceled. John and I are going to have to walk and talk, I'm afraid."

"Got it." Sharon busied herself with the sheriff's order.

"Trouble?" Decker asked.

"You bet. Fancy a ride along?"

"Sure." Decker nodded. He waited while Sharon transferred

his coffee to a to-go cup and put his Danish in a brown bag, then followed Bill outside. "Want to tell me where we're going?"

"Park ranger found a guy dead in his truck a few miles out of town. Sounds like an animal attack." Bill glanced around. "Where did you park?"

"On the street. The blue rental." Decker pointed to his car.

"Metered parking's only good for two hours. After that you'll wind up with a ticket. Between you and me, the department makes most of its money from fines," Bill said. They arrived at a brown and white SUV with a light bar strapped to the roof. Bill pulled his keys out and unlocked the doors. "I'll tell my sergeant your car will be there awhile. That way you won't get any nasty surprises when we get back."

"Much appreciated." Decker climbed into the passenger seat.

Bill pulled out and made a U-turn in the road. He stayed silent as they rode along Main Street. It was only after they left the town behind that he spoke again.

"I heard about Wolf Haven."

"I expected as much." Decker wondered if every cop in the country knew what had happened.

"The news channels must be desperate for content. A werewolf, of all things? How on earth did the media even come up with that? Talk about far-fetched."

"It was real."

"Yeah, right." Bill chuckled. "I wasn't born yesterday."

"I'm not joking." Decker kept his eyes straight ahead. He didn't want to see the disbelief on his friend's face. He knew that look all too well. "Little old lady turned into a wolf."

"Boy. No wonder they fired you. Is that what you put in the report?"

"More or less. Not quite in those words." Decker felt a tinge of regret. Had he done the wrong thing in coming here? "There were several witnesses."

"Uh-huh. Weren't you in the middle of a hurricane at the

time? Lights were off, I suppose. You sure you didn't see one thing and think it was something else?"

"It was real, Bill." Decker felt weary. He was tired of defending himself to everyone. "Damned monster killed the mayor. Ripped him apart like a hunk of raw steak. Tore open his throat."

"Yeah. I heard about that. Hard to believe it was some old woman. The strength she would have needed. Incredible. But still, a werewolf?"

"Locals call it a Loup Garou," Decker said. "It sounds crazy, even to me. Must have sounded even worse to the board of inquiry. They weren't exactly on my side. Plus, my deputy was more than happy to throw me under the bus to get my job."

"Sorry," Bill said.

"Me too." They were traveling along a rural road with dense woodland on both sides.

"How's the vacation?"

"Good. Nancy's having fun." Decker looked out of the window and watched the scenery zip by. "She needed to get away."

"And you?" Bill turned onto a narrow dirt road. "What do you need?"

"I wish I knew," Decker said. "That's kind of why I'm here. I need some advice."

"Well, shoot." Bill steered around a deep rut. "Must be pretty important for you to take time away from the beach."

"It is. I've had a job offer, and I'm not sure if I should take it."

"Sounds ominous," Bill said as the trail closed in around them. Branches scraped the sides of the SUV. "Tell me more, and I'll tell you what I think."

EIGHTEEN

EMILY BRIGHT WATCHED Alex send yet another useless command to the stricken ROV in the vain hope it would respond, which it didn't. She leaned back, disinterested. There was nothing to do. With the sub out of action, activity at the waterhole had decreased to nothing. The divers were nowhere to be seen. Carlos, the crane operator, was lying on the embankment near the water, shirtless, sunning himself. Apparently, the mosquitos and horse flies either didn't worry him or he was not tasty enough for them to feast on. Emily, however, had spent the best part of the morning swatting away bugs.

"Do you think the professor will pull the plug?" Alex spoke for the first time in over an hour.

Emily sat up straight. "He said we have two days."

"What if he changes his mind when he talks to the university?"

"Then we pack up and leave," Emily said. "I've known Professor Howard for a long time, and I've never seen him go back on his word. He wants to find out what happened as much as we do. Besides, if he goes back with his tail between his legs, missing a forty-million-dollar piece of equipment, it will be a huge dent to his reputation. He might not get another field assignment for a long time, if ever."

A shadow fell over the desk. "That's why I requisitioned three sets of cave diving gear first thing this morning. Bottles, lights, lines, gas mix, the works. It wasn't cheap, but what's the point of having funds if our project is stuck at the bottom of a sinkhole."

Emily and Alex turned in unison to find the professor standing there, arms folded.

"I thought you said it was too dangerous to send divers in," Alex said, although his voice contained a hint of relief.

"And I stick by that assessment, for now. I emailed footage of the attack to the university this morning," Howard said. "I have an old friend in the zoology department. I asked him to be discreet, so that we don't raise any eyebrows. We'll see what he thinks, and we'll go from there."

"See?" Emily smiled. "I told you we could trust the professor."

"I hope he doesn't take too long," Alex said. "Every hour LISA is down there could be compounding the damage. What if her hull was breached? There might be water seeping into vital components. Not to mention the cameras, the SONAR array, a whole host of other systems."

"She was built to handle these types of situations," Howard said. "She'll be fine, don't you worry."

"LISA wasn't built to handle being attacked," Alex said. "This situation is outside of our operational parameters."

"Not true, my boy. We have no idea what the conditions are like on Europa or what a submersible might encounter there."

"I'm pretty sure it wouldn't encounter an ROV-eating monster with big teeth."

"Why not? Who knows what we'll find on that frozen moon? There's a whole liquid ocean under the ice. That's why this is such a big deal. What if LISA encountered some kind of hostile life? There wouldn't be any divers to bring her back."

"Except that we're not on Europa, we're in Florida, and this isn't part of our brief."

"But it could be," the professor replied. "Don't you see? This is a golden opportunity."

"No, I don't," replied Alex. "What I see is a hopeless situation."

"Nonsense. We've already gleaned valuable data, even if it wasn't what we expected."

"Is that how you're going to spin this to NASA if we lose their toy?" Emily said.

"I have no intention of spinning the narrative, nor losing LISA, for that matter." Howard slapped Alex on the back. "We have the best ROV technician on the continent working on the problem. And if that fails, our new scuba gear will be here in the morning. LISA will be back on dry land before you know it."

NINETEEN

CHARLIE WATCHED the state trooper exit the cruiser with a mixture of relief and fear. The cop had a gun, which meant that Charlie was now safer than a few moments ago. At the same time, Charlie didn't like the way the trooper's hand lingered at his holster, as if he expected trouble.

"Would you mind telling me what you're doing out here, sir?" The state trooper observed him from behind dark sunglasses. "You live in the woods?"

"Yes, sir." Charlie resisted the urge to tell the cop about the attack and the beast that lurked in the woods. All that would get him was a one-way trip to a holding cell on a drunk and disorderly, or worse, a visit to the state hospital. The truth sounded crazy, and since Charlie would not have believed there was a monster in the woods if the situation were reversed, he was sure the cop would not believe it either. "Did I do something wrong?"

"A concerned motorist flagged me down and said you might need assistance." The cop adjusted his sunglasses. "This is a welfare check, that's all."

"I'm fine." Concerned motorist? Not a chance. At least, not concerned for him. More likely one of the drivers he'd tried to flag down had reported that there was a drunk in the road.

"Have you been drinking, sir?"

And there it was. All the confirmation Charlie needed. He shook his head no.

"You sure about that?" The cop moved closer.

"Yes." Charlie felt his stomach tighten. He should be getting further away from the homeless camp, and that monster, not be stuck here talking to a cop. "Can I go now?"

"Not just yet." The trooper motioned to Charlie. "Would you mind approaching the car, sir?"

"Why?" Charlie did not want to get any closer than he already was.

"I just want to make sure you don't have any weapons on your person." The cop motioned again. "If you would be so kind as to put your hands above your head and step toward the car."

"You can't arrest me; I haven't done anything wrong." Charlie could feel the panic rising within him. He had to get out of here, and this stupid cop was delaying that.

"I'm not arresting you. Please follow my instructions." The cop's hand rested on the butt of his gun. His fingers twitched.

"I don't want to." Charlie took a step away from the officer, not toward him.

"Don't do that, sir."

"I have rights. Leave me alone." Charlie turned away from the trooper.

"That's far enough."

Charlie froze. He risked a backward glance.

The cop stood legs apart, gun drawn, the muzzle pointed in Charlie's direction.

The two men stood there, each waiting for the other to make a move.

A twig snapped amid the trees, the sound sharp and loud.

But it wasn't the snap that sent Charlie cold with fear. It was the silence afterward. Even the birds had ceased their twittering.

"We shouldn't be here." Charlie prayed he wouldn't see the creature coming toward them. "It's not safe."

"Why not?" The state trooper was on alert now, spooked by Charlie's odd behavior. "Is there someone else out here with you?"

"Not someone," Charlie mumbled. "Something. A monster."

"A monster?" The cop shook his head. "Are you sure you haven't been drinking?"

"I'm not drunk," Charlie said. "It's back."

"What's back?" the trooper asked.

But Charlie didn't answer. He didn't have time.

From the undergrowth a low rumbling snort reverberated.

"What was that?" The cop swiveled, his gun waving in wild fashion.

Another angry snort drifted from within the trees.

"Get in the car." The trooper backed up toward the cruiser. "Hurry up."

For the first time in his life, Charlie didn't mind climbing into a police car. He hurried forward and pulled the passenger side rear door open, and tumbled in.

The trooper kept his gun leveled at the woods, and then turned and sprinted for the driver's door. He jumped in. The car jolted forward. But not fast enough.

Something big and agile erupted from the woods, crashing out of the brush in a blur of speed.

Charlie whimpered and recoiled in his seat.

The beast stopped in front of the car, reared up on two legs, blocking the trooper's path.

"What the hell is that?" The trooper gasped.

"Get moving." Charlie said. "What are you waiting for?"

"Right." The trooper snapped back to action, tearing his eyes from the monstrous visage. He gripped the wheel and pushed the accelerator to the floor. The engine screamed. The car shot forward. The trooper swung the wheel in wild fashion, desperate to avoid the creature in their path.

But it had no intention of letting them escape. The beast lowered its head and lunged at the speeding vehicle. It struck the front passenger door.

The side window imploded with a pop.

Charlie lifted his arms to protect his face from the flying glass.

The cruiser tilted, wheels spinning in air. Then they were tumbling onto the driver's side as the car rolled off the road.

They crashed down a small embankment, barely missing tree trunks, until the front of the car snagged a boulder. The world lurched sideways. The front of the car stopped. The back, carried by its own momentum, kept on going. There was a sickening feeling of weightlessness as the vehicle performed a perfect end over end somersault. Charlie's stomach rushed to meet his mouth. He reached out and braced himself. Then the roof caved in, and everything went black.

Charlie swam back to consciousness, hanging upside down, the seatbelt all that was stopping him from collapsing onto the crumpled roof.

He tried to move but changed his mind when pain shot through him like red-hot knives. His legs were clearly broken, and he had taken a hard knock to the head. Blood flowed into his eyes and obscured his vision. A deep gash down his left arm had exposed raw muscle. But his wounds were not the real danger. There was the more pressing issue of their attacker. Charlie took a moment to regain his composure and then assessed the situation. The gun, which he was sure the cop was still carrying when he got into the car, was nowhere to be seen, thrown from the vehicle somewhere between the road and their final resting place.

And then his eyes turned to the cop.

At first, he thought the trooper was dead.

His limp form hung upside down, his face a mess of blood and shattered bone. It was only when the cop gave a low, terrified moan, that Charlie realized otherwise. Not that it mattered, because he could see what was approaching the wrecked cruiser. And this time, there would be no escape.

TWENTY

THE SCENE of the animal attack was a natural spring deep in the woods. Bill pulled up behind a white panel van with CORONER stenciled along the side in thick black letters. Behind them a squad car guarded the head of the trail, blue and red lights flashing. The deputy who had waved them through leaned against the passenger side door, arms folded. He looked bored.

Up ahead was a shimmering circle of deep blue water, specks of sunlight glinting across its lapping surface. A cluster of people, some uniformed and others in white coveralls, buzzed around a battered pickup truck that was parked on a rise away from the pool.

Bill cut the engine and glanced toward Decker. "If I were you, and this is just my personal opinion, I'd take that fancy government job. Sounds like it's your only valid option."

"You think so?" Decker unclipped his seat belt and pulled on the passenger side door handle.

"Sure." Bill climbed from the car and waited for Decker to join him before speaking again. "You know what they say, when life gives you lemons…"

"Yeah." Decker wiped a bead of sweat from his brow. "Maybe I don't like lemons."

93

"Look here." Bill turned to Decker. "You didn't ask for all that bull crap to happen in Louisiana, and sure, you got a raw deal, but this job offer could be a lifeline. They want you precisely because of what happened. I don't know if I believe in witches and monsters. It all sounds like a bunch of hooey to me. Then again, what have you got to lose?"

"My morality." Decker met Bill's gaze. "This outfit, they do things differently."

"Please. You worked homicide in New York. Are you telling me that you never took a short cut, did what had to be done?"

"I bent the rules once in a while, sure, but only when I knew it was for the right reasons," Decker said. "This is different."

"Is it?" Bill raised an eyebrow. "You'll still be helping people. Just in a different way. And I'll bet the pay is better."

"A little," Decker admitted.

"Then take the job." Bill adjusted his belt, his palm coming to rest on his gun. "If you hate it, you can quit, but until then, you'll be putting some green in the bank, and you can't tell me you don't need that."

"I won't argue with that."

"Problem solved then." Bill motioned for Decker to follow him before taking off toward the pickup. "Come on."

They approached the truck, with Decker a few steps behind the sheriff. As they drew close, a figure in a white hazmat suit turned to greet them.

"This is a doozy, Bill." The coroner was a stocky woman in her fifties with a tangle of wiry silver hair and a face that looked like it had seen its share of the misery humans inflict upon each other. She looked at Decker, one eyebrow raised. "What do we have here, a new face? The mayor finally let you hire some help?"

"Nah." Bill shook his head. "You know better than that. This here's John Decker, an old friend from the academy. John, say hello to Margaret Gibbs, the best medical examiner in the state."

"Please." Margaret looked genuinely abashed.

"You can't argue the truth," Bill countered.

"Well, then I won't." Margaret turned to Decker. "A pleasure to meet you. Any friend of Bill's, and all that..."

"Likewise." Decker extended his hand.

"Yeah, you don't want to shake this," Margaret said, indicating her gloved hand. "Not after where it's been for the last fifteen minutes."

"Speaking of which." Bill stepped forward. "What do we have here?"

"I'm so glad you asked." The medical examiner moved aside, allowing a better view of the truck. She pointed a gloved finger. "I hope you didn't stop for lunch on the way up here, or it might be coming back up."

Decker leaned forward, his eyes settling on a most unusual, and unsettling, tableaux. A man in a full wetsuit sat propped in the driver's seat, his face twisted into a terrified death mask. The body sat upright, as if it could somehow drive the vehicle away. Except it was missing one arm and a good portion of its chest area. Not to mention the congealed blood coating the dash, seats, and headliner. The truck looked like it had been pounded by a wrecking ball. The driver's side door was pushed inward, the glass shattered into small balls that crunched underfoot. The passenger side door was missing, along with some of the cab's roof. Sunlight filtered through the jagged hole onto the corpse.

"Whoa." Bill's voice had lost some of its pep.

"Nicely put," Margaret said. "Succinct."

"Sure does look like an animal attack." Decker leaned in further, careful not to touch anything.

"Yup. Although I'm not sure I could give you a suspect." She squinted against the sun. "I'm no wildlife expert, but as far as I know, there's nothing in these woods that could rip the roof off a truck."

"What about the corpse?" Bill asked. "Any idea what was munching on him?"

"Something nasty," Margaret said. "I'd say an alligator, but it would have to be mighty big. Based on the bite marks, at least twice the size of your average gator. And that doesn't explain the poor state of the truck. I'll know more when we get this fellow back to the lab, but one thing I can tell you, I wouldn't want to run into whatever had this man for lunch."

"He's wearing a wetsuit." Bill rubbed his chin and glanced toward the water. "Must have been diving the aquifer."

"Not the safest of pursuits at the best of times," Margaret said. "I can't count the number of stupid divers who have come across my table over the years after a swim in the caves."

"Except that caves don't take bites out of people." Bill turned and started toward the water.

Decker followed, casting a glance back toward the corpse as the coroner went back to her job. He felt uneasy, his mind turning to the Loup Garou and the bloody trail the Cajun werewolf had left the previous year in Louisiana. He shook the grim thoughts off and hurried to catch up with his friend.

"Look here." Bill was standing near the water's edge with his hands on his hips.

"You got something?"

"I'd say so."

Decker followed Bill's gaze and saw a face mask, the glass cracked and bloody. "I guess this confirms that our guy went for a swim before he got eaten."

"Not only that." Bill sidestepped the mask, approached a pile of discarded clothing. He nudged the heap with his foot. "Two pairs of trousers, two pairs of shoes. Two shirts."

"A second diver."

"Yeah." Bill glanced out over the serene water. "So that raises the question: What happened to him?"

TWENTY-ONE

ALEX WEIR WAS FRUSTRATED. He leaned on a tree near
the water and gazed upon its mottled surface. A sudden breeze
whipped into the clearing, turning the usually glassy pool into a
surrealist rendition of the surrounding woodlands, rippling with
watery brush strokes. LISA was down there somewhere, cold
and immobile, whatever charge remained in her batteries slowly
draining until the last of her systems blinked out and died.

They should be sending the divers in after her, not sitting up
here waiting for... just what were they waiting for? He was sure
the university would provide no answers regarding the
recording the professor had sent them, and for all they knew the
creature was a hundred miles away by now.

The more he thought about it, the more he came to the only
conclusion that made any sense. It was nothing more than a
scared and confused gator that had fallen into a sinkhole and
gotten sucked down into the aquifer. There was nothing else that
matched what they had witnessed on their monitors. Those
teeth, the way it swam, it all added up. But none of that was any
help. LISA was gone, and he wondered if he would ever see her
again.

"Penny for your thoughts?"

Alex turned to find Emily standing a few feet away, regarding him with cool dark eyes.

"I was thinking about LISA. I'm not sure how much longer her batteries will hold up. If they go dead before we retrieve her, we might lose any data she didn't get a chance to transmit."

"The new diving gear will be here soon, and then we'll be able to get her back."

"If the professor deems it safe."

"He wants to retrieve LISA just as much as you," Emily said. "You know that."

"This was supposed to be a safe dive. A quick shake down," Alex said, a glum expression on his face. "What rotten luck."

"Come on." Emily took his hand, a sudden mischievous grin on her face. "You need a distraction."

"Fat chance of that," said Alex, allowing himself to be led across the clearing. "Where are we going, anyhow?"

"My tent," Emily said over her shoulder.

"Really?" Alex perked up. "Right now, in the middle of the day? Finally giving in to your passion, huh?"

"We're not doing that." Emily suppressed a laugh. "Sorry to disappoint you."

"Then what are we doing?"

"You'll see." They reached the tent. Emily unzipped it and ducked inside. She rummaged through her pack, and then backed up, extricating herself. "Found them."

"Found what?" Alex wondered what was going on.

"These." Emily opened her hand and Alex saw two fat slugs of wrapped paper, tapering off at the ends.

"Joints?" His eyes widened.

"Yup. Brought them along for a special occasion." Emily grinned. "This seems as good a time as any to make use of them."

"You know the professor will fire us if he sees these."

"Then we'd better make sure he doesn't see them." Emily held a joint out between two fingers. "Take it."

98

Alex wavered. "I don't know."

"Come on. It won't kill you. Hell, it's legal in half the states now." She produced a lighter and proceeded to light up. "And anyway, we don't have anything else to do."

"If we get caught, I'm blaming you." Alex took the joint and put it to his lips but didn't inhale. The last time he'd smoked weed was in college, and even then, he'd only done it a few times at parties.

"What are you waiting for, an invitation from the queen?" Emily drew on her joint, releasing a column of white, sweet smoke.

"Fine, but I'm doing this under duress." Alex sucked on his own joint, resisting the urge to cough.

"There's my boy; a few minutes and everything will be better," Emily said, drawing back another hit. "I have to warn you though, I'm really funny when I get high."

"I find that hard to believe." Alex could feel the first creeping effects of the drug. His lips were going numb, and his vision seemed a little softer.

"Come on," Emily said, leading him away from the tent in the direction of the sink hole. "We should do this somewhere more private."

"Why can't we smoke in your tent?" Alex asked.

"Because I don't want my tent smelling like weed for the rest of the expedition." She led him around to the opposite side of the water, past the crane and three parked pickup trucks, toward a storage area containing extra fuel for the generators and the specially outfitted flatbed trailer that had transported LISA up to the clearing.

They slipped behind the trailer, out of sight of the main camp. Alex let out long, deep breaths as the drug took hold of him. He glanced over at Emily. He hadn't noticed before, but she was probably the most beautiful woman he'd ever seen, and she was here, alone with him. Not that it would do any good. The talk was that she had been in a relationship with the professor for several months. That was how she got to be his research assistant. Although he'd never seen anything untoward with his own eyes, and it might be nothing more than malicious gossip. Colleges were like that, especially when it came to prestigious appointments. Petty jealousy was a fine motive to start a hurtful rumor. Regardless, he didn't stand a chance with her, despite their frequent playful innuendo. It might not be totally innocent on his part, but he felt sure she had no romantic feelings toward him.

They smoked in silence for a while, each lost in their own thoughts. For his part, Alex found that the marijuana did indeed calm his chattering brain, and soon he felt a warm fuzziness descend upon him. Finally, after several more minutes, he spoke again, his eyes raised toward the heavens. "Do you think they'll ever actually send LISA to Europa?"

"Who knows? It won't be our LISA though," Emily said. "She's just a prototype."

"Wouldn't that be a sight to see, a robotic submersible we helped design exploring the depths of an alien planet."

Emily corrected him with a self-gratified snort. "Europa's a moon, not a planet. "Thought you would have known that, mister smarty pants."

"Are you questioning my knowledge of the cosmos?" Alex wanted to feel slighted, but he really didn't care, which he found strange. "I'll wager I can name more planets than you."

"I have no doubt. You can probably name more episodes of Star Trek than me, too."

"Of that, there is no question." He grinned and took another drag. "I am the king of the nerds."

"Dork." She feigned a punch to his arm.

Alex sidestepped the playful jab and was about to respond when he noticed that she wasn't smiling anymore. There was an expression of fear on her face. His own smile dropped away. "What's wrong?"

"Look." Emily was staring at the ground a few feet away, her eyes wide. "Over there."

Alex followed her gaze, his eyes coming to rest upon a peculiar indentation in a patch of soft earth near the trees. He caught his breath. It looked like a footprint, a wide oval depression with four spread toe marks ending in deeper holes, as if claws had dug into the soil. The print was large, at least twice the size of a human foot, and he could see the faint impression of scales. "Holy crap."

"There *is* something out here." Emily's voice was low now, as if she were afraid that whatever had left the footprint might hear her. "I knew it."

"Whatever left that print, it's big." Alex was in awe, while at the same time he felt a creeping sense of danger.

"We shouldn't stay here." Emily didn't sound stoned anymore. She turned to leave. "It's not safe."

"Hold up." Alex gripped her arm. "Don't tell the professor about this, okay?"

"What?" There was disbelief in Emily's voice. "Why?"

"If Professor Howard sees this, he'll never let divers go into the water," Alex said. "Let's keep this to ourselves, at least for now."

"There are more important things than a chunk of metal and wires."

"Please," Alex implored her. "If we can get LISA back, we might be able to record this thing, get video of it in its native habitat. Think of the publicity. That track is much too big for a regular alligator. Besides, alligators are ectothermic. They can't control their body heat. There's no way a gator is living down there in such a cold environment. We might be talking a new species here. Don't you want to be a part of that?"

"I want to keep us all safe."

"Give me twenty-four hours, that's all I ask. If it shows up in camp again, we'll tell the prof about the footprint," Alex said. "But if not, no harm done."

"I'm not making any promises." Emily whirled and walked away. "Are you coming or not?"

"Right behind you." Alex took one more look at the footprint and then turned to follow Emily. When he glanced toward the woods, and the darkness between the trees, a shiver ran up his spine. Was there something out there right now, watching them, waiting? He quickened his step, eager to be back on the other side of the clearing, and the relative safety of the camp.

But even when they reached the control tent, he still felt a nagging feeling of foreboding that refused to subside, and for a brief moment he wondered if maybe they should tell the professor what they had found. But then he thought of LISA, crippled and lifeless in the caves, and his resolve returned. After all, whatever was out there hadn't caused any trouble so far, except for disabling their submersible, so how dangerous could it really be?

TWENTY-TWO

DECKER SAT in the passenger seat of Bill Gibson's SUV and waited for his friend to talk. They had left the crime scene behind several minutes before and were now making their way back into town. Eventually, when the waterhole was nothing more than a speck in the rearview mirror, Bill finally spoke.

"This is some bad business, John. I've seen some stuff in my time, gator attacks and the like. They're rare, but they do happen. This one though, the ferocity, it feels too brutal for an animal."

"Are you asking for my advice now?" Decker glanced sideways. "Because if you are, I feel I should warn you, my professional opinion isn't much sought after in law enforcement circles these days."

"Am I asking you if a werewolf did this?" Bill said. "Well, I'm not. Don't take me the wrong way, but I just don't believe in werewolves and vampires and things that go bump in the night."

"I can't help what I witnessed," Decker said.

"I'm not disputing what you saw. You're a good cop. Level-headed. That's why I didn't question your version of events with that cult in New York. And I'm not questioning you now."

"I should have done the same in Wolf Haven as I did in New York."

"Made the official report a little easier on the eyes?" Bill said. "More mundane?"

"Right," Decker said. "Then I would have kept my job."

"Yeah." Bill glanced at Decker. "But I'm glad you're here, because I just can't get my head around this. The only thing big enough to go after a man in that fashion would be an alligator, but there's no way a gator could do so much damage to the truck. Maybe a bear, but the bite marks don't add up."

"Maybe the bear chased the guy, tore into his truck, and then a gator came along and finished the job."

"If you believe that, you're crazier than I thought." Bill chuckled, although there was not much mirth to it.

"All I'm saying is that there's usually a rational explanation. I think my experience in Wolf Haven was an anomaly."

"Then I can strike a pissed off witch from my list of suspects?"

"Probably. Still, something was pretty angry when it went after that truck. The top was peeled back like a sardine can."

"Yeah." Any levity had left Bill's voice. "Question is, am I looking at the start of a killing spree?"

"Only one way to know that," Decker said. "Time."

"I'd rather not wait until some other poor unfortunate gets themselves eaten."

"You might already have a second victim."

"The other diver?"

"There was only one body up there, and it seems pretty obvious that two people went into the water."

"You think the other diver is still underwater?" Bill asked. "That the original attack was in the aquifer?"

"It's a distinct possibility." Decker knew only too well that bodies had a habit of piling up. "It would explain the lack of another body, and if the second diver is still alive, why hasn't he shown up to report the attack?"

"Or in the hospital," Bill said. "But if another diver is down there, we'll never know. The aquifer is huge and mostly unexplored."

"And you don't want to send more men into an unmapped and hostile environment if there's a chance a wild animal might be using it as a hunting ground."

"Good point. Although I've never heard of anything living in the caves. I'm not even sure that it's possible."

"And I'd never heard of witches that could turn themselves into wolves, but it happened."

"If you're trying to cheer me up, you're doing a lousy job." Bill slowed the car as they came around a bend and crossed into Leland.

"I'm not trying to cheer you up," Decker said as Bill pulled into a reserved space outside of the sheriff's office. "In my experience things like this don't just go away on their own, supernatural or otherwise."

"I know that." Bill put the SUV in park and sat back. He rubbed his eyes. "If this gets out of control, I can call in the state police, but I'd hate to go that route unless there's no other choice. In the meantime, I'll talk to the forest service and see if they can shed any light on it. They spend all day in the woods; maybe they've seen something."

"If you want any help—"

"What, and ruin your vacation? No way," Bill said, opening his door. "It's not happening, buddy. I haven't even met Nancy yet. I'd hate to make her mad before we're even introduced."

"Well, the offer is there." Decker pulled his door open and stepped out. "You know where I am."

"We'll handle it." Bill closed the door and locked the truck. "You enjoy the Florida sun. If you take that job, you'll have all the adventure you can handle by the sound of it."

"I'm still not sure about the job."

"Well, don't take too long to come to a decision. Time waits for no man."

"So true," Decker agreed. "And like I said, the offer of help is there if you want it."

"I appreciate that." Bill leaned on his car. "Now get yourself back to the beach and forget about all this."

"Keep me posted?"

"Sure thing." Bill paused, collecting his thoughts, and then spoke again, his voice softer now. "Nice seeing you again, John."

"You too." Decker turned and walked to his car, the grisly sight at the waterhole fresh in his mind. He didn't know why, but he had a feeling that it was the start of something much bigger and that he wasn't finished with it. Not just yet.

TWENTY-THREE

WHEN DECKER ARRIVED BACK at the hotel, he made his way to the elevators and rode up to the eighth floor. When he entered the hotel room, Nancy was taking a shower. He sat near the window and waited until he heard the shower turn off. A moment later she exited the bathroom, wrapped in a white towel.

"Hey, you. How did it go?" She leaned in and kissed him. She smelled of coconuts and Aloe Vera. Wet hair clung to her shoulders in silky auburn strands. "Did you get the answers you were looking for?"

"I did," Decker replied.

"Good." Nancy smiled.

"Bill was on his way out when I arrived. He asked me to ride along," Decker said. "Some poor guy got himself chewed up. Nasty business. Reminded me of Wolf Haven."

"You're not saying—"

"Heavens, no. I don't think there's a werewolf running around the Florida woodlands. This is more likely an animal of the regular variety. Still, I think Bill might have his hands full on this one."

"And you?"

"What about me?"

"Come on, John. I know you well enough. Did you volunteer to help him?" Nancy pursed her lips.

"I'm not a cop anymore. Remember?" There was a tinge of regret in Decker's voice despite his best efforts to conceal it. "Even if I was, I don't have jurisdiction here."

"Doesn't mean you didn't offer." Nancy wiped a strand of sodden hair from her brow. "And besides, you don't need jurisdiction. The police hire specialists all the time."

"I know."

"So?"

"I might have said he could call me if he got in a bind. Only for advice though, nothing more. I don't want to get involved." He looked away, hoping Nancy would not notice his white lie. She often knew when he was fudging the truth. Today was no exception.

"I knew it. You want this." A look of satisfaction crossed Nancy's face. "That's why you need to take that job with the government. You're never going to be content on the sidelines, and you know it."

"I'm closer to a decision," Decker said. "Today helped. I just want to make sure I'm doing the right thing."

"You always do the right thing. That's what made you a good cop," Nancy said. She shrugged the towel off and walked to the suitcase laying open on the luggage rack. She rummaged through, pulling out underwear and a bright tee. "Now, why don't you get out of those sweaty clothes and take a shower. Then you can buy me dinner. I'm starving."

TWENTY-FOUR

AT 10PM THAT night Louie Walker settled onto his air mattress and closed his eyes. He would not sleep, he knew, but that was fine. He had been thinking all day, formulating a plan. He would wait until the others were well and truly asleep, and then make his move. By the time they woke he would be miles away, and they'd never find him. It was a good plan; not great, but sufficient. And best of all, he would finally be free of Frank. The man was insufferable.

Louie lay on his back and feigned sleep. When he heard Jerry start to snore, he opened his eyes and stared into the darkness. His gaze settled upon the ceiling, where a fat black spider prowled, barely visible in the weak moonlight filtering through the room's narrow window. The arachnid poked out of the rafters, then scuttled back in. Louie wasn't disturbed. On the contrary, he admired the eight-legged creature. It was singular in its intent, a deadly killer that struck without remorse. Louie could relate to that. He viewed himself in the same vein. Cold and calculating, unmoored from the tedious emotional responses that plagued the vast majority of the population. He did what had to be done without guilt or regret.

Now Louie sat up and glanced toward the other mattress

where Jerry lay on his side facing the other way, a blanket covering all but the top of his head. With all the stealth he could muster, Louie slipped out from under his own blanket and climbed to his feet.

A floorboard creaked under his weight.

Louie froze and waited, but Jerry only let out another rumble of a snore and shifted position. Satisfied that he hadn't roused his roommate, Louie tiptoed to the door, which hung half open on seized hinges. He peered out to make sure the corridor was empty, then stepped from the room. Everything was going to plan. Soon he would be free of Frank and the others for good.

But first came the hard part. Louie had no intention of leaving empty-handed. He'd worked for that loot, risked his life and freedom to take it, and he was damned if he was going to leave it for the others to share.

Louie took a deep breath.

Across the corridor, opposite his door, was the larger room where Liz slept. Along with her, stashed in what remained of the built-in closet, was the bag containing the stolen cash. All he had to do was get his hands on it. No small feat. Liz kept her shotgun within reach night and day, even when she was sleeping. It would be tucked next to her pillow, an easy grab should the need arise. If he woke her, he ran the very real risk of catching a load of buckshot in the chest.

Louie took a moment to steady his nerves. This would have to be done in complete silence if he wanted to make it out of the cabin alive. He pushed the fear down and controlled his breathing until it was shallow and quiet. Ready at last, he reached out and gripped the doorknob leading to the larger bedroom.

"What are you up to?"

The sudden voice made him jump. Louie spun around, his heart hammering in his chest. Frank stood in the space between the front room and the corridor, wearing nothing but a pair of sweat-soaked boxers. His beady eyes bore into Louie.

"Nothing." Louie whispered his reply. Did Frank know what he was up to? "I have to pee."

"Did you get confused?" There was a hard edge to Frank's voice. His hand was out of sight behind the doorframe. Was he holding a gun? "Bathroom's the far door on the left."

"I forgot, that's all." Louie tried to keep the fear from his voice. If Frank suspected he was trying to steal the money, it was all over. "I'm not used to this place yet, and it's dark."

"I guess you also forgot that the toilet doesn't work. No running water," Frank said. "You start using that thing and it'll smell the whole place up before you know it."

"Oh, right." He cursed himself for not thinking faster. They had been taking toilet breaks out in the woods since arriving at the cabin. Frank's appearance had flustered him, and Louie had said the first thing that came into his head. Regardless, he'd have to follow through now and pretend like he'd just forgotten.

"Off you go." Frank stepped aside to let Louie pass.

"Thanks," Louie mumbled, heading for the front door. All the while, he could feel Frank's suspicious gaze eating into his back. What if he told Liz? There would be hell to pay. She was even more paranoid than Frank.

Louie descended the porch steps and stopped beneath a large pine tree. The night was humid, but there was a cooling breeze whipping through the woods. It felt good after the stifling heat inside the cabin. And now that he was here, he discovered that he really did need to pee, which would only bolster his story if Frank was watching from behind one of the dark cabin windows. Even so, he would have to rethink his plan. He'd almost gotten caught tonight. He would need to be more careful next time.

TWENTY-FIVE

ALEX WOKE to the smell of fried eggs and bacon wafting into his tent. He sat up, rubbed the sleep from his eyes, and crawled from his sleeping bag. He hadn't slept well, his dreams haunted by a shadowy creature that pursued him through a dark and endless forest. More than once he was jolted from his sleep, only to lie in the blackness, unable to shake the image of that giant footprint they had discovered behind the storage area. Had he made the right decision, asking Emily to keep their discovery secret? He had no idea. What he did know was that the professor would probably evacuate the camp if he knew about the footprint, and that would doom LISA. That wouldn't happen, Alex thought, as he dressed and exited his tent. The diving gear would arrive today, and a rescue mission could be mounted just as soon as Professor Howard deemed it safe to do so.

Alex arrived at the mess tent just as the support crew were leaving. He stepped inside to find Emily and the professor deep in conversation. After loading a plate with bacon and maple sausage from the propane grill, and scrambled eggs from a pot on the burner, he took a seat.

"Glad you could join us." The professor fixed Alex with a stern stare.

"Sorry. I overslept." Alex scooped eggs into his mouth.

"For that you earn washing up duties, my boy."

"Really? I did it yesterday," Alex protested.

"You know the rules. We all pitch in with the cooking and cleaning. You weren't here to help prepare breakfast, so you can redeem yourself by clearing up."

"Fine." Alex knew better than to argue. "Any news on the diving gear?"

"It will be here this afternoon." The professor rubbed his hands on a napkin. "A courier is bringing it from town."

"And the university?" Alex asked. "Did you hear back about the video?"

"Not yet." Howard patted Alex on the shoulder. "If anyone needs me, I'll be in my tent. I have paperwork to catch up on. We might not have a sub right now, but that doesn't mean I can skip this expedition's more mundane tasks."

Alex nodded, watching the older man depart.

Emily hadn't said much so far. When she was sure Howard was gone, she finally spoke. "We need to talk about what we found yesterday."

"We did already," Alex said. He stood and poured a coffee from a metal urn, then returned to his seat. That was one thing about being on an expedition. There was always plenty of coffee. "We agreed to keep quiet about it, remember?"

"I've thought about it, and I'm not sure that's the best thing to do." Emily scooted close to him, her voice barely more than a whisper. "If there really is a dangerous animal out there it would be stupid not to mention what we found."

"There's nothing dangerous in the aquifer," Alex countered, trying to sound convincing.

"LISA would beg to differ."

"Whatever attacked the sub is probably long gone by now. We only saw one measly footprint, and it was heading toward the woods."

"That doesn't mean it didn't return." Emily took a deep

breath. "I saw something go into the water the other night. I'll bet it was whatever left that track."

"Emily—"

"You can't know what's down there."

"I agree, but if there is an animal down there, don't you want to be the first to discover it? A creature that size living in the aquifer would be unprecedented."

"At what cost?" Emily asked, her voice hoarse. "What if one of the divers comes in contact with it? What if someone gets killed?"

"No one is going to get killed," Alex replied, although Emily's fear was starting to rub off on him.

"We can't take that chance. You saw what it did to the sub."

"You're right." Alex sighed. "Of course. But the professor already knows there's an animal in the caves. He was there when the sub got attacked. He saw the video just like we did. All our footprint proves is that it can move around on land too."

"So why keep it from him?"

"Because if he sees that footprint, he might close us down. This isn't about whether it's safe to dive the aquifer anymore. It's about whether the professor thinks we're in jeopardy."

"And that's a valid concern," Emily said.

"We don't even know if the footprint is connected."

"You really believe that?"

"We've been fine so far. Nothing has attacked us, and my guess is that nothing will. Even if there is a large animal living in the aquifer, and that is a big if, there's no proof that it's dangerous to us," Alex said. "If we find more footprints or there's any indication that we aren't safe, then I'll tell the professor myself. You have my word. Until then, we need to keep this on the down low, just like we agreed."

"If it wasn't for the fact that I want LISA back as much as you, I'd be packing up my gear right now."

"I know," Alex said. "And I'd be right behind you. I'm not exactly the hardy outdoors type."

"I don't like keeping secrets," Emily replied. "If I think for one second that we're in any danger we tell the professor, and then we get the hell out of here, sub or no sub. Agreed?"

"Agreed," Alex said, and he meant it. Because despite his desire to recover LISA and make a discovery that would guarantee fame and fortune, a part of him just wanted to get as far away from the aquifer as possible.

TWENTY-SIX

BILL GIBSON PARKED a block from the station. It was a gorgeous morning. The sky was a deep azure blue with only the barest hint of wispy clouds, which no doubt would burn off as the day progressed. He was not, however, in a good mood. The park ranger's grisly find had left him feeling uneasy.

He adjusted the rim of his hat to shield his face from the sun and walked toward the Grounds and Grains Coffee Shop. It was a daily ritual. A tall iced coffee with two sugars and a dash of caramel flavoring, accompanied by an almond croissant. Not exactly healthy, but a small concession to his sweet tooth. Besides, the coffee shop was a good way to stay accessible to the local community, many of whom shared his predilection for caffeine and sugary treats.

"Morning, Sharon," Bill said, entering. He stepped up to the counter. On the way he tipped his hat at Johnson Tapper, who owned the scrap yard on the way out of town. The man nodded in acknowledgment, a wary look passing across his face, before grumbling a half-hearted greeting as he charted a course for the front door, coffee in hand.

Bill watched him go, keenly aware that the other man knew

he was being observed. Johnson Tapper had run afoul of the law on more than one occasion, mostly for drunk and disorderly, but twice he had been arrested for selling stolen car parts out of the junk yard. Both times he swore innocence, claiming that he'd pulled the parts from wrecked cars. The second time resulted in a conviction and a six-month suspended sentence. Bill wanted Tapper to know he was keeping an eye on him, which was why he watched him until Tapper climbed into his beat-up tow truck. Only then did he turn his attention back toward the counter.

"What will it be today, Sheriff Gibson?" Sharon asked while he was still halfway across the floor.

"Like you need to ask," Bill replied.

"Just checking, Sheriff," Sharon said. "Never know when you'll up and change your order on me."

"Not while you're still making those damned irresistible croissants." Bill leaned on the counter. "How long have I been coming in here, Sharon?

"How long have you been sheriff?"

"And yet you still won't call me Bill."

"You know very well why that is." Sharon's eyes twinkled with mischief as she prepared the coffee. "What if I need you in a professional capacity one day, and here we are on a first name basis. I wouldn't want folk to think you were giving me special treatment because we're friends and all."

"I assure you I'll be more than professional even if you use my first name. Scout's honor."

"I think I'll stick to sheriff, if that's all the same with you. Feels more civil somehow." She placed the coffee on the counter and slid a croissant into a brown paper bag. "That'll be three-fifty, with the law enforcement discount."

"It's a steal," Bill said. He pushed a five over the counter. He picked up the coffee and brown bag containing his pastry. Before he could leave, however, Sharon spoke again.

"Well, is it true?"

117

"Is what true?" Bill asked.

"There's a rumor going around town that some park ranger found a chewed-up body out in the woods. People are saying it was the work of a rogue gator."

"I can't possibly comment on that." Bill put on his most officious voice. "If there was an incident, and I'm not saying there was, mind you, it would be police business."

"At least until Reggie Wallace down at the Leland Gazette gets ahold of the story; then it will be front page news."

"Well, then, we'd better hope that doesn't happen." Bill made a move toward the exit. He juggled his coffee in one hand and was about to open the door when his radio squawked.

It was Halley Wills in dispatch.

He stopped and put his breakfast down on the nearest table. "Go, Halley. What you got?"

"Sorry to call before you even step foot in the station, Sheriff," Halley said. "I'd rather not interrupt your breakfast run with bad news, but we have a situation."

"Talk." Bill felt a tingle of apprehension. This town was too quiet for two lots of bad news in as many days.

"Motorist out on Route 30 came across a car in the woods. Looks like it went off the road."

"Dang it," Bill cursed. "Anyone hurt?"

"Two fatalities."

"Aw, hell."

"And it gets worse. The car belonged to a statie."

"A state trooper?" Bill grimaced. "Crap."

"That's not all. It's banged up to hell apparently. And the bodies look like…" Halley trailed off.

"Say it, Halley. What do the bodies look like?"

"They look like something ate them."

"I'm on it." Bill scooped up his coffee and pastry. He yanked on the door, then looked back at Sharon. "You didn't hear any of that. Am I right?"

Sharon shook her head. "Didn't hear a thing."

"Thank you." Bill left the coffee shop and hurried toward his car. When he got there, he placed the coffee on the hood, took out his phone, and made a call. He only hoped John Decker would answer.

TWENTY-SEVEN

"ARE YOU READY YET?" Decker lingered outside the bathroom door, buttoning a short-sleeved cotton shirt. "I'm starving."

"Just a minute." Nancy's voice came from beyond the closed door. "Putting makeup on."

"You look fine as you are," Decker said, partly because his stomach was rumbling and he wanted breakfast, and also because he didn't think she needed makeup. She was already beautiful as she was. "Let's go."

"I'm on vacation. You don't need to rush me." The door opened, and Nancy stepped out wearing a light summer dress that ended just below the knees. It clung to her body, the thin cotton fabric accentuating her curves.

Decker, as usual, was taken aback by the way she looked. He grinned. "Wow. You're one hot piece of—"

"Can it, mister." Nancy cut him off. She laughed and put her arms around his neck and kissed him. "You could try to be a little more romantic."

"Sorry." Decker slid his arms around her waist and looked into her eyes. "I shall do my best to be the gentleman you expect."

"That's better." Nancy laughed as they left the hotel room.

They rode down to the lobby in silence. On the floor below, a family stepped into the elevator. Father, mother and two pre-teens, a boy and a girl. The kids spoke to each other in hushed whispers. The parents kept their eyes straight ahead, as if acknowledging Nancy and Decker would open them up to some kind of forced social interaction. It was strange, Decker noted, how people didn't like to speak in such situations. As if it was an invasion of personal space.

Decker watched the kids chatter back and forth, and somewhere deep inside, he felt a pang of regret that he'd never taken the time to have children of his own. Part of this was a fear that he would turn out like his father, who had retreated into alcohol and insanity after his mother's death. But not all of it. There was also Nancy. He'd abandoned her all those years ago in Wolf Haven, left her there while he ran from his demons under the guise of pursuing a career in the big city. He knew he'd hurt her back then. Now, all these years later, she was by his side anyway. Her love had never really faded, and neither had his. If he had stayed in Wolf Haven, things would have been different. Taylor would have been his daughter, not the child of some jerk who couldn't even be bothered to stick around and raise the kid.

But none of that mattered. He'd made his decisions, and he couldn't undo them. As the elevator door swished open, he stepped out, then turned to Nancy, gripped by a sudden urge to tell her how sorry he was for all the mistakes he'd made. And then, before he could say anything, his phone rang.

It was Bill Gibson. A feeling of dread enveloped him. Bill would not be calling unless something was very wrong.

"Are you going to answer that?" Nancy asked. "It might be important."

"Sure." Her words snapped him out of his fugue, and he accepted the call. Bill's familiar voice filled his ear. Decker listened to what he had to say, and then hung up, slipping the phone back in his pocket.

He turned to Nancy. "I have to go back to Leland."

"What?" She looked confused. "Why?"

"There's been another attack," Decker said. "Bill wants my advice."

"When?"

"Right now," Decker said. "I'm so sorry."

"Don't be," Nancy replied. "But you're not going alone."

"I don't think that's a good idea." Decker shook his head.

"Don't argue with me," Nancy said, her eyes narrowing. "I'm coming."

"Wouldn't you rather stay here and enjoy the hotel pool?" Decker said. "I don't want to ruin your vacation."

"And sitting here alone, worrying about you the whole time, wouldn't ruin it?" Nancy replied. "I'm coming along, and that's all there is to it. Besides, I might be useful. You're not the only one who has experience with monsters. That is what you think this is, right?"

"Not a werewolf, but something out of the ordinary," Decker admitted.

"Then what are we waiting for?" Nancy was already turning back toward the elevators. "We'll pack an overnight bag and grab some food along the way."

Decker wavered, wishing he could dissuade her, but then he let out an exasperated sigh and hurried to catch up. Whatever was waiting in Leland, they would deal with it together.

TWENTY-EIGHT

THE CABIN WAS STIFLING HOT, the air thick and humid. Frank Denning wiped a bead of sweat from his forehead and wished he was anywhere else on the face of the planet. Florida was not a pleasant place to be without modern comforts such as air conditioning, which was why most of the other structures in the state possessed it, except for their decrepit hunting cabin.

"I can barely breathe." Louie fanned himself with an old magazine he'd found in one of the bedrooms. The pages were tattered, but it still served as a moderately passable way to move some air. "Feels like a sauna."

"Better than prison." Frank glanced up from his book.

"I don't know how you can sit there reading in this heat," Louie said.

"What else am I going to do?" Frank replied, turning his attention to the book again.

"I wish we had internet to pass the time. A TV would be nice. I'd even take a radio." Jerry was lying on his back, sprawled across an air mattress. "I'm not sure how long I can put up with this."

"For as long as I say you do." Liz appeared from the rear of the cabin. "Speaking of which, we have a problem."

"What now?" Louie looked up.

"The van," Liz said. "The cops are looking for it."

"That's not possible," Frank said. "No one even knows the van is missing yet."

"Yeah, well, Jerry's cousin didn't bother to wait before reporting it stolen. Worse, the cops have cell phone footage of us fleeing the scene. Apparently, some kid on a bus recorded the whole thing. Once they figured out Jerry was in that car, they connected the stolen van to the robbery."

"Crap." Frank had looked right up at the kid, saw him point the phone in their direction. That meant the cops had not only connected Jerry to the heist, but him too. Suddenly another stint in prison looked likely. "I thought you said the police had no idea who robbed the bank."

"That's what the news said yesterday. I guess the cops weren't sharing their info." Liz stomped into the middle of the room, her cell phone in one hand. She held up the phone. "Every news site from here to Timbuktu is carrying the story."

"Relax." Jerry was still on the mattress. He seemed unconcerned by this new development. "Big deal. They know we took the van. They still don't know where we are."

"They know enough to be looking in Florida," Liz said. "Apparently we were picked up on traffic cams."

"We should have stuck to back roads," Louie said. "No cameras there."

"It would have taken hours longer," Liz replied. "Besides, if Jerry's cousin had waited to report the van stolen, like he was supposed to, the cops wouldn't have figured it out. They wouldn't expend resources searching all sorts of CCTV footage for a stolen van, but a bank robbery, that's a whole other ball game. And don't forget that they only connected the van to us because of that damned kid capturing Jerry's ugly mug on video."

"Shit." Frank stood and paced. "Our faces are probably all over the news. What are we going to do now?"

"We have to get rid of the van." Liz glanced toward the front door. "It's a liability. If someone sees it here, they'll lead the police right to us."

"Who's gonna see it?" Louie asked. "We're in the middle of the woods."

Liz shrugged. "A hunter. Park ranger. Some guy out walking his dog. You want to take that chance?"

"Liz is right," Frank agreed.

"And what if we need to leave in a hurry. How are we going to do that without wheels?"

"That van is slower than molasses. We wouldn't last five minutes in a chase." Frank peered out of the window toward the stolen vehicle stashed under a rambling oak. "Better to ditch it. There's only one road in or out of this place anyway. The van won't be worth crap to us if the cops come up here. Our best chance of escape would be out the back and through the woods."

Louie started to protest. "I still think—"

Liz cut him off. "This isn't up for debate. Frank, you want to take care of it?"

"Sure thing, boss," Frank said. "Piece of cake."

"You're going to let him drive away with the van, just like that?" Louie said.

"Yeah. Just like that," Liz said. "You got a better idea?"

"No." Louie shuffled his feet, looked down at the floor. "But what if he keeps driving, doesn't come back? What if he gets caught?"

"I'm not going to get caught," Frank said.

"That's right." Liz nodded. "And as for not coming back, I trust Frank."

"Which is more than we can say about you." Frank eyed Louie.

"Go to hell." Louie took a step forward.

"That's enough, boys." Liz placed herself between the two

men. "Frank will come back. Like I said, I trust him. And anyway, he has no choice if he wants his share of the cash." She turned to Frank. "You want to take someone with you?"

"No." Frank shook his head. "I'll be faster alone."

"Okay," Liz said. She reached into her pocket and tossed the keys in Frank's direction. "Here you go."

He snatched the keys from the air. "Give me ten minutes, and then I'm out of here."

TWENTY-NINE

IT TOOK an hour to reach Leland. Decker barely spoke on the journey, his face stoic, eyes focused forward. But when they arrived at the coordinates Bill Gibson had given them, a quiet out of the way road a few miles out of town, he spoke up.

"Are you absolutely sure you want to do this?"

"I think they need you," Nancy replied. Ahead of them the road was blocked by a throng of police cars, two fire trucks, and paramedics. "It looks bad."

"Sure does." Decker pulled up and parked behind an idling fire truck.

They had barely left the car when Bill Gibson approached. He looked haunted and weary.

"John," Bill said, offering a hand in greeting. "I'm glad you're here."

"What's going on?" Decker shook his hand.

"It's a mess." Bill glanced toward Nancy, hesitating to talk further.

"Don't worry," Decker said. "She's tough."

"Yeah." Bill nodded. "Even so, I'd rather not go into detail here. I think you should see for yourself."

"Okay," Decker said. He turned to Nancy. "Stay here?"

Nancy nodded.

"I won't be long." Decker gave her a peck on the cheek and then followed Bill past the police units and fire trucks.

"It's over here, in the woods," Bill said, scrambling across a roadside drainage ditch. "Car went off the road and flipped, ended up wrapped around a boulder."

"I thought you said it was an animal attack?" Decker pushed through thick undergrowth. When he looked down, his feet were covered in beggar's ticks, small green seeds that stuck to everything they encountered.

"It is. The crash appears to be secondary to the attack."

"Are you saying that this animal actually caused the accident?"

"It would appear so," Bill replied. "You'll see."

They were coming up on the vehicle now. As they neared the crash site, Decker saw with some surprise that it wasn't just any vehicle. There, ahead of them, was an upside-down police cruiser. Judging by the path cut through the foliage, it appeared to have tumbled off the road and flipped onto its roof after contacting a large boulder. But it was the victims that really shocked him.

Laying a few feet from the car were the remains of not one but two people. The bodies were torn up. In fact, they looked like they had been put through a mangle. The closest of the two, whom Decker identified as a state trooper by the remains of his uniform, was missing an arm and part of his upper torso. His head was also gone, leaving behind a bloody, ragged stump. The other body hadn't fared much better.

"Holy crap." Decker came to a halt.

"It's a sight, huh." Bill surveyed the crash scene. "We figure the initial attack took place up on the road, and then the attacker pursued the vehicle in here and dragged the victims out to finish the job."

"I don't suppose you have any witnesses?"

"Nope. This stretch of road is pretty quiet. No one even noticed the wreck until this morning."

"Shame."

"Yeah." Bill folded his arms. "The forensics guys who examined the vehicle think the initial damage was caused by something ramming the car. That's why it left the road."

"You think there's an animal out here big enough to chase down a moving vehicle and force it off the road?"

"The evidence would appear to suggest just such a scenario." Bill didn't sound happy. "What that could be... your guess is as good as mine."

"I don't have a clue." Decker's eyes roamed over the scene, at the torn-up bodies, the battered cruiser. "It would have to be mighty big to do this."

"We have bears, gators, and even the occasional Florida panther," Bill said. "But I just don't see any of those animals being capable of this."

"Panthers and alligators wouldn't have the capacity to attack a moving car," Decker surmised. "A bear would have the strength, but neither the speed nor inclination. And it would maul its victims, but not eat them."

"Yup. That's what I figure." Bill sounded desperate. "When I consider the last attack, the diver in the truck, I can only think of one logical conclusion."

"There's a large, unknown predator roaming these woods," Decker said. "Something fast and deadly, with a bad temper."

"Bingo." Bill sighed. "I think I need some help on this, John."

"Are you asking for my assistance?"

"That's exactly what I'm doing," Bill replied. "We have at least three victims. Four if you count the missing second diver. I'm certain there will be more attacks. These things don't just go away. It would be nice to have someone on the team who's dealt with this kind of situation before."

"I'm not sure that a werewolf can be considered a similar situation."

"I am," Bill said. "I'm not saying this here is a werewolf. But it is out of the ordinary, and that seems to be your shtick in recent times."

"It does indeed," Decker replied ruefully.

"Well, are you in?"

"He is." Nancy's voice piped up.

Decker turned to find her standing behind him. "I thought I told you to stay put."

"I'm your girlfriend, not your deputy. I don't take orders."

"Figures." Decker knew when he was beaten. "How long were you standing there?"

"Long enough." Nancy pushed her hands into her pockets. "I guess we'll be needing a place to stay."

"Already done," Bill said. "The Southern Winds Guesthouse has a room ready and waiting. I figured you'd say yes and took the liberty. The Leland Sheriff's Department is picking up the tab."

"Am I that obvious?" Decker asked.

"I could tell you were itching to get involved when we rode together yesterday."

"You could, huh?"

"Absolutely." Bill put a hand on Decker's back. "Why don't you go and get checked in, and we'll get together later to figure this out." Then, as an afterthought, Bill said, "Grab a bite to eat too. You must be starving. The Grounds and Grains has good pastries. If you're in the mood for something heartier, the Sunshine Diner on Route 10 does a mean breakfast steak. Just tell them to bill the department. It's on me."

"Sure thing," Decker said, but after seeing those mangled bodies, he wasn't sure he could even look at a steak, let alone eat one.

THIRTY

LOUIE WALKER STOOD on the front porch and watched Frank drive away in the plumber's van. He cursed under his breath. Without wheels it would be that much harder to make his escape when the time came. Hiking out of the woods on foot did not appeal to him. But the van was hot, so perhaps it was for the best. Besides, he could still get a good head start on the others, even without wheels.

There was still one problem though. The last time he'd tried to steal the cash and slip out unnoticed, Frank had been there to get in the way. Good old reliable Frank. The man was insufferable. Worse, Louie wondered if Frank somehow knew what he was up to or at least suspected. Going out the front door was not an option, that much was clear. With Frank bedding down in the front room, Louie didn't stand a chance of escaping unnoticed. Likewise, getting his hands on the loot.

There had to be a better way.

And then a thought struck him.

Louie turned back to the cabin and slipped inside. Jerry was sprawled out on Frank's air mattress, dozing now. Liz had her eyes glued to the burn phone, no doubt trolling the internet for any tidbit of information regarding the robbery. She was thorough, Louie had to give her that. If anyone could evade the police and get them out of this without a ten-year stretch, it was her. Except that Frank and Jerry's mug shots were probably in the hands of every police department from Key West to Atlanta. All thanks to that damned kid on the bus and his cell phone. If Frank got nabbed, he would give up Louie in a heartbeat. The man hated him. Louie wasn't sticking around for that.

He lingered a moment in the front room, trying to look casual, then he sauntered off toward the back bedrooms. But he didn't stop there. He continued on to the wrecked bathroom. After a quick glance to make sure no one was paying any attention, Louie ducked inside.

The bathroom was small, with only a toilet and sink. Neither one worked. The sink wasn't even standing upright anymore. It had dropped down through a patch of rotten floorboards and now rested on the dirt underneath the cabin. Louie grinned. The hole was big enough to scramble through. He wouldn't have to go out the front after all.

But that still left the cash. The whole plan was pointless if he couldn't get his hands on the money. He had an idea on that score too. Louie knelt down and ran his hands over the wall separating the bathroom from the master bedroom, where Liz slept. He probed gently, feeling the rough wooden boards under his palms, until he found what he was looking for.

Satisfied, Louie straightened up again and padded from the bathroom back toward the main living area. No one had noticed his excursion. Jerry still slept, and Liz didn't even look up when he entered. Perfect. Tonight, he would put his plan into action, and by the time they realized he was gone, it would be too late.

THIRTY-ONE

PROFESSOR DANIEL HOWARD stood behind Alex, watching the younger man tap away on his keyboard.

"Do we have a connection yet?"

"Don't be so impatient." Emily, standing next to him, placed a reassuring hand on his arm. "We're in the middle of the woods. You can't expect perfect internet."

"Actually, the signal is pretty strong, considering," Alex replied.

Behind them, on the north side of the clearing, was a VSAT dish antenna connected to a government telecommunications satellite in geostationary orbit. It wasn't as stable as a wired fiber-optic network, but it was still surprisingly good. "I uploaded a bunch of data to the servers this morning, and I was getting 2mbps and higher for most of the transfer. Not bad."

"Well, hurry up then." Howard pushed his hands into his trouser pockets and glanced toward the large screen above the desk.

"I'm doing my best," Alex said, then looked up as the screen flickered and a man's face appeared. "Voila!"

"Professor Howard?" the man on the screen said in a clipped

British accent. "I'm Professor Jonathon Gladwell with the biology department. I must say, it's awfully nice to meet you. I've heard so much."

"Pleased to make your acquaintance, Professor Gladwell," Howard said. "You reviewed the footage we sent you?"

"I did." Gladwell nodded. "I must admit, I've never seen anything quite like it before. At first, I thought I was looking at a garden variety alligator, which in itself would be unusual, considering the environment in which you say the animal was filmed, but when I looked closer, it didn't make sense. No, not at all."

"You don't think the creature on our footage is a gator?" Emily took a step closer to the monitor. She glanced at the webcam positioned on top, its lens pointed upward toward them.

"I don't," Gladwell replied. "The features are not consistent with the American alligator. For one thing, the snout is long and narrow, while Alligator Mississippiensis has a wide snout. Also, the teeth are wrong. I took the liberty of showing the video to a colleague in the paleontology department and he agreed."

"Paleontology?" Emily furrowed her brow. "Why?"

"I think it would be best if I show you. This is a still image I pulled from your video." The screen split to display Gladwell on one side and an image of the creature's gaping mouth on the other. "This is the best angle I could get of the jaws. Note how the premaxillary teeth are recurved, slender, and serrated. The posterior process is much longer than a modern crocodylian. Now we come to the maxillary teeth, which are sharp and finely serrated, like convex steak knives. This isn't the case with modern crocodylians, but is consistent with older, extinct specimens. There are other features that better represent a creature from the fossil record too, but I won't go into those here for the sake of brevity. They're all in the report I've emailed you. Suffice to say, this is a most unusual animal."

"Surely you're not suggesting that we've discovered a living example of an extinct crocodile, "Emily said. "Nothing that ancient could still be around, It's impossible."

"On the contrary." Gladwell raised an eyebrow. "There are known cases of extinct animals being rediscovered. The Coelacanth is a good example. A fish thought to have died out sixty-five million years ago. A specimen was found off the South African coast in 1938. It caused quite a stir at the time."

"A fish?" Emily said. "That hardly compares with something of this size."

"The Coelacanth grows pretty big, upwards of six feet. Not bad for something thought to be a fossil."

"But we're not talking the deep ocean here," Howard said. "This is Florida."

"Right you are. But the aquifer is mostly unexplored. Who knows how deep those caves go? And don't forget, the aquifer extends right under the Gulf of Mexico and even the Atlantic in some places. Who's to say there aren't openings where these animals can come and go from the ocean?"

"I still don't buy it," Emily said. "There can't possibly be an extinct crocodilian roaming around Central Florida."

"There's one way to find out," Gladwell replied.

"What's that?"

"Get more footage of this beast. Preferably the entire shebang. Tip to tail."

"That might be easier said than done," Alex said.

"Really? I thought you had a fancy submersible at your disposal. What better way to prove its worth than to rediscover a lost species?"

"If only it were that simple—"

"We do have a submersible." Howard cut in. He glared at Alex. "But I'm not sure it falls within our mission parameters."

"That's a shame," Gladwell said. "If you do happen to get more footage, send it along; I'd love to explore this further."

"We'll do that, Professor," Emily agreed.

"And now, if you don't mind, I have a class to teach," Gladwell said.

"Not at all. You've been most helpful," Howard replied a moment before the screen went dark.

THIRTY-TWO

FRANK DENNING UNLOADED the gas cans from the rear of the van. Having the gasoline on hand was fortuitous, even though it had seemed like a wasted effort when they discovered the cabin's missing generator. But sometimes things just work out, and Frank was pleased to have an easy way to dispose of the stolen vehicle. Not that he was looking forward to the six-mile hike back to the cabin. He had driven around for almost an hour looking for a good spot to dump the Transit, and eventually decided on a narrow, out of the way dirt road surrounded by dense woodland.

Frank uncapped the first container and approached the van's cab, splashing the clear, pungent liquid inside, making sure to thoroughly soak the seats, steering wheel, and dash. It would not do to leave fingerprints or fibers that could definitively tie the vehicle to Frank. Fire was a good eradicator of such things. He dumped the last of the gasoline and threw the empty container inside before retrieving a second gas can and dousing the exterior of the vehicle. Next he opened the rear doors and sprinkled gasoline throughout. Satisfied that the entire van was drenched, he placed the remaining full can on the driver's seat for good measure. This would, hopefully, explode when the flames reached it, all but guaranteeing no clues would be left behind.

Next he took a bundle of rags that he'd found in the rear of the van and wadded them up, lighting one end with a match before tossing the burning bundle into the cab.

At first, nothing happened, and Frank wondered if he'd done something wrong. This was his first time torching a vehicle. It looked easy in the movies, but in practice it was difficult. He wondered what he would do if the van wouldn't catch fire, but then a bright orange glow lit up the cab, followed by hungry, licking flames.

Thick black smoke laced with lighter white wisps, was curling up now, pirouetting skyward on a hot updraft. The unpleasant smell of burning rubber permeated the air.

Frank took a step backward, then another, suddenly aware of the possibility that the van's gas tank might blow. He didn't want to be anywhere nearby when that happened. He retreated down the same dirt trail he'd driven in on, following it until the van was out of sight. At a safe distance, he glanced back, noting how the plume of acrid smoke was barely visible above the trees. Further away, beyond the woods, the smoke would be much more obvious, but tracing its source in such a remote location would be almost impossible. He felt a surge of satisfaction. This was a job well done. Now all he had to do was return to the cabin without being seen.

Frank walked for forty minutes, following the trail. Up ahead was the main road. It was lightly used, and he had seen only a few cars speeding in the other direction while he was looking for a good spot to dump the van. He would have preferred to wait until that evening and ditch the van under cover of darkness, but that would make returning to the cabin impossible until dawn, and he had no desire to spend a night alone in the woods. Regardless, the risk of the van being recognized was low, and even if one of the vehicles he had passed did call the cops, the van would be long gone before they responded.

But being on foot was another matter. People would certainly remember a lone figure walking out here so far from civilization, and Frank didn't look like a hiker. His clothes were all wrong, and even though he wore a small backpack containing bottles of water, he did not have a sleeping bag or tent. This was why, while the road was still a little way off, Frank stepped off the trail into the woods.

The going was slower now. The ground was rough and clogged with underbrush. Not only that, but the dense foliage soon became disorienting, and even though Frank had a good sense of direction, he found himself second guessing the route back to the cabin.

Despite this, he pressed on, keeping parallel to the road until it veered off toward a small town several miles distant. He delved deeper into the woods, hoping to reach the trail leading to the cabin before dusk. It was then, after another half an hour of walking, that he heard voices. The sounds were indistinct. He couldn't make out actual words, but he knew it was not his own companions. He was still at least three miles from the cabin. Still, if someone was out here, this close to their hideout, it could mean trouble.

He stopped and listened.

The voices were off to his right where the land rose steadily to a small ridge.

Frank cursed under his breath.

It was most likely backpackers or campers enjoying the woodlands, but that didn't matter. If someone stumbled across the cabin, who knew what would happen? Liz was already jumpy, and she kept her shotgun close at hand. The last thing Frank needed was a couple of dead bodies to take care of. With a grunt of frustration, he changed course and headed toward the sounds, keeping low to avoid being spotted. He reached the crest of the rise, flattened himself out on the ground, and peered over.

The voices did not belong to either hikers or campers.

Instead, Frank saw a wide clearing with a glistening pool of water in the middle. Several tents were set up on one side, two of them bigger than the others. The furthest of the two big tents had its sides drawn up and tied to reveal what looked like a canteen complete with a propane range and seating for several people. Equipment and crates lined the shore. A track crane sat a few feet from the water, a thick sling hanging from its boom.

At first, he didn't see any signs of life, but then an older gentleman appeared from within the largest of the tents, followed by a younger man and a slim, attractive woman wearing tight jeans and a white shirt. They were deep in conversation, heading toward the canteen tent, but even so, Frank ducked low as they passed.

When he looked up again, they were gone, and the canvas sides of the canteen tent had been dropped to enclose the area, no doubt in an effort to keep mosquitos at bay.

He briefly harbored the idea of slipping from his hiding place and sneaking into the clearing for a closer look, but then he spotted a burly man loitering near the crane with a cigarette in his hand. But it was what Frank saw behind the man that made him smile. There, parked in the shade at the edge of the clearing, under the trees, were three quad-cab trucks.

Frank watched for a few more minutes, assessing the situation, and then as silently as he'd arrived, he retreated, giving the clearing a wide berth as he resumed his trek back to the cabin.

THIRTY-THREE

THIRTEEN-YEAR-OLD MARCUS FENTON hurried along the sidewalk in the direction of his house in the Thousand Pines subdivision, legs pumping as fast as they possibly could. The Leland First Baptist had wrapped up Sunday morning service fifteen minutes ago. Usually, he would be overjoyed to be released to his own devices, especially on a day like this, when his mother went straight from church to her double shift at Carter's Convenience Store in Collierville, two towns over. She pulled a double at least twice a week and was never home much before 9PM. That meant he had pretty much the whole day and evening to do as he pleased. Today, though, was different. He had responsibilities.

"Hold up." Barry Choy, his best friend, was struggling to keep up, thanks to his heavy frame and an aversion to anything that might resemble physical exercise. "What's the big hurry?"

"I have to walk Mister Licks." Marcus reached the corner of Willard and Main. He changed direction, turning onto the side street without missing a step. "If I don't take him out soon, he'll take a crap on the living room carpet."

"You still have that dog at your house?" Barry was winded, his breath coming in short, rasping gasps.

141

"Aunt Bethany is going to be away for a few more weeks, so lucky us, we get the dog."

"Do we have to run though?" Barry asked. He was losing steam. "I mean, seriously."

"Like I said, the stupid thing is on a timer. It poops at noon every day. Doesn't matter where or on what."

"Damn. This I've gotta see." Barry sniggered despite the pain needling his right side when he drew breath.

"It's not funny. Mom will kill me if that dog makes a mess inside again." Marcus slowed as they approached the house. He swung the gate wide and hurried to the front door, lifting a terracotta flowerpot and retrieving the front door key. He turned to Barry. "Wait here."

"You won't get any arguments out of me." Barry flopped down onto the front steps, gasping for breath. He watched his friend disappear inside and leaned back with his elbows on the next step up.

A dog barked, the sound high pitched and excited. Then Marcus reappeared with a scruffy brown mutt in tow. He wrestled the animal down the steps and paused when he reached Barry. "Say hello to Mister Licks."

The dog flicked its tongue out and ran it down Barry's face. He recoiled and waved at the slobbering dog. "Yuck. Get that thing away from me."

"He's just being friendly."

"Well, he can be friendly on someone else's face. Guess we know how it got its name." Barry stood and hopped down the steps. "What are you feeding him anyway? His breath smells like days old cabbage."

"Dunno. Mom handles that stuff." Marcus shrugged. "Some kind of hard brown pebbles. She gets them at work with her discount. They don't look very appealing."

"Convenience store dog food." Barry opened the gate and waited for Marcus to exit with Mister Licks. "Your dog sure lives the high life."

"I told you, he's not my dog."

"Does he know that?" Barry glanced down at the mutt tearing in circles around his friend's legs, the leash coiling and threatening to trip him on each pass. "So where is your Aunt Bethany anyhow?"

"Not sure. Mom said she's on vacation, but I heard them talking on the phone. She's really in some sort of hospital. Something about getting off the sauce."

"Sauce. I don't get it. Is she sick?"

"I don't think so." Marcus eased up when they reached Main Street. He reigned the dog in and stopped. "Where do you want to go? The park?"

"Nah. There's a junior league game this afternoon. Todd Jenkins might be there."

"So?" Marcus said.

"He got in trouble for cheating on a test, and he thinks I squealed on him."

"But you didn't, right?"

"Do I look like I'm nuts? Of course not. That won't stop him practicing his swing with my head though."

"You think of somewhere then."

"I know where we can go." Barry took off along Main. "Follow me."

"Where?"

"You'll see." Barry led them along Main until they were almost out of town and then turned right onto a winding dead-end road that terminated in a pair of formidable metal gates, beyond which stretched the town's only junk yard. A narrow path led off to the left, skirting the perimeter of the junk yard. Rusting hulks of old cars and trucks loomed over a chain link fence topped with wicked-looking barbed wire. A tow truck sat idle near a portable cabin in the middle of the yard, a large iron hook hanging from a davit affixed to the rear bed.

Marcus paused when he reached the path, Mister Licks waiting at his side, tongue out and panting.

Barry turned and motioned. "Come on. What are you waiting for?"

"I don't like this place. It gives me the creeps."

"It's fine," Barry said. "Hurry up."

Marcus hesitated a moment longer, then followed his friend. The dog raced forward, pulling him along, and soon they were at the far corner of the junk yard where the path took a turn to the right and followed the back fence.

Marcus relaxed now. Soon the wrecker's yard would be behind them. But then, from somewhere between the gutted cars he heard a bark, low and guttural. Mister Licks let out a returning woof, but then fell silent when the answer came back as a menacing growl.

"That dog can't get out, right?" Marcus peered through the fence, nervous.

"Nah. I don't think so. Besides, my dad says it's pretty much blind. No good at guarding anything."

"Still has teeth though." Marcus hurried after his friend, pulling Mister Licks along as fast as he could. Beyond the wrecker's yard the landscape fell away into dense woodland. He looked around, nervous. "We shouldn't be here."

"Says who?" Barry was heading for a narrow trail barely discernable between the trees.

"Says that." Marcus pointed to a plastic sign fixed atop a leaning metal post.

Ricketts Pond.
Closed Due to Algae Bloom.
No Access Beyond This Point.

Barry snorted. "That's nothing. We're not swimming anyway."

"I don't know. What if we get caught?"

"No one's going to catch us." Barry pushed ahead toward an opening in the trees, beyond which a circle of cool blue water shone in the afternoon light. "Besides, it means we'll have the place to ourselves."

"I guess," Marcus said, following Barry toward the pond, which was, in reality, a spring.

The water, cool and deep, connected to a myriad of other springs in the area by the caves of the aquifer system. There were probably near on a hundred such water holes in the surrounding landscape, and many more across the state. Marcus could vaguely remember coming up here with his mother years ago. Back then, there would have been scores of kids swimming on a lazy Sunday or diving off the far shore where the land rose higher. Not now though. The clearing was empty, thanks to the algae bloom. A car tire, attached to a low hanging branch by a length of fraying rope, turned lazily in the breeze. Gnats hung in the air. A pair of dragonflies darted in and out of the trees, weaving around each other in a playful dance.

"There you go, boy." Marcus leaned down and unclipped the dog's leash. The animal gave a snort of pleasure and bounded off.

"Should you let him run free like that?" Barry watched the dog tear around the clearing and disappear into the underbrush on the other side of the pond.

"He's fine. He'll come back." Marcus picked up a pebble and threw it toward the water with practiced ease. It hit flat and skipped several times before plopping into the pond and sinking.

Barry found a stone and flicked it with his wrist. Instead of bouncing, the pebble hit with a plunk and disappeared. "Dammit."

"You suck." Marcus found another flat stone and repeated his feat, watching it skip three times. "See. Nothing to it."

"Not fair," Barry protested. "Your stone was better than mine."

"It's just a stone. There's plenty more. I can't help it if you pick lousy pebbles."

"This is boring." Barry kicked the dirt. "There must be something better to do."

"We could go back to my house and watch TV."

"Or…" Barry had a grin on his face, "we could go over to Coulson Street. I bet Sharon will be there. She always swims when it's hot."

"She's never there this early." Marcus shook his head. Coulson Street was close to his home. And Sharon's house bordered the woods, which was perfect. They could peek through the perimeter fence without being seen. "She doesn't get off work at the coffee shop until later in the afternoon. You know that."

"Yeah."

"We could go this evening. My mom won't leave work until nine. As long as I'm back before her, it'll be fine."

"Can't do it," Barry said, a look of disappointment on his face. "Mom said I have to do my chores this afternoon, and then I have homework."

"Rats." Marcus liked peeking on Sharon Roberts. She was a friend of his mom's, but that didn't matter. She had a rocking body and liked to swim in the skimpiest of bikinis, which she did almost every afternoon after work in the summer. He fought back his frustration. And then he had an idea. "Wait."

"What?"

"You can tell your mom that we need to study. She'll believe that."

"I don't know. She's pretty good at spotting a lie."

"It'll work. I guarantee," Marcus said. "I can even call my mom at work and tell her we have a big test tomorrow at school. I'll ask her to call your mom. It'll be easy."

"We're not really going to study though, right?"

"No." Marcus rolled his eyes. "Of course not. We're going to Coulson Street. You can be such an idiot at times."

"It might work," Barry conceded.

"It has to," Marcus said, already anticipating the evening's adventure.

Barry, for his part, seemed similarly distracted. A silence descended upon them, both boys lost in thought, a quietness broken a few minutes later by a frightened squeal, animalistic and high pitched, from somewhere within the woods.

"W-w-what was that?" Barry asked, the words coming out as a stutter, something he only did when he was either very excited or very scared.

"I don't know." Marcus looked around, nervous. Suddenly, being up at the pond, just the two of them, didn't seem like such a good idea. "It sounded like a dog."

"M-Mister Licks?" Barry's voice trembled.

"I hope not." Marcus took a step forward.

Barry shot an arm out and grabbed him. "What are you doing?"

"What do you think I'm doing?" Marcus cupped his hands and called out as loud as he could. "Here, boy. Come on back."

"Don't do that."

"We have to find Mister Licks. What if he's hurt?" Marcus said. He called out again, louder this time.

"What if it wasn't Mister Licks that made that noise?" Barry shuffled from foot to foot. He glanced back at the trail, clearly eager to leave. "Have you thought of that?"

"We still need to find him." Marcus examined the clearing, hoping the dog would appear, but there was no sign of Mister Licks.

"I'm g-going back," Barry stuttered. "I don't want to b-be here anymore."

"Don't be such a wuss," Marcus said. "I'm going to look for him, and you're coming with me."

"Like h-hell I am."

"Suit yourself." Marcus started toward the trees. He skirted the circle of shimmering water until he was on the other side of the clearing. When he glanced back, Barry was standing there, watching him. Marcus hesitated a moment, and then stepped into the woods.

It was dark and gloomy under the canopy of trees. A fat gray squirrel with a bushy tail scurried away into a tree.

"Here, boy." Marcus called out. His voice sounded different, smaller, now that he was surrounded by woodlands. "Mister Licks?"

Only the chirp of birds and the rustle of leaves answered him. A tingling dread enveloped Marcus. What if the dog really was hurt, or worse? There were black bears in the area as well as bobcats. A small dog would not fare well if it ran into either one. Marcus walked and shouted the dog's name again, then paused, ears straining for the dog's telltale woof.

Nothing.

He stifled a sob. What would he tell his mom if the dog came up missing? She would surely not be pleased. Not to mention Aunt Bethany, who would lose it. He didn't want that to happen. Aunt Bethany was a dragon at the best of times. He would find Mister Licks, even if it took the rest of the day.

Marcus moved with a renewed sense of urgency, pushing through a tangle of bushes, the branches raking at his skin. The trees closed in around him, claustrophobic and disorienting.

Then he heard it.

Something crashing through the underbrush.

Something big.

Marcus froze, his heart pounding.

Branches snapped. Twigs cracked under the weight of whatever was out there. Then Marcus found the will to move. He turned and fled back in the direction of the clearing, feet pounding the ground. He didn't care that the branches snagged his clothing and scratched the bare skin on his arms. In his blind panic, all he wanted to do was get away from whatever was out there. And then a dark shape appeared up ahead, blocking his way forward. Marcus felt a scream bubble up in his throat. He tried to stop, but his foot caught on a jutting tree root. He tumbled forward, hitting the ground hard enough to send the wind rushing from his lungs. He lifted his head, saw the shape crouching low. And then, before he could scream again, it lunged forward.

THIRTY-FOUR

EARLY IN THE AFTERNOON, after they checked into the Southern Winds Guest House, Decker and Nancy strolled along Leland's Main Street toward the Grounds and Grains Coffee Shop.

It was a beautiful day with a light breeze and the temperature tipping eighty under a gorgeous blue sky. Birds sang in the trees overhead, and butterflies crossed their path, wings ablaze in orange and yellow. The peaceful tranquility provided a stark contrast to the horrors Decker had witnessed over the last twenty-four hours.

When they entered the coffee shop, Decker recognized the same server from the day before. He recalled that her name was Sharon.

"Back again already?" she asked, looking up from an open book laying on the counter. "You must have liked that Danish."

"I wish that was my only reason for being here," Decker replied.

"Well, whatever brings you back, we're happy to have you." Sharon smiled and looked to Nancy. "You brought a friend too."

"This here is my better half. Nancy."

"I'm Sharon. Pleased to meet you."

"Likewise." Nancy glanced around at the tables with white tablecloths, the dandelion-yellow walls adorned with vintage photos of Leland, and the classic juke box sitting near the door. "Cute place you have here. I like it."

"Thank you." Sharon beamed. "Designed it myself. Always fancied being an interior decorator. Then I found my true calling. Serving coffee ten hours a day in a backwater town."

"I hear that." Nancy laughed.

"You meeting Bill again?" Sharon asked.

"No." Decker shook his head. "He did say our order was on him though. The Leland Sheriff's Department is picking up the tab."

"I think we can arrange that." Sharon closed the book and put it under the counter. "What'll it be?"

They ordered two iced coffees, a pair of egg bagel sandwiches, and a Danish to split, then took a seat near the window.

Leland was a lot like Wolf Haven, Decker thought as he gazed out toward the street. It had that same small-town charm. A close sense of community that he'd never felt during his time in New York. He would miss his hometown, he realized, despite the way those he had considered friends had turned on him.

"What're you thinking?" Nancy asked after she had finished her bagel. "You're miles away."

"Wolf Haven," Decker said. "This place is so much like it."

"Sure is," Nancy replied. "There's even a monster running around killing people."

"Don't remind me," Decker said. He leaned over and took her hand. "I'm sorry about this. We should be back on the coast sitting by that hotel pool."

"Are you kidding me?" Nancy laughed. "You hate that stuff."

"That's not true."

"It absolutely is."

"Okay, maybe I do find sunbathing a bit boring, but there are other things we could do."

"Like what?"

"There's a museum down the coast in Sarasota full of circus stuff; I saw the brochure in the hotel lobby. That might be worth a visit after we finish up here."

"A circus museum?" Nancy giggled. "John Decker wants to walk around a museum dedicated to clowns?"

"Not clowns. The circus." Decker suppressed a smirk.

"Same thing." Nancy turned her attention to the Danish. "And by the way, clowns are creepy."

"Yes, they are. And if we run into any, I'll be sure to defend you from them."

"You know what. With your habit of finding monsters everywhere you go, running into a killer clown isn't that far-fetched," Nancy said. "For you, it would just be another day at the office."

THIRTY-FIVE

MARCUS RAISED his arms to fend off the black shape hurtling toward him. A desperate cry escaped his lips. He found his feet, staggered backwards in a blind effort to escape, but it was not enough. The beast hit Marcus square in the chest, sending him toppling back to the ground. The next thing, a wet tongue was sliding down his face, covering him in drool. And then he realized what had floored him.

"Mister Licks." Marcus laughed and wrestled the dog to one side. "Get off me."

Mister Licks gave a frustrated woof and watched Marcus haul himself up on his elbows.

"Can we go now?" Barry leaned against a tree.

"Great. Now you show up, when the danger's over." Marcus got to his feet, clipped the leash onto Mister Licks. "I thought you'd gone home already."

"And leave you alone out here?" Barry asked. "What kind of friend would I be?"

"The kind who refused to come with me into the woods," Marcus retorted, but he wasn't mad with his friend, just relieved that his attacker was the dog. "Where did you find Mister Licks, anyway?"

"He came running out of the woods a few minutes after you disappeared," Barry said. "I waited for you to come back. When you didn't, we came looking for you."

"What were you running from, anyway?"

"I thought there was something out here," Marcus said, remembering the sounds in the woods. "Did you hear anything?"

"Nope," Barry replied. "Just you, wailing like a girl, and making enough noise to wake the dead."

"I'm sure something was out here. It sounded big," said Marcus, steering the dog back toward the pond.

"Na-uh. I bet it wasn't big." Barry trailed behind, kicking at the ground and sending clumps of dirt into the air as he walked. "Things sound larger in the woods. I thought there was a monster in our back yard once, but it was a racoon. It was making a hell of a racket in the bushes."

"It wasn't a raccoon," Marcus replied, but now that he thought about it, he wasn't sure what he'd heard. In his panic, he imagined a huge bear lumbering out of the woods toward him, but in reality, it could very well have been something as small as a raccoon, or even a rabbit. Not that he wanted to stick around and find out. "Let's get out of here."

"Suits me. I'm starving." Barry picked up the pace as they entered the clearing. "What is there to eat at your house?"

"Dunno." Marcus shrugged. They passed the pond and left the clearing behind. Mister Licks pulled at his leash, sniffing eagerly as they trotted back toward town. "I think we have chips."

"Can we make peanut butter and jelly sandwiches?"

"Sure. Mom brought a fresh jar of peanut butter home a few days ago." Marcus quickened his pace as the dog pulled him along. "We have to clean up after ourselves though. She'll kill me if I mess up the kitchen."

"Cool," Barry said as they reached the junk yard and skirted it, ignoring the guard dog's menacing growls on the other side of the fence. "And then the real fun begins."

THIRTY-SIX

"THERE'S a whole camp set up down there," Frank Denning said. He had arrived back at the cabin an hour ago, and after eating a sandwich of canned tuna on stale sliced bread, proceeded to tell the rest of the group what he had found. "It's a pretty substantial operation."

"How many people?" Liz was worried.

"I don't know. At least four," Frank replied. "Maybe more."

"I don't like it." Jerry rubbed the back of his hand across his forehead, dislodging beads of sweat. "We were supposed to be alone up here."

"Relax," Frank said. "They're miles away. They won't find us tucked away up here."

"We should still be careful," Liz said. "Where exactly did you see them?"

"A few miles off the road we drove in on, before the turn for the dirt trail to the cabin. I'd say due north, at least a few miles."

"So they probably don't know about the cabin. That's good." Liz paced back and forth. "Still, I would be happier if we didn't have neighbors."

"You're missing the point." Frank pulled a bottle of water

from a pack in the kitchenette and twisted the top off, taking a gulp.

"And the point is?" Liz waited for him to swallow.

"They have trucks. Three quad-cabs fitted with mud tires. Much better than that slow-ass plumber's van."

"Great. We'll steal one of the trucks," Jerry said.

"Not so fast." Liz waved a hand. "If we do that, they'll report the theft to the cops. You want the police poking around the woods?"

"We don't need to steal a truck," Frank said. "We know where they are, and that's just as good."

Louie spoke for the first time. "I don't see how."

"Because if we need to leave here in a hurry, we have a plan now." Frank took another swig of water. He was still dehydrated from the hours-long trek back in the brutal heat. "A truck doesn't do us any good up here anyway. We've been over this already. There's only one road in and one road out. If the cops show up, they aren't going to leave the trail open. No way out except on foot. But now we know where those trucks are, we can hightail it away from here and lose the cops in the woods. Then we'll double back to that camp and take what we need. It won't matter if they report the truck stolen by then. It only has to get us far enough away to find a less conspicuous ride."

Liz nodded in agreement. "Frank's right. We have a solid exit strategy. I like that."

"Or we just go down there right now and take care of those people the easy way." Louie eyed the shotgun leaning next to the cabin door.

"You can't be serious." Frank felt a tingle of revulsion. "You want to murder a bunch of people in cold blood just for a truck?"

"If they're dead, they won't report the truck missing, will they?" Louie said. "And I bet they have supplies too. Some decent food, drinks. Maybe a cold beer or two. You said they have a propane stove. We could actually eat something hot for a change instead of canned tuna and potato chips."

"We're not shooting them." Frank exchanged a worried glance with Jerry. "What the hell is wrong with you?"

"It's not your call to make." Louie folded his arms. "You aren't in charge here."

"No." Liz stepped in. "I am, and I have no intention of murdering a bunch of innocent people just to get their wheels. Not unless there's no other option."

"You're making a mistake."

"And you aren't thinking straight." Liz's voice was even, but her face flushed with anger. "We have no idea who might be out in these woods. You really want to attract attention with a bunch of shotgun blasts? That isn't going to help anything."

"I'm only saying—"

"Don't," Liz said. "I'm calling the shots, and I say we leave that camp alone until such time as it becomes necessary to do otherwise."

"This is ridiculous." Louie turned and stomped off in the direction of the bedrooms. A moment later the sound of a door slamming reverberated through the cabin.

Frank pursed his lips, looked first at Jerry, then at Liz. "He's going to be trouble. I guarantee it."

"I can handle Louie," Liz replied, although she didn't sound very sure. "He might be a petulant asshole, but he's not going to do anything stupid."

"I'm not so sure about that." Frank walked to the window and looked out over the woodland. "He's unpredictable. A hothead. I don't know why you even brought him along on this."

"Yes, you do," Liz said. "I had no choice. Believe me, if I had the option, Louie would be last on my list."

"Exactly," Frank said. "Which is why I'm going to keep an eye on him."

"Be my guest." Liz shrugged. "But play nice. We might need Louie if things go south, and I'd rather have him covering my back than shooting at it."

THIRTY-SEVEN

SHARON ROBERTS ARRIVED home a little later than usual and went straight to the bedroom. After leaving the Grounds and Grains coffee shop, she had stopped by Pizza Chef on Main, her favorite dinner spot because it was quick, affordable and easy. Not to mention being the only Greek pizza within a thousand miles. While there, she had run into Meredith Blackwell, who worked at the Shoppers Mart grocery store. A hopeless gossip, Meredith had kept Sharon talking for half an hour.

Now all Sharon wanted was to sooth the aches of the day with a dip in the pool. She slipped off her work clothes, discarded them in a pile on the bedroom floor, and put on a white bikini. That done, she grabbed a towel and padded through the house to the kitchen, where she opened a bottle of wine and poured a glass before heading out to the pool. This was the best part of the house, and the reason she had purchased this property. The yard backed up to a wooded area, and the other houses were far enough away, on the other side of a six-foot fence, that no one could see in.

She dropped the towel on the nearest patio chair and took a

sip of wine before placing that down too. A moment later she was at the edge of the pool. She paused and closed her eyes, enjoying the way the breeze played over her exposed skin. Then with practiced aplomb, she bent her knees, raised her arms, and dove into the cool, clear water.

THIRTY-EIGHT

AT SEVEN O'CLOCK that evening Marcus left his house in the Thousand Pines subdivision and made his way to Coulson Street, where Barry was waiting.

After a round of high fives, their usual greeting, the boys cut through a vacant lot into the woods. A narrow path skirted the edge of the subdivision, and soon they came to a white PVC privacy fence, beyond which Marcus could see the rooftops of houses.

"Do you remember which yard it is?" Marcus asked as they followed the fence.

"Sure, I've been here a hundred times," Barry replied, jumping up to peek over the fence. When they reached one section with a gate set into the fence, he stopped. "This is it."

"For real?" Marcus pressed his eye to a gap between the gate and the fence. The back yard was rectangular, with bushes lining the perimeter. In the middle sat a kidney shaped swimming pool, its water clear and blue. A table with a red sun umbrella occupied a patio at one end. Two Adirondack chairs stood on the grass at the other. A set of sliding glass doors led into the house.

Marcus beamed. "Told you I knew which yard it was."

"I don't see her." There was a fleck of disappointment in Marcus's voice. "Maybe she's not going to use the pool tonight."

"Are you kidding me? It must be a hundred degrees," Barry said. "She's going to use the pool. She always swims when it's hot."

"I don't know. It doesn't look like anyone's home."

"She's home," Barry said. "I can feel it. Besides, what else is there to do? You want to go back and study instead?"

"No." Marcus shifted position to gain a better vantage point. "But we could rent a movie. I know Mom's parental lock password on the cable box. I bet there's something good on one of the pay-per-view channels."

"You know she'll see that on her bill, right?" Barry, as usual, was the voice of reason. "And since you're the only other person in the house, who is she going to blame?"

"Well, have you got a better idea?"

"Yeah. We wait and see what happens here. This is better than TV."

Then, as if on cue, the patio doors slid open, and Sharon Roberts emerged, wearing a white bikini. A towel was draped over one arm, which she dropped on the closest chair.

"Holy crap." Marcus drew a sharp breath.

"What did I tell you?" Barry grinned. He squinted through a gap in the fence. "Come on. Let's get a better view."

"What?" Marcus asked. "How?"

"We need to get higher up." Barry pointed to a sprawling live oak with twisted, reaching limbs.

"You want to climb up that tree?"

"Why not?" Barry asked. "Unless you're chicken, that is."

THIRTY-NINE

AFTER DINNER, Alex, Emily and Professor Howard retreated to the control tent to discuss what to do next. The call with Professor Gladwell had left all three shaken, and despite their reluctance to accept such an outlandish theory, none of them had come up with an alternative.

"It doesn't make sense," Emily said. "It's impossible."

"A prehistoric crocodilian roaming the aquifer?" Alex swiveled on the chair. "Animals that size don't evade discovery. Someone would have seen it before now."

"Maybe not," Professor Howard said. "There are many precedents for crypto-zoological creatures. People see them all the time. Think of the Loch Ness Monster, Big Foot, Champ in Lake Champlain. There are reports of big cats roaming areas they should not be living in. Only a few decades ago the giant squid was thought to be a myth."

"Seriously?" Alex jumped to his feet. "Most photos of Nessie are hoaxed. Big Foot is nothing more than fanciful thinking. You're talking about these creatures like they're a proven fact when the truth is most sea monsters and hairy apes are nothing more than the work of overactive imaginations. We might as well say UFOs and pixies are real at the same time. At least if we're basing our assessment purely on eyewitness accounts. And might I remind you that eyewitnesses are notoriously unreliable."

"Just because these creatures haven't been found doesn't mean they aren't there. You saw that beast attack the submersible. We all did. What's your explanation?"

"I don't have an explanation, but I'm not jumping on the fairytale bandwagon just because we saw something odd. We'll end up as laughing stocks."

"Not if we get proof," Emily said. "We know a large creature is down there. If we can capture it on tape, we'll have the find of the century."

"The century?" Howard chuckled. "It will be the find of the millennium. A genuine prehistoric beast, and not some fish swimming around at the bottom of the ocean, but a creature that shared the earth with actual dinosaurs, snacked on them."

"And what better way to test NASA's submersible than to discover a living fossil," Emily said.

"Except that LISA is DOA in a flooded cave," Alex said. "We can't discover anything if we don't have her."

"Which is why we shall get her back online, my boy." Howard was excited now. If he could prove that a prehistoric genus of crocodilian had somehow evaded extinction, it would make his career. It would make all of their careers. There would be money. Buckets of it. Grants. Funding. He might even make the cover of National Geographic. Not only that, but the publicity would spark excitement in their little submersible. NASA would ride the wave of publicity all the way to Jupiter and its ice moon, Europa. If they were lucky, Howard and his team would secure cushy positions on the mission staff. After all, they were the ones who field tested LISA. Howard patted Alex on the back. "We need that sub up and working."

"One problem, professor," Alex said. "The only way to get LISA back is to dive down and repair her."

"We have cave diving gear now," Emily said. "It arrived this afternoon. I inventoried it myself. We even have a third suit and tanks just in case."

"I'm not sure we should send divers down." Howard rubbed his chin. "Not just yet."

"How else will we get LISA operational again?" Alex asked. "It will be a short dive, an hour at most."

"And what if that creature comes sniffing around, what if it attacks the divers like it did LISA? Do you really want to put them in jeopardy?"

"No. But we can't just sit here waiting for the sub to repair itself." Alex was frustrated. "We either go down and get her, or we pack up and admit defeat."

"It's the only way, Professor," Emily said.

"You're right, of course." Howard nodded. He turned to Alex. "I want you to keep working on LISA. Do what you can. I would prefer not to send the divers down unless there is no other choice."

"I'll try." Alex took his seat again. "But just so you know, LISA's main batteries are probably drained by now. The auxiliary power supply might still function, but that only keeps her vital components ticking over in the case of a catastrophic failure of main power. It won't be enough to operate thrusters or bring her back to the surface."

"We don't know that the batteries are dead."

"No. But given the time she's been down there, I can make an educated guess," Alex replied. "Besides, we haven't had any communication from LISA since the attack. Even if there is power, something else is very wrong. For all we know, the sub might be toast."

"And for all we know, it isn't," Howard said. "I have faith in you, Alex. If anyone can bring LISA back, it's you."

"And if we can't get the submersible working remotely?"

"Then I'll send the divers in." Howard folded his arms. "You have my word. But I rather hope you won't put me in that position."

FORTY

THE TREE PROVED HARDER than it looked to climb. Marcus made two attempts to clamber up the trunk but lost his grip both times. It was only on the third attempt that he managed to secure enough purchase to make a clumsy ascent onto the oak's lower branches. Barry followed behind, aided by a helpful hand offered from above, and soon both boys were perched eight feet up, their legs straddling a thick branch. When they looked back toward the pool, Sharon was still there, swimming long, lazy laps.

"Where's your phone?" Marcus asked, keeping his eyes on the swimming pool.

"Give me a minute, will you?" Barry pulled his phone out, opened the camera, switched to video, and pointed the phone toward the swimming pool.

"Awesome." Marcus turned his attention back to the pool. Sharon was still doing laps, her lithe body cutting through the water with ease. She might be his mother's friend, but regardless, Marcus was growing excited. He imagined what it would be like to touch her, his hands roaming over her wet, bare skin. Of course, that would never happen. She barely knew he existed, and even if she did, she wouldn't want to be with a boy of his age, especially one who sat in trees watching her swim. Still, there was no harm in dreaming.

"Are you still recording?"

"Yes." Barry huffed his disapproval at such a stupid question. "You think I'd miss this?"

"Jeez. Just asking," Marcus said.

"Well, don't. You're ruining the video by talking over it."

"Am not." Marcus shifted position on the tree branch. "Besides, who cares about the sound? It's the picture that's important."

"Shush. Be quiet."

"Don't tell me to be quiet," Marcus said.

"I mean it," Barry hissed. "I thought I heard a noise."

"Like what?"

"I don't know. Something moving in the woods." Barry cocked his ear. "There it is again."

"I don't hear anything," Marcus said. Only that wasn't true, because now he heard it too. A rustling, as if something big was moving through the undergrowth, snapping twigs.

"Told you." Barry's voice trembled. "Something is down there. Take a look and see what it is."

"No," Marcus said in a hoarse whisper. "I've already gotten scared half to death once today. You look this time."

"How about we look together?"

"Fine," Marcus said. "After three."

The rustling was closer now, right beneath them.

"Forget counting. Just look," Barry hissed.

"Okay, keep your shirt on," Marcus said, peering down toward the ground. At first, he didn't see anything out of the ordinary. There was an old cola can, its red and white graphics faded to a pale yellow by the sun. But then, just when he was about to berate Barry for hearing things, he saw it emerging from the understory. And what he saw made his stomach clench with fear. A creature that looked for all the world like one of those dinosaurs he'd seen in movies, like a velociraptor or a small T-

Rex. Only not quite. It was at least twelve feet, with a thick armor-plated hide and three rows of oblong bumpy scales running the length of its back. Its head was wide and heavy, with a long snout packed full of gleaming white teeth. But the most frightening thing was how the beast walked — on a pair of muscular hind legs. Where the front legs should have been were two short arms that ended in webbed, vicious claws.

"I-is that an a-a-alligator?" Barry asked, his eyes wide with fear.

"I don't think so." Marcus kept his voice so low that he wondered if Barry could even hear him. "It looks more like a dinosaur."

"W-what are we g-g-going to do?"

"Shhh." Marcus held a finger to his lips. The creature was at the base of the tree now, moving with slow, ponderous footsteps. Marcus held his breath, afraid that even the tiniest of sounds might draw the beast's attention. After a while, his lungs started to burn, and he wondered how much longer he would be able to go before he was forced to breathe.

And then he felt Barry move.

Marcus ripped his eyes away from the beast in time to see his friend leaning forward at a precarious tilt with the phone, aiming it downward toward the creature. His hands were shaking, the resulting image nothing more than a fuzzy blur.

"Don't do that," Marcus whispered, afraid that Barry would tumble from the tree. He reached out to offer a steadying hand. Instead, his fingers knocked his friend's arm and set him off balance. Barry scrambled to stay in the tree, reached out for a branch, and in doing so, he dropped the phone.

Marcus suppressed a horrified shriek.

The phone fell toward the ground, barely missing the prowling creature, and landed face down amid the fallen leaves.

The beast paused, startled by the sudden intrusion.

For a brief, terror-filled moment, Marcus thought they were goners. All the beast had to do was look up…

But it didn't. Instead, it moved off again.

"I d-don't think it saw us," Barry whispered, his voice thick with fear.

"Where's it going?" Marcus asked, even though he already knew the answer, because the beast was at the fence now, roaming along, looking for a way in. And when it came to the gate, it found one.

FORTY-ONE

"LOOK OUT!"

Sharon heard the desperate cry as she turned to complete another lap of the pool. She paused, treading water, and looked toward the source of the warning. A pair of teenaged boys perched in an oak tree on the other side of the fence. Her first instinct was to grab the towel and cover up. She could feel her cheeks burning. How long had they been there, watching her swim? More to the point, had they done it before? Sometimes, when it was really hot and she was in the mood, Sharon didn't even bother with the bikini. The thought of being watched while she enjoyed such private moments was mortifying. But then another thought occurred to her. What was so urgent that the boys had risked discovery to shout their warning?

They were waving wildly now. One of the boys almost lost his balance and would have tumbled from the tree had his friend not been holding him. But it was the source of their consternation that made her stop and stare.

On the other side of the yard, halfway through the back gate, was something that looked just like a giant alligator. Except that this gator was walking on two legs. And it was entirely too big.

Sharon's breath caught in her throat.

She was gripped by a crippling uncertainty, torn between attempting to flee and staying still in the hope that it hadn't yet seen her.

Except that the beast was through the gate now, and it was moving toward the pool. Not only that, but it had ignored the boys, its attention focused on easier prey.

Her.

Sharon wanted to scream, but her throat had contracted, and all that came out was a choking sob. She backpedaled toward the edge of the pool, afraid to even take her eyes from the monstrous visage that was skulking along on the far side, watching her with hungry yellow eyes.

When she reached the edge, Sharon pulled herself up, clambering out onto the deck without her eyes ever leaving the beast.

It had paused now and was watching her, in no hurry to close the gap between them.

She had the unnerving feeling that it was toying with her, relishing the moments before it attacked. Was that even possible? An image of her childhood cat playing with a mouse came to mind, the way it drew out the kill.

She took a step backwards, retreating slowly, afraid that a sudden movement would antagonize it. The beast followed, keeping pace but not drawing closer.

When she risked a glance back at the boys, they were on the move, scrambling down out of the tree. She felt a rush of relief. They were coming to her aid, for sure. They disappeared behind the fence. Sharon waited for them to appear at the gate. But instead, they ran past it, heading toward the woods. They weren't going to help her. They were fleeing. Sharon let out a terrified whimper and looked toward the house. Twenty feet away, the sliding glass doors meant safety. If she could get inside, it might not be able to follow. Her cell phone was in there too. She could call for help.

The creature snorted.

Sharon sensed that something had changed. It was about to attack. She felt a rush of fear and knew there was only one thing she could do.

Sharon turned and ran.

She bolted toward the sliding doors, reaching out to open them as she drew near. But behind her, the creature was moving.

It shot forward, nipping at her legs.

Sharon felt a searing crush of pain, and she was tumbling forward, straight into the glass, which shuddered under the impact, held briefly, and then gave way.

Sharon toppled forward through the opening and landed hard, crying out as shards of glass cut into her. She tried to rise and escape those snapping jaws that even now were pushing through the opening, but she couldn't. In a horrified instant she realized why. Her legs were gone, bitten clean off at the knees. Where her shins should have been, there was nothing but air. And then Sharon found the will to scream.

She screamed as the beast dragged her out of the shattered doorway and back toward the pool. She screamed as it pulled her into the cool waters. Finally, she screamed when sharp teeth bit higher and higher, crushing her chest. At least until those teeth punctured her lungs. Then she didn't scream any more. But it would be another minute before the darkness would, mercifully, claim her. And that final minute was the worst one of Sharon Robert's short life.

FORTY-TWO

DECKER RECEIVED the call just as he was about to suggest that he and Nancy take a drive through town in search of a good dinner spot. When he saw Bill Gibson's name on the screen, he groaned. He'd hoped that there wouldn't be another attack so soon.

He was wrong.

Ten minutes later he and Nancy were leaving the hotel room on their way across town to the address Bill had given them. A house in the Thousand Pines sub-division. When they arrived, there was a uniformed officer standing next to a squad car at end of the road. Decker stopped and rolled his window down.

"I'm here to see Sheriff Gibson."

"Name?" the cop asked in a bored voice. No doubt he was frustrated with being put on such menial duty while his fellow officers were at the crime scene doing the real work.

"John Decker."

"One minute, sir." The cop turned away and spoke into a radio. There was a moment of silence, then a squawk of static. The cop paced back and forth in front of the car, conversing, before approaching again. "All right, you're clear to proceed."

"Thanks." Decker rolled his window up and pulled away. Up

ahead were three police units and a paramedic. A small crowd of neighbors had gathered on their lawns, looking on with mouths agape. The whole scene was lit by strobing red and blue lights.

Decker parked behind the paramedic. "Stay here, okay?"

"You must know me better than that by now." Nancy was already halfway out of the car.

Decker shrugged. "Stay behind me then. Cops can get pretty annoyed by civilians tramping over their crime scene."

They made their way across the lawn to a fenced back yard, through the open gate, and across a patio area with chairs and a table. Beyond this was a swimming pool surrounded by various uniformed figures. Two men in black jackets were wheeling a loaded gurney in their direction. From the shape of the bag, it appeared to be occupied. Decker stepped aside and allowed them through, eyes searching the milling throng of cops and medics until he saw Bill Gibson.

"John." Bill waved and beckoned to him.

"Wait here." Decker told Nancy. "I mean it this time."

He hurried toward Bill, skirting the pool. When he drew close, he noticed the streaked blood and several chewed up scraps of meat, which he realized were the last few remains of whoever had been wheeled out on the gurney.

"Am I glad to see you," Bill said as Decker approached. "This one hits a bit close to home."

"How so?" Decker could see the distress on his friend's face.

"You remember Sharon from the coffee shop?"

"Sure." Decker had a feeling he knew where this was going.

"She's our victim." Bill removed his hat. "I feel just awful about this, John. She was a good friend."

"I'm so sorry," Decker said.

"Thanks." Bill rubbed the bridge of his nose, his brow furrowed. "I'm not looking forward to telling her family."

"Been there," Decker said. "You got any leads?"

"Oh yeah." Bill rubbed at the days-old stubble on his chin. "I'll be damned, John, it's getting weird. With a capital W. We have two witnesses. Couple of horny boys up a tree on yonder side of the fence, watching Sharon take a dip. Apparently, they like peeping on half-naked woman more than they like playing video games in the safety of their own homes. Little pervs."

"Where are they now?" Decker glanced around but didn't see any sign of the boys.

"At home, with their families. We've already taken statements."

"And?"

"God, John. This is going to sound nuts. Still, if anyone will believe their story, you will." Bill paused. He glanced around, as if he was afraid that someone would overhear what he was about to say. "They say a dinosaur came in here and attacked Sharon."

"I'm sorry?" Decker frowned. "Did you say a dinosaur did this?"

"Yup. That's what the boys claim they saw. Told you it was weird."

"Could they have been mistaken? What about an alligator?" Decker asked, but he was already thinking about the wrecked police cruiser he'd seen earlier in the day. The torn and mangled bodies. No alligator could have done that.

"They were pretty adamant. It was a dinosaur. Walked on two legs and everything. They even recorded it on their cell phone. It's pretty blurry. Damned kid couldn't keep his hands still. You can barely make anything out. I guess it looks like a dinosaur. Of course, it could be someone out for a walk in the woods for all I know. It's impossible to tell, especially since the kid ended up dropping the phone out of the tree before he could get more than a few seconds of shaky footage."

"That's bad luck."

"Is there any other kind in this job?"

"I assume you're keeping this on the down low." Decker said.

"Naturally. I swore the kids and their parents to secrecy," Bill said. "If this leaks out, the town will panic. I'd rather avoid that if I can. At least for now."

"Good idea," Decker said. "And if I were you, I wouldn't talk too loud about dinosaurs eating people. You don't want to end up like me, railroaded and out of a job."

"For sure." Bill grimaced.

"You mind sending that video to my email?" Decker asked. "I'd like to take a look over it for myself."

"Sure thing. I'll do it right away," Bill said. "I'll take you over to the morgue in the morning to examine the body, and we'll brainstorm where to go from here, how to stop this thing. In the meantime, you should head back to the guesthouse and get some rest. There's nothing you can do here tonight."

"I'll do that," Decker said. He turned to leave, then looked back at Bill. "I'm sorry about Sharon. It's tough to lose a friend, especially like this."

"Thanks, John. That means a lot," Bill said. He put his hat back on, straightened it. "Now get along back to the hotel. I need you bright and fresh in the morning if we stand a chance of beating this."

FORTY-THREE

LOUIE WALKER GLANCED at his watch. It was a little past two in the morning, and he was still wide awake. A few feet away Jerry Biggs snored loudly. Louie climbed to his feet and slipped from the room.

In the corridor Louie paused. He didn't want to run into Frank again. He would have no excuse for prowling the cabin in the small hours two nights in a row. He peeked into the front room. Frank was lying on an air mattress, facing away. He appeared to be asleep, but Louie was glad he didn't have to go through the room to make his escape.

Instead, he turned and went to the bathroom, treading as softly as he could. Liz was in the other bedroom, and she was at least as formidable as Frank, probably more so. If she thought Louie was about to betray her, she wouldn't hesitate to kill him.

That was why this next step in the plan had to be executed quickly. He knelt down and felt along the wall until he found what he was looking for.

A loose panel.

He pried it out, wincing when a tight nail gave a rusty squeak as it came free. He placed the panel to one side and tugged on the next one. The wood was rotten. The board came away easily. Soon there was a hole big enough for him to reach through. He grinned. The bedroom closet was on the other side of this wall. He poked his head through the hole, looking around until he saw the duffel bag of stolen cash tucked into the corner of the closet. Liz's shotgun leaned next to the bag. His own weapon was still in the front room, too close to Frank to be worth retrieving.

He reached over and tugged the bag toward him, then lifted it through the newly made hole. He curled an arm back around and grabbed the gun. No point leaving it behind; he might need some firepower if the others caught up with him.

Louie grinned. Success.

He opened the bag and peered at the tightly packed stacks of $100 bills, then reached behind the busted toilet and pulled out a backpack stashed earlier in the day. This contained a change of clothes. He transferred the cash from the duffel to the backpack. It was a tight fit, but the duffel would be too unwieldy in the woods. He scooted over to the opening in the floor where the sink had fallen through and swung his legs into the gap.

He shuffled forward, dropping down through the space where the floorboards had rotted away, then poked an arm back through the hole and dragged the backpack through. Louie was now in a tight crawlspace under the cabin. He squirmed forward on his belly, ignoring the silken cobwebs that stuck to his face, and tried not to think about what might be down there with him. Spiders were bad, but there were worse things, like snakes. If he got bitten by a cottonmouth, that would be it. Curtains. They were too far from the nearest hospital even if Liz was willing to get caught to save his life, and since Louie had double crossed her, that was never going to happen. She would just shoot him. Or worse, let the poison do its work.

Relieved to be free, Louie crawled out of the tight space and stood up. He was at the back of the cabin now, near the old generator shack. He brushed himself off, slipped the backpack on, and hurried away from the cabin. He had a long walk ahead, and he wanted to put as much distance between himself and Liz as possible.

The plumber's van would have been his best option for a quick escape, but that was long gone. It would be a charred husk by now. That was a shame, and he'd had to alter his plan to account for it. But thanks to Frank's discovery earlier in the day, Louie now had a new plan. He would sneak down to that camp and steal one of the trucks. He had no idea what was going on around the waterhole, and he didn't care. It was a stroke of luck, and if anyone gave him trouble, well, he had a gun. By the time Frank and the others realized he was gone, Louie would be a hundred miles away.

He grinned, feeling happier than he had in a very long time. Finally, life was going his way, and he had a hunch that it was only going to get better from here.

FORTY-FOUR

JOHN DECKER SAT at in the darkened room and peered at his laptop screen. Behind him Nancy slept, her light breathing a comfort in the unfamiliar room. He should be sleeping too, he knew, but all he could think about was the bodies he'd seen that day. Including Sharon Roberts, who he had met twice in the last twenty-four hours. Which was why he had slipped out of bed and gone to the small desk sitting in the corner of their room at the Southern Winds.

Bill had emailed the video over before Decker and Nancy had even returned to the hotel. He included two attachments. The video that was now up on Decker's screen and a recorded interview with the two boys. The interview told him little that he didn't already know. The video clip was a different matter. It was short, only lasting a few seconds until the phone fell. However, now that he looked closer, he saw something he hadn't noticed before. When the phone tumbled to the ground, it landed screen down, but before that, for just a split second, it was facing toward whatever was skulking under the tree, and if he was lucky, it had captured a better image than the indistinct blur the boy had recorded. He ran the video back frame by frame, until he reached the moment before the phone hit the ground. And there it was, staring at him from the screen. The image still wasn't great, but it was good enough for Decker to see the beast. And what he saw sent a chill through him.

The creature resembled an alligator, with a long snout and scaly hide covered in thick horny plates. But it didn't look like any gator Decker had ever seen. He couldn't see the whole body, given the camera's angle as it fell, but even so, he sensed the size of the beast, and it was much too big. But it was the other obvious feature in the still image that really sent a shudder through Decker. It was walking on two legs.

Decker leaned back in the chair, staring at the image. The boys had been right. It really did look just like a dinosaur. But how was that possible? Decker knew that alligators shared the prehistoric world with their more famous counterparts, but could this really be what they looked like?

Decker opened a browser window and ran a search for *Prehistoric alligator*. He ignored the first few hits. They weren't relevant. The third was different. It was an article that talked about fossilized crocodiles discovered in South Carolina, millions of years old. Decker skimmed through the article, but it was the accompanying illustration that made him stop and stare. There, on the screen, was a bipedal croc that looked suspiciously like the beast caught on the cell phone video. He moved the video so that it was positioned alongside the browser window displaying the illustration, then compared the two animals. It wasn't an exact match, especially given the poor quality of the still image he'd captured, but the features were close enough for Decker to come to a startling conclusion. Whatever had killed the diver and attacked that poor woman should have been extinct long ago.

He sat back in the chair and let that thought sink in.

A prehistoric creature roaming the woods. It was ridiculous —too unlikely to be believable. Yet the evidence was right there in front of him.

"John?"

Decker turned to find Nancy sitting up in the bed. "I thought you were sleeping."

"I was." She sat up. "What are you doing?"

"Couldn't relax," Decker said.

"You're watching that video again." Nancy's eyes roamed past Decker to the computer screen.

Decker shrugged. "I couldn't stop thinking about it."

"Did you find anything useful?"

"Actually, I did." He scooted his chair back to allow Nancy a better view of the screen. "I managed to find a single frame that showed the creature clearer than the others. Then I did a search online and came up with some startling results. What do you think?"

For a while she said nothing, her eyes flitting from the boy's frozen cell phone video to the illustration in the browser window. "They look similar."

"That's what I thought," Decker said.

"I've never seen an alligator like that."

"It's not an alligator. It's a crocodile. A huge croc that walked on two legs and could run as fast as a car."

"Sounds nasty."

"It was. 112 million years ago," Decker said. "It's extinct. Except—"

"Except that it looks an awful lot like the creature in that video, the one that tore apart that poor woman in her swimming pool." Nancy finished the sentence.

"Right." Decker glanced back toward the screen. "I don't think that our killer is the same species. It isn't an exact match from what I see here, but I'm pretty sure this thing should have been dead and gone a very long time ago."

"112 million years?" Nancy asked. "Is it even possible that a prehistoric alligator could have survived all the way to the present day?"

"Well, modern alligators are just the descendants of animals that lived alongside the dinosaurs. If they survived, why not another similar creature?"

"Because no one has ever seen one," Nancy replied. "You'd need a fairly large population just to breed over the millennia. I'm pretty sure something like that would have been noticed by now."

"Unless it lived somewhere out of sight. Like deep in the aquifer."

"Alligators need to breathe air. They aren't fish. And besides, what would it eat?"

"Who knows?" Decker yawned. He was tired now. "Maybe it adapted. It might live mostly in the caves and swim out into the ocean to hunt."

"So why is it coming onto land now? Why is it killing people?"

"I wondered that," Decker said. "The water levels in the aquifer are dropping. We're pumping it out at an alarming rate to use as drinking water. Maybe the levels dropped to a point where this thing couldn't reach its normal hunting grounds anymore."

"It sounds far-fetched," Nancy said. "I mean, prehistoric crocs?"

"I agree. It sounds nuts," Decker said. "Still, far-fetched seems to be my stock-in-trade these days, and after what happened in Wolf Haven and Alaska, I'm not such a skeptic anymore."

"I hear that," Nancy said. "There's nothing you can do right now though. Come back to bed."

Decker nodded. "I should call Bill, tell him what I've found."

"He'll be asleep. It's only a few hours until dawn; it can wait until then."

"Yeah." Decker took a last lingering look at the screen, then closed the laptop and climbed into bed beside Nancy. He lay awake for a while, too disturbed to drift off, but he eventually fell into a fitful sleep and dreamed of impossible creatures that stalked him through a gloomy forest.

FORTY-FIVE

LOUIE WALKER PICKED his way through the woods with only a flashlight for guidance. It was darker than he expected, and he stumbled several times, once scraping his knee on a fallen tree trunk and drawing blood.

Louie did not know the exact location of the camp Frank had found, but he had a good idea of the route Frank had taken, steering clear of the main roads and woodland trails as he walked back to the cabin after ditching the van. He'd feigned little interest in Frank's retelling of the return journey, but in reality, he was noting each and every clue regarding the whereabouts of the camp and the all-important trucks.

Louie pressed on, acutely aware that until he found a vehicle and put some distance between himself and the cabin, he was in real danger. He might be discovered missing at any time, and while he figured Liz and the others wouldn't notice until dawn, he could not rely on that assumption. Once they figured out that he'd stolen the loot, it wouldn't take a genius to guess where he was going.

And Frank was smart. Too smart for Louie's liking, even if he didn't like to admit it. He was also under no misconceptions regarding Liz's reaction should she catch up with him. She valued loyalty and rewarded betrayal with the same callous fervor. He didn't want to end up on the receiving end of her fury.

That was why he was relieved when he spied a glimmer of light between the trees up ahead. It wasn't much, just a faint twinkle, but it was out of place in the dark woods.

He slowed his pace, proceeding carefully. The light grew brighter, and before long he was standing at the edge of a wide clearing, peering through the foliage toward the camp Frank had stumbled across.

It was bigger than he'd expected, with tents pitched around a circle of shiny black water. One side of the clearing, where most of the tents were located, was illuminated in the dim yellow glow of a strand of low powered lights strung across a central walkway. The other side of the clearing was swathed in darkness, but from what he could see it was some sort of staging area, with a crane and other assorted equipment.

Louie wondered what they needed so much gear for, but he didn't dwell on it, because he'd seen what he wanted. Parked near the trees were the trucks Frank had mentioned. If he was lucky, one of them would have the keys in it. If not, it wasn't that big a deal. Louie had picked up a few tricks over the years.

Ten minutes, and he'd be riding in style. More important, he would be putting some miles between himself and the rest of the gang back in the cabin.

Louie crept around the perimeter of the clearing, keeping close to the trees. There didn't appear to be anyone around. They were probably tucked in safe and sound in their sleeping bags, but it never hurt to be cautious.

Louie was near the trucks now. He came to a halt and peered into the clearing one more time, just to be sure he was alone. Even so, he raised the gun as he stepped out from the safety of the trees. If it came to it, he wasn't averse to a little violence to get his way.

But there was no need. This was as easy as escaping the cabin. A few more minutes and he could drop the pack full of money from his back. It was heavy, and his back ached. Not that he cared. He was carrying enough cash to keep him going for a year, two if he was lucky. After the disastrous getaway, the dye packs exploding, they only made off with a fraction of what they stole. The rest was abandoned, useless and stained, to be recovered by the cops. A four-way split meant barely enough cash for any of them. Taking all the money for himself made the heist worthwhile. Not that Liz and the others would see it that way.

Louie hurried to the closest vehicle and tugged on the handle. It was unlocked, but there were no keys. The next truck was the same, but on the third one he hit the jackpot. The keys were just lying there, sitting on the dash. Louie grinned. He stepped back and took a quick look around to make sure the camp was still quiet.

Then he heard it.

A low shuffling sound, faint, but different enough to set his nerves on edge.

His first thought was that someone from the camp, maybe a site security guard, must be walking around after all. He scanned the gloom between the tents, but he saw nothing.

Probably just his imagination.

Louie turned back toward the truck.

Except there was something there now, a black shape near the trees. He tried to make sense of what he was seeing. It was too bulky to be a person. A bear perhaps?

Louie swallowed hard, his heart thudding in his chest. He aimed the gun.

The shape lunged forward.

Louie pulled the trigger.

There was an empty click.

Louie looked at the gun in horrified disbelief. Liz must have removed the ammunition. Clearly, she didn't trust anyone enough to leave a loaded weapon lying around.

Louie took a step backward, swinging the gun like a baseball bat.

There was a blur of movement and something slammed into him. The gun was wrenched from his grip.

Louie grunted and staggered backwards.

His attacker followed, slipping from the shadows into a pool of moonlight.

The beast was large, with a snout full of deadly teeth. It stood upright on two massive, muscular legs that supported a lizard-like body. And in its mouth, the shotgun.

The creature bit down on the weapon, then flicked its head to the side, discarding the crushed and useless gun.

Louie felt his bladder loosen. Hot liquid streamed down his leg.

The creature paused, sniffing the air. It watched him with a calculating stare that sent ice through Louie's veins.

Then it barreled forward with unbelievable speed.

Sharp teeth bit down on Louie's shoulder. It hauled him off the ground. Searing pain like a thousand knife cuts overwhelmed him. The creature swung its head from side to side, jerking Louie around like a rag doll. The shoulder popped from its socket. Bones cracked. A wave of blackness enveloped Louie, and for a moment he thought he might pass out. The beast tilted its head one more time, swinging Louie around, and then it let go, tossing him toward the water. For a moment he hung in the air, arms flailing, before he hit hard. Then he was going under, the backpack full of cash pulling him inexorably down.

Louie gulped in a frantic lungful of air, held his breath as the water closed over his head and he sank into the murky blackness. He twisted to dislodge the pack, despite the agony of broken bones. But the straps were tight, and the heavy wads of hundred-dollar bills acted like an anchor, dragging him deeper. He struggled, lungs burning, and then he could hold on no longer. The last breath of his life rushed out in a torrent of bubbles. His final flickering thought was of Liz, and how good it felt that she would never find the money.

FORTY-SIX

PROFESSOR DANIEL HOWARD woke with a start. He lay in the dark, chest heaving, a sheen of sweat coating his brow. Something was wrong. He couldn't explain it, couldn't pinpoint the source of his foreboding, but it was there. Had he heard a noise to rouse him so? If he had, it was gone now. Regardless, the strange sensation lingered.

He pushed his way out of the sleeping bag, crawled to the front of the tent and unzipped the flap.

Crickets chirped. Frogs croaked their throaty mating call. In the distance an owl hooted, the haunting sound drifting on the humid night breeze.

Daniel stepped from the tent, letting the flap fall closed behind him. He glanced around, noting that the other tents were silent and dark, their occupants fast asleep. There was no sign of movement from within the camp.

He took a step forward, moving toward the placid circle of water in the middle of the clearing. On the far shore he could make out the hulking shapes of the crane and the cluster of trucks they had used to haul gear to the camp, silhouetted against the darker expanse of the dense woodland beyond.

He saw something else too.

A figure at the edge of the clearing.

At first, he thought it must be one of the support crew out for a walk or catching a quick smoke. But that was unlikely. It was the middle of the night. Why would anyone be out at such a late hour? Besides, it didn't look like anyone he recognized.

So that left two possibilities. A lost hiker looking for help, or someone up to no good, trying to steal a truck. The best course of action would be to retreat to his tent and place a call on the satellite phone, get some cops up here to take care of the matter.

Then Daniel saw the weapon.

The intruder was carrying a shotgun. And he was raising it, like he was going to shoot. A surge of panic raced through Daniel. He backed up instinctively, ready to flee, but then he realized that the gun wasn't pointed at him. The stranger was aiming off into the woods.

Daniel watched, transfixed, even though alarm bells were ringing inside his head. He could feel his heart thumping. He risked a glance back toward the tents, but no one else had stirred. He considered shouting to bring the rest of the camp running, but then the intruder would see him for sure, and he didn't fancy their chances against an armed assailant. Better to retreat back to the tent and make that phone call. Before he could move, a loud splash drew his attention back toward the intruder.

Except the man was gone.

Had the intruder stepped into the woods? And what had made the splash? Something had gone into the pool for sure. Daniel could clearly see the ever-widening ripples making their way across the surface.

Then he noticed the silence.

It was like someone had turned the volume down. There were no crickets, no frogs. Even the breeze had died, quieting the rustling leaves. It was eerie. Unsettling.

Daniel edged toward the relative safety of the tents, gripped by a primitive urge to flee. There was danger here, lurking unseen in the darkness. He could feel it. Watching. Waiting.

He took another quick step back.

A twig snapped in the underbrush to his left, the sound stark and loud.

Daniel caught his breath. His eyes darted toward the source of the sound.

Something was there, crouching between the trees. A low, hulking shape that watched him from the shadows.

A bear perhaps or a bobcat?

No. This was something else. And it was stalking him, waiting for the perfect moment to strike.

Daniel froze, caught in a rare moment of panicked indecision. Was it better to stand his ground, confront whatever was out there, or turn and flee? He wavered between the two options, afraid to stay where he was, but terrified to turn his back and run.

And then it made a sound. A low, guttural hiss that sent a chill down Daniel's spine. He was seized by a blind terror. He willed his legs to move, stumbled backwards, but not quickly enough.

It lunged in a blur of movement.

Daniel felt a rush of displaced air, a blast of fetid carrion tainted breath. He recoiled, turning to flee even as powerful jaws closed around him and teeth tore through his skin. Then, as the life was crushed out of him, Professor Daniel Howard found the breath to scream.

FORTY-SEVEN

THE FIRST SCREAM jolted Emily awake. By the second scream she was already climbing out of her sleeping bag and scrambling to find her pants. A moment later she was tearing at the tent flaps, fumbling for precious seconds before finally pulling them back and stepping outside.

The normally quiet camp was erupting into chaos.

One of the support divers, a man named Ozzie, raced past her, knocking her sideways as he went. She was about to call after him and ask what was going on, but then she saw.

It was Professor Howard.

Even in the dark of night she recognized him.

But it was the creature that held him in its jaws, dragging him into the cold black water, that made her stop and stare in horror. It was like nothing she had ever seen, standing on two legs, with a long, bony tail and a pair of glowering eyes above a vicious, elongated snout.

She watched, horrified, as the beast retreated into the pool, the professor struggling feebly. His terrified shrieks dropped to a gurgling hiss, and then, finally, to awful silence.

On the shore, keeping a distance between themselves and the beast, the two divers hesitated between a desire to help and an unwillingness to risk their own lives on what they surely perceived as a fool's errand.

Emily felt no such conflict.

She started forward, sprinting to the water's edge.

One of the support divers, realizing her intention, reached out and grabbed her shoulders. "It's no use. He's dead."

"Let go of me." Emily spun out of the man's grip and stepped into the water.

It was shallow at the edge, but it would drop off sharply, she knew, the sandy bottom falling away into a precipitous chasm that plunged downward. She only had a few feet of stable ground left.

The professor was limp, his body hanging from the beast's jaws like a broken doll. His arms lolled down. His head drooped.

Emily waded toward the retreating beast and reached out. "Professor, take my hand."

At first Howard didn't move, and she feared he might already be dead.

Precious seconds ticked away.

"Take my hand." She tried again, moving deeper into the water, praying that the bottom held out.

Still nothing.

Emily stood, helpless, as the beast moved further away. Then, at the last moment, just when she feared it was too late, Howard raised his head.

Their eyes met.

He lifted an arm, a feeble gesture, but enough for their fingers to graze, and then the sandy shelf fell away under the beast and it sank lower, pulling the professor under until all that was left to show he had ever been there were a few gently ebbing waves and a thin ribbon of blood weaving through the water.

Emily gulped back a choking sob, her arm still outstretched, empty fingers reaching for thin air.

There was a splash.

A hand tugged at her elbow. A familiar voice cut through the shock.

"He's gone," Alex said. "It's not safe. You need to come out of the water."

"I almost had him," Emily said, her voice barely above a whisper. She turned to Alex and allowed him to lead her back to the shore. "He was still alive, Alex. He looked at me."

"I know." Alex put an arm around her. "You did all you could."

"It wasn't good enough." Emily felt red hot tears sting the corners of her eyes. She scanned the now placid water. "We should have packed up and left when we found that footprint."

"We couldn't have known." There was a tinge of regret in Alex's voice.

"What happens now?"

"We call in the cavalry, which is what we should have done right from the start," Alex replied, "and then we get the hell out of here before that thing comes back for seconds."

FORTY-EIGHT

THE PHONE WAS RINGING.

Decker responded to the shrill sound before he was even fully awake. It was still dark. There was only one reason for a call at this time of night.

Bad news.

He reached for the nightstand and fumbled until his hand landed on the phone.

"Hello?"

"John." It was Bill Gibson.

"What's going on?" Decker was sitting up, reaching for his pants. "Another attack?"

"Looks that way." There was a pause on the other end of the line. "I hate to wake you up like this."

"Don't give it a second thought," Decker said. He pulled a gray polo shirt from his travel bag and slipped it on. "I told you I was here to help, and I meant it."

"You can't have gotten more than a few hours sleep."

"Comes with the job," Decker said before he realized that this wasn't, in fact, his job. Not anymore. "Want to fill me in?"

"Not yet." There was a pause on the other end of the line.

"How about I swing by the hotel and pick you up? I'll bring you up to speed on the way."

"On the way to where?"

"The woods outside of town. We're going for a little field trip."

"Sounds intriguing. Give me fifteen minutes?"

"Sure thing, buddy." The line went dead.

From behind him in the bed, Nancy stirred. She sat up. "What's going on? Was that Bill?"

"Yes." Decker nodded. "There's been another attack. Go back to sleep."

"You know me better than that. I'm not letting you out of my sight." Nancy was already heading for the bathroom.

"What?" Decker shook his head. "You're not coming with me. Not this time."

"Like hell I'm not." Nancy peeked around the bathroom door, toothbrush in hand.

"It might be dangerous."

"Really?" Nancy stepped back into the room. "Like when Annie Doucet was running around the high school trying to kill my daughter? I think I can cope. Besides, the attack has already happened, am I right?"

"Yes."

"There's nothing to be worried about then."

"Nancy—"

"Look, I know you'd rather be playing policeman than sitting on a beach in Tampa; that's why I encouraged you to pursue this. But I'm a big girl, and I get bored too."

"That's just it. You're not a cop. You don't have the training."

"You're not a cop either, remember?" Nancy was pulling on her boots. "And I'm pretty sure you don't have any more training for chasing monsters than I do."

"Fair point." Decker nodded. He slipped his phone into his back pocket and headed for the door. "Come on then."

They made their way down through the lobby and outside. It

was raining, a steady drizzle that filled the air with a fine mist of water. They stood under the hotel portico until a pair of headlights sliced though the darkness. Moments later Bill pulled up in an unmarked Jeep.

He rolled the window down. "Get in."

"No sheriff's vehicle tonight?" asked Decker.

"Came straight from home." Bill glanced at Nancy. "We got us a ride along?"

"Looks that way," replied Decker. "I tried to talk her out of it. Said she should stay at the hotel and get some sleep."

"And I told him what I thought of that idea." Nancy climbed into the Jeep's back seat behind Decker. "You want John, you get me too. We're a team."

"I figured as much." Bill glanced back over his shoulder. "You promise to keep an eye on her, make sure she doesn't trample my scene?"

"Sure." Decker clicked his seat belt. "How about you tell us where we're going."

"Love to." Bill shifted into gear and steered the car out of the hotel parking lot.

"And I have something of my own to say," Decker replied, "about that video you sent me."

"Great. I'll go first," Bill said. "And listen good, kids. I only have time to say this once."

FORTY-NINE

"WAKE UP."

Someone was shaking Frank, pulling him from a deep slumber and a dream where he was on a tropical island, being served Margaritas by beautiful dark-haired women. In the fantasy, he was free and clear and beyond the reach of the authorities. Never again would he have to endure an eight-by-ten cell or be bundled into the back of a van to clear trash from the side of the highway. Now, as the dream slipped away, he found himself back in the cruddy, too hot cabin lying on a half-deflated air mattress.

Liz stood over him.

Jerry lingered a few steps behind.

"What's going on?" Frank licked his lips. When he swallowed, there was barely any saliva. He was dehydrated. His head hurt.

"He's gone." Liz was dressed in a pair of camo pants and a black tee. A hunting knife hung from her belt.

"Who's gone?"

"Louie. He took the cash and scarpered."

"Took a gun too," Jerry added.

"My gun," Liz added, ruefully.

"What the…" Frank jumped up, grabbing his pants in a fluid movement and pulling them on. "I thought you had the loot stashed safe."

"Me too." Liz nodded toward the back room. "It was in the closet. He broke through the back."

"He can't have gone far." Frank looked around and saw his shotgun leaning against the wall. "We'll find him."

"And then we take care of him," Liz said. "And get our money back."

"And it'll be one less way to split the loot," Jerry said. "Bonus."

"What do you mean?" Frank looked at him with narrowed eyes. "You're suggesting we kill him?"

Liz answered before Jerry had a chance. "Wouldn't be the first time I've had to take care of things." Her eyes shone with cold indifference. "I'm sure it won't be the last."

The words hung in the air. Frank wondered who Liz had killed, and when? The situation felt like it had just gotten much more dangerous. He decided to watch his back lest his companions decide that a two-way split was better than three. The seconds ticked away. After a while, he turned to Jerry. "You should get dressed. Every minute we waste, Louie's getting further away."

————

They departed the cabin an hour before dawn and trekked in the direction of the camp that Frank had seen earlier. This was, Liz surmised, the most likely place Louie would go, since it was the only viable location to quickly secure transportation. Frank agreed with her. Louie would want to snag a truck, something that would get him out of the area in a hurry. Frank knew now that he should have kept quiet about what he'd seen, taken Liz to one side and told her in private. Maybe then they wouldn't need to hoof it through the woods in the dark, risking capture. Or maybe Louie would have taken the loot and run off anyway. The man was a liability from the start. If anything, it was Liz's judgment in bringing Louie along on the job that had resulted in this situation. That made him feel a little better.

"At least Louie didn't take all our ammunition," she said as they followed the trail deeper into the woods. "And my gun wasn't loaded. None of them were. That should make it easier when we catch up with him."

"If we catch up with him," Frank said. "We're not entirely sure he went this way."

"Just because your gun wasn't loaded doesn't mean he didn't take any ammo," Jerry said. He slowed and turned to Liz. "Why weren't the guns loaded anyway?"

"Insurance," Liz replied. "I didn't want anyone getting a case of cabin fever and going off on the rest of us." Liz patted her gun. "They're loaded now though, and when we find Louie, he's going to know it."

"I get it. You don't trust us," Frank said. "But we would've been screwed if the cops had shown up and we were firing empty guns at them."

"I had the ammunition tucked away safe and sound," Liz replied. "Anything went down, I would have distributed it."

"When did you even take the ammo?" Jerry asked.

"While you were sleeping."

"Perfect. Instead of keeping watch, you were sneaking around making sure you had the drop on us if things got testy."

"I was making sure no one did anything stupid," Liz said. "You would have done the same."

"Not likely." Jerry snorted and slowed so that he was walking in stride with Liz. "We're supposed to be a team."

"And how did that work out?" Liz asked. "After all, we're trudging through the woods in the middle of the night chasing one of our own."

"Let it be." Frank shot a warning glance toward Jerry. "Let's find that son of a bitch before he gets himself arrested and snitches on us. After that, we can sort out our differences."

"After that, I'm out of here," Jerry said. He looked at Liz. "You can spend the next few weeks shacked up in that crap hole of a cabin if you want, but I'm done. You hear me?"

"Yeah. We hear you," Liz replied. "Loud and clear."

"And now, with that settled, can we all just shut the hell up?" Frank said. "We'll be coming on that camp pretty soon, and I'd rather not advertise our presence ahead of time."

"Agreed," Liz replied.

"You got a plan for when we get there?" Frank kept his voice low. "We'll probably have to show ourselves, and I'd rather not spook the occupants of that camp. Don't want anyone calling the cops on us."

"I know what to say. Just follow my lead," Liz said. She patted her gun, a grim look on her face. "And if it all goes south, we'll just make sure there's no one left to identify us."

FIFTY

EMILY WAS STILL SHAKING. She sat in the control tent gripping a mug of hot tea that contained an extra kick. A fifth of scotch. Next to her, Alex fiddled with the joystick that controlled the robotic sub, even though the machine was lost somewhere in the depths below them. It was a distraction, something to do with his hands so that he wasn't simply doing nothing.

"I can't believe he's gone." Emily wiped a tear from her cheek. "How could this happen?"

"I don't know." Alex sounded defeated. "We should have packed up and got the hell out of here once we realized that creature was coming up onto land."

"We *should* have told the professor what we found." Emily forced back a sob. "Maybe then he wouldn't be dead."

"There's nothing we can do about it now." Alex stood and paced the tent. "Christ. This is a nightmare."

"I don't want to be here anymore." Emily watched him walk in circles around the tent. She felt numb and wanted to scream, both at the same time. It was shock, she knew. "Why are we even still here?"

"You know why," Alex said. He picked up the bottle of scotch and poured a generous amount into a tin mug, then downed it with a grimace. "We can't do anything until the cops get here and release us."

"And how long is that going to take?" Emily asked.

"Beats me. Not long, I hope. Screw the sub. I don't care if I never see this place again."

"Me neither."

Maybe this is them now." Alex was peering through the tent's open flap toward a Jeep that bumped into view from the access road and swung into the clearing.

"Thank heaven." Emily was already on her feet. She stepped outside with Alex close on her heel. The divers and Carlos had relit the campfire and were huddled around it in silent shock, as if that would protect them from whatever had dragged off their leader. Now they turned their heads to watch the approaching vehicle.

When the Jeep came to a halt, three people stepped out, two men and a woman, all in civilian clothing. They did not look like cops. Emily felt her hope dwindle.

"Who's in charge here?" The Jeep's driver asked with an air of authority that didn't fit the jeans and denim shirt he wore.

One of the divers broke from the fire and pointed toward Emily. "I suppose she is. Now."

"And you are?"

"Emily Bright. I'm Professor Howard's research assistant."

"I assume Professor Howard is the reason we're here?" The denim clad man crossed the space between them, followed by his companions.

"Yes." Emily wanted to say more, but her throat tightened, and she thought, briefly, that she was about to cry again.

"Sorry. I didn't mean to upset you."

Emily nodded and bit her lip.

Alex stepped out from her shadow. "Would you mind telling us who you are?"

"Of course." The stranger looked sheepish. "I should have

introduced myself already. I'm Bill Gibson, the town sheriff." He motioned sideways. "This here is John Decker."

"And I'm Nancy Cassidy," the woman said.

"You're all cops?" asked Emily. Out of the three, Decker looked closest to her idea of a real cop. He was lean and muscular, with a rugged jawline, whereas the actual sheriff was flabby and unshaven.

"No." Decker shook his head. "I'm consulting with the Leland Sheriff's Department. Nancy is here as an observer."

"Oh." Emily wasn't sure what to make of that. "You're some kind of wild animal specialist?"

"Some kind. Yeah." He glanced around, eyeing the equipment and the cluster of tents. "What exactly are you guys doing up here anyway?"

"Research project," Alex replied.

"Archaeology?"

"Scientific. We're testing a robotic sub in the aquifer."

"Or at least, we were," Emily said.

"What does that mean?" Decker asked.

"We lost it a few days ago."

"Technical hitch," Alex added.

"It wasn't a technical hitch." Emily snapped at Alex, her anger rising. After all that had happened, he was still trying to keep secrets. "You know that."

"Would someone mind filling us in?" This was the sheriff.

"Fine." Alex sighed. "We ran across something down in the aquifer. Some kind of aquatic creature. It took the sub out."

"And killed Professor Howard," Emily said, choking up afresh as she did so.

"You lost the sub a few days ago," Decker said. "Your boss was only killed a few hours ago."

"So?" Emily knew what was coming.

"Why didn't you leave after the attack on your submersible? Surely you realized it was dangerous."

"We had no idea it would come up onto land," Alex said.

Emily shot him a glance. That was a boldfaced lie. She considered coming clean and telling the sheriff about the tracks they'd found, but what good would that do except make them look worse than they already did? Instead, she said, "We thought it was worth studying. We were wrong."

Sheriff Gibson waved a hand. "We can get into all of that later. First things first. Why don't you show us where the attack happened?"

"Sure," Emily said. "We can do that."

"Don't you want to wait for the rest of your people first?" Alex said.

"Our people?" the sheriff looked confused.

"Yeah." Alex nodded toward the woods. "Those guys."

Emily followed Alex's gaze to see a tight group emerge from the trees. Two men and a woman. They all held shotguns. She felt a tingle of apprehension.

The sheriff had seen them too. He tensed, hand resting on the butt of his service weapon. When he spoke, his voice was thick with concern. "Those *aren't* our people."

FIFTY-ONE

DECKER WATCHED THE STRANGERS APPROACH, his eyes drawn to the guns the trio carried. Beside him, he felt Nancy take a step closer.

"They don't look too friendly," Nancy whispered, her hand resting on his back.

"No, they don't," Decker agreed. He glanced toward Bill. "I don't suppose this is just a gaggle of adventurous townsfolk out for an early morning stroll?"

"Nope, can't say that it is. I know everyone in town. I've never seen these people before." Bill positioned himself between the group and the strangers. "And I don't like the look of those guns."

"Me neither." Decker could feel the hairs on his neck rising. There was something about the way the strangers carried themselves. He'd gained a sixth sense for trouble years ago when he was a cop in New York, and that sense was jangling right now.

"I assume you're not carrying?" Bill asked.

Decker shook his head. "I'm not a cop anymore, and this was supposed to be a jaunt in the woods to investigate an animal attack."

"Shame." Bill's eyes strayed toward the Jeep. "If I was driving the cruiser there would be a rifle in the trunk, but—"

"Yeah." Decker edged further in front of Nancy. "I think we should find out just who we're dealing with and what they want."

"Way ahead of you." Bill stepped forward to meet the strangers. He unclipped his holster, but kept his gun sheathed. He held up one hand in greeting, keeping the other close to his weapon. "Can I help you, folks?"

"Maybe." It was the woman who spoke. She drew to a halt ten feet from the sheriff. "We've been camping in the woods the last few days, doing a spot of hunting, and one of our group has wandered off and gotten themselves lost."

"Hunting, huh?" Bill said.

"That's right," The woman nodded.

One of her companions, the taller of the two, spoke up now. "Wild hog. They're all over these woods."

Decker was still eyeing the strangers' weapons. He'd seen a lot of shotguns in his time, and he knew that anything with a barrel less than sixteen inches was illegal. He figured these guns fell into that category. Not only that, they looked like they had been sawn.

"Those are some mean looking pieces you have there," he said. "I would have thought a rifle would be better for taking down hog."

The woman patted her gun. "These work just fine."

"Is that so?" Bill said. "Shotguns for hunting hog. Huh. Who knew?"

"Right?" This was the taller guy again. "Sounds crazy, but it works."

"I see." Bill scratched his forehead absently. "I don't suppose I could see your hunting licenses?"

"Licenses?"

Decker saw a flicker of panic cross the woman's face, but then it was gone. "Is that a problem?"

"Well..." The woman paused. "To tell the truth, we don't have them with us. They're back at the camp. Besides, we're not hunting right now, just looking for our friend."

Bill's hand moved closer to his gun. "We'll still need to see those licenses. We can accompany you back to your camp if you like."

"We won't be doing that." The woman's hand tensed on her own gun. "We don't need to show our permits to you. Unless you're with Florida Fish and Wildlife, that is, and I'm pretty sure you aren't."

"No, we aren't," Bill said. "But I am the sheriff around these parts, so I think I may have a little jurisdiction."

"You're a cop?" The shorter of the two men spoke for the first time. His eyes flew wide with fear.

"Yeah. I'm a cop." Bill had seen the man's sudden panic. His hand curled around the butt of his service weapon. He started to draw it from its holster. "And I'm going to ask you to put those shotguns on the ground, nice and slow, so that we can have a friendly chat."

"I don't feel like being friendly anymore." The woman brought her gun to bear in a fast, fluid motion.

The next few seconds passed like a blur to Decker.

Bill pulled out his handgun, brought it up, but not fast enough. A boom split the air. Decker saw a flash as the woman's shotgun went off. He pushed Nancy sideways, twisting away from the gunfire and landing heavily on the ground. From somewhere off to his left, Bill cried out in pain. When Decker looked around, the cop was on his back in the dirt, clutching his shoulder. Blood seeped through his fingers.

Bill had dropped his gun when he fell. The woman stepped forward and kicked it out of his reach. One of her companions, the taller of the two, picked it up.

She motioned to the shorter man. "Go take a look around. Make sure there's no one hiding out anywhere. I want everybody where I can see them."

"Why me?" He groaned and nodded toward his companion. "Can't Frank do it?"

"Nice going, genius." The other man, now identified as Frank, grimaced. "Since we're using names, I think you should run along and do as you're told, *Jerry.*"

"Dammit, Frank." Jerry turned on his companion. "What did you do that for?"

"If we get caught, I want you back in that cell right along with me."

"What makes you think you're going to last long enough to get caught?" Jerry turned his gun on Frank.

Decker held his breath, expecting the gun to discharge at any moment.

Instead, the woman stepped between her squabbling companions. "Shut it, both of you. Nobody's getting caught. We talked about this already. We follow the plan."

"This is getting out of hand," Jerry grumbled. "Just like Atlanta."

"Enough. Every time you open your mouth, you make it worse." The woman glared at Jerry. "Now, do as you're told and search the camp. I don't want any more surprises."

FIFTY-TWO

DECKER HELD NANCY'S HAND.

They were huddled together in the middle of the clearing. Decker and Nancy, along with Bill, sat together. The girl who had introduced herself as Emily, the nerdy-looking Alex, and three burly men who looked like laborers, sat in their own tight group. One of the men, Decker surmised, was probably an operator for the squat crane that sat near the water line.

They were being watched over by the woman and the man named Frank. Jerry, the third member of the interlopers, was off looking for unaccounted-for camp personnel and, presumably, whoever they were chasing.

Emily observed the strangers with fear in her eyes, although she seemed to relax just a little when Alex slipped a protective arm around her. Decker wondered if they were a couple.

"Who do you think these people are?" Nancy asked, glancing toward their captors. "And why are they here?"

"Beats me." Decker eyed the twin shotguns leveled at them. He briefly entertained the idea of leaping up, attempting to overpower one or both of them. But he knew it wouldn't work. All he would get for his efforts was a heap of pain. Even if the guns were loaded with birdshot—lightweight, small projectiles that would scatter and lose effectiveness at a distance. That wouldn't matter. At close range, birdshot would still pack a mighty punch. Enough to kill him. Besides, it was unlikely the guns were loaded with such a light fare. These guys meant business, as evidenced by the sawn barrels and willingness to take hostages. More than likely, the guns were loaded with larger, deadlier 00 buckshot. He quickly discarded the idea of rushing their captors.

"Whoever they are, they mean business." Bill grimaced and held his wounded shoulder. "We're in a heap of trouble."

"They mentioned Atlanta." Decker spoke in a whisper. "A group like that, packing pump actions, I'm thinking robbery."

"Or worse." Bill groaned. A thin line of blood seeped down his arm.

"Let me take a look at that." Nancy scooted over closer to Bill.

"I'm fine," Bill said. "It's nothing."

"You took a shotgun blast to the shoulder. It's not nothing." Nancy reached out and pried his hand away from the wound. She inspected it. "But I think you'll live."

"Pleased to hear it," Bill said. "Thank the Lord that bitch was a crappy shot."

"That wasn't bad aim," Decker said. "If she wanted you dead, you'd have a bunch of holes in your chest right now. She wanted to disarm you, nothing more. You got lucky."

"I don't feel lucky." Bill let Nancy rip a swath from the bottom of his shirt and wrap it around the wound. When she pulled it tight, he let out a moan. "That hurts." "Don't be such a baby," Decker said. Bill's wound, a tightly spaced pepper of small holes, was confirmation that the guns were loaded with shot. If he'd been hit by a slug at that range, there would be a lot less shoulder to bandage. "Most of the spread missed. You only took a few pellets."

"Still stings like hell." Bill didn't seem comforted by Decker's assessment. "I've never been shot before."

"Let's hope you don't get shot again." Nancy was finishing up with her makeshift nursing. "You'll need a hospital once this is over. Those pellets are still in your shoulder."

"Perfect." Bill looked miserable.

"It might be a while before we can get to a hospital," Decker said. "Assuming these guys don't just kill us as soon as they get what they want."

"Anyone ever told you you're a real downer?" Bill asked.

"Once or twice," Decker replied. "But that doesn't change the fact that we're in trouble."

"No. It doesn't. You got any ideas?"

Decker shook his head. He was angry at himself for letting Nancy come along on this jaunt. If he'd insisted that she stay at the hotel, she would be safe right now instead of staring down the barrel of a shotgun. Of course, he wasn't expecting a bunch of trigger-happy thugs to take them hostage. They were supposed to be investigating an animal attack. "If we're going to do anything, we'd better do it while there's only two of them."

"Too late." Nancy nodded toward the waterhole and the lone figure strutting toward them.

Jerry was back, and he didn't look pleased.

FIFTY-THREE

THE FIRST THING Frank noticed when Jerry came striding toward them was the extra shotgun he now carried. The second thing he noticed was the scowl on his associate's face.

"Found this on the other side of the water hole." Jerry held the gun up. "The barrel's bent, and there's a crack through the stock."

"My gun," Liz said, snatching it out of Jerry's hands. "You found this by the water?"

"Yeah." Jerry nodded toward the pickup trucks parked on the opposite shore. "I didn't see anyone else around the camp, so I went looking for Louie. I figured he'd make straight for those trucks, and it looks like I was right. Not that there's any sign of him now."

Liz turned the gun over, leveled it and looked along the barrel. "It would have taken a lot of pressure to do this. I've never seen anything like this."

Frank reached out and ran his hand down the barrel. He stopped at a series of deep gouges in the metal. "These look like bite marks."

"That's ridiculous," Liz said.

"Just pointing out what I see," Frank replied.

"There's more." Jerry dug into his pocket and came up with a couple of torn and dirty fifty-dollar bills. "I found these too, near the waterline."

"Jerry was here all right," Frank said.

"Question is, did any of those people see him?" Liz nodded toward the huddled group. "And if they did, do they know what happened to him?"

"And the money," Frank added.

"Only one way to find out." Liz tossed the useless gun aside and hoisted her own very much working weapon. "Let's ask them."

FIFTY-FOUR

DECKER STOOD in the control tent where they had been herded moments before. One of their captors, Jerry, was busy using zip ties he'd found in a supply crate to secure their wrists. The three interlopers apparently felt that there were a few too many people to keep adequately in line despite the firepower they possessed.

When everyone was secure, the woman, who Decker surmised was in charge, addressed them.

"Someone in this tent knows what happened to our associate. He was here. We've found his weapon. Who wants to go first?"

"No one knows anything about your friend." This was Alex, who spoke up despite the tremble of fear in his voice. "If you let us go, we won't tell anyone about this."

The stockier of the two male intruders, the one named Frank, laughed. "Sure, you won't. I bet you'll just forget all of this ever happened. Right?"

"Yes." Alex nodded, a little too vigorously.

"We're not going anywhere," the woman said. "And neither are you. At least, not until we get what we came for."

"Alex is telling the truth," Emily said. "We don't have a clue who you're looking for or why you are here. We have problems of our own."

"Your problems are only just beginning." The woman lifted her gun, pressed the barrel against Emily's forehead. "Someone had better start to talk, and soon."

"You don't want to do that," Decker cautioned. "Right now, you're looking at false imprisonment charges. You pull that trigger, it's first-degree murder."

Emily whimpered and screwed her eyes closed.

"You think I care about that?" the woman asked. "If we get caught were done regardless. We aren't seeing the outside of a cell for the rest of our lives."

"And you already know our names." Jerry blurted out. "That should be enough to prove we have nothing to lose."

Frank gave him an angry look. "You aren't helping."

"He's right. You aren't helping," the woman agreed. "But since we're proving our desperate nature, I might as well go with it. My name's Liz. We hit a bank in Atlanta. Armed robbery. It doesn't matter what we do here, because if we get caught, it's game over."

"So why would we bother to help you?" Emily asked despite the gun pressed to her head. "You'll kill us anyway."

"Not necessarily. Maybe we'll just hogtie the lot of you and make our escape."

"I doubt it."

"Why?" Liz asked. "You think I want to kill everyone? It's messy. I hate messy. Regardless, even if I'm lying, you might as well talk. What do you have to lose?"

"We can't tell you what we don't know," Emily replied.

"Well, you'd better tell me something, or I might decide that messy is worth it." Liz pushed the gun tighter against Emily's head. Her finger flexed on the trigger.

"Don't hurt her." Alex's eyes were wide with fear. "Please, put the gun down. I'll tell you what we know."

"See?" Liz lowered the gun. "You give a little, you get a little. Now talk."

"We really are telling the truth," Alex said. "None of us know anything about your friend. We haven't seen him. But I have an idea what might have happened."

"Keep going," Liz said. "I'm listening."

Alex took a deep breath. "There was an incident this morning before you showed up. An attack. Something killed one of our co-workers."

"Our boss," Emily said. Her eyes glistened wet. "Professor Daniel Howard. It dragged him off into the water. Killed him."

"What do you mean, dragged him off? How could anything in these woods drag a grown man away and kill him?" Liz asked.

"An alligator," Frank said. "That could pull a man into the water."

"It wasn't a gator," Alex answered. "This was bigger, meaner. It looked almost… prehistoric."

"I don't get it," Jerry said. "Prehistoric? Like a dinosaur?"

"Something like that, yeah." Alex nodded.

"Great." Frank groaned. "They're making this up, messing with us. We're getting nowhere."

"I agree." Liz raised the gun again.

"No, honestly. I'm telling the truth." There was panic in Alex's voice. "You have to believe us. That's why the cops are here."

"So, they're not here because of Louie?" Frank asked.

"No." Bill spoke up now. He was still holding his damaged shoulder, but at least the bleeding had abated. "We were called out regarding an animal attack. It wasn't the first one either. The kid's telling the truth. There really is something dangerous out here. We've seen it on video."

"And I'll bet that whatever took Daniel also attacked your man," Emily said.

"She's right," Alex agreed. "You found that gun with bite marks on it, didn't you? What do you think did that?"

"I really don't care what did it," Liz said. "If Louie's dead, it saves me the trouble of doing the job. I *do* care about what he was carrying."

"The money from the bank heist," Decker said. He'd seen Jerry show his companions the fifty-dollar bills. "Your colleague double-crossed you. Took the cash and fled. That's why he was here, wasn't it? He was looking for a means of escape."

"Yeah. He took the money, and I want it back."

"Turning on each other over the loot," Decker said. "Never changes."

"I'm pleased we lived up to your expectations," Liz remarked dryly. "Doesn't help us get the money back though."

"Sorry to disappoint you," Emily said, a subtle smile playing across her lips. "But if that creature took your man, then the money is probably with him at the bottom of the aquifer. You'll never get it back."

FIFTY-FIVE

LIZ FELT her anger boil over. After the botched robbery, the crappy hideout, the days of squabbling, it came to this. Louie dead at the bottom of some waterhole in the middle of nowhere with all their hard-earned cash. It was an insult. It highlighted her own failure to control the situation. Worse, this bratty, precocious girl was smirking at her, taunting her with that very failure.

She almost lifted the gun up, put it to the girl's head, and pulled the trigger. Almost. Because another part of Liz, the calculating part, knew it would do no good. The money was gone either way. Still, there was one silver lining. Louie had apparently suffered an ignominious and painful death.

"What are we going to do now?" Jerry moaned. He glared at Liz. "This was all pointless. There's nothing left to split. We don't even have the cash that wasn't ruined by the dye packs, thanks to you."

"It's not Liz's fault." Frank came to her defense, and she felt a moment of gratitude amid the rage.

"It is my fault," Liz said. "I planned this whole thing. I put the team together. I should have anticipated better."

"You should have taken care of Louie before he could double-cross us," Jerry shot back. "Any fool could see that he was too high strung."

"Enough." Frank stepped between them. "What's done is done. We need to get that money back. It's at the bottom of a pond. Big deal." He glanced toward their captives. "Seems to me that these people must have a way to get down there; otherwise, what are they doing out here?"

"There's scuba gear at the back of the camp in a tent. At least three suits, maybe more," Jerry said. "I saw it when I was looking around."

"There you are." Frank nodded in satisfaction. "We go down, scoop up the money, then take one of those pickup trucks and get the hell out of here. Easy as pie."

"And who's going to go into the water?" Jerry asked. "Might I remind you that something apparently ate Louie. You can count me out."

"None of us need go into the water," Liz said. She motioned to their captives. "That's what we have these people for."

FIFTY-SIX

DECKER FELT HIS STOMACH CLENCH. The situation had just gotten much more dangerous.

"Who does that scuba gear belong to?" Liz asked. "I'm willing to bet there are a couple of trained divers among us."

The group remained silent.

"Well?" Liz looked from one face to the next.

Still no one spoke up. It seemed there was little appetite to help, considering they were all more than likely to get shot anyway.

"I don't have time for this," Liz said. "Someone needs to talk, or I'll just pick a couple of random folks to go for a swim."

From off to his left, Decker heard Nancy's breath quicken. He gave her a reassuring glance. If it came down to it, he would volunteer to go in. He'd received some dive training years ago in New York as part of a joint initiative with the NYPD Harbor Unit.

"Fine, have it your way." Liz perused the group, then made her first pick. She pointed at Emily. "You."

"Me?" There was terror in Emily's voice. "I can't do that."

"Sure, you can," Liz said. She fixed Alex with a cold stare.

"And why don't we have your boyfriend accompany you? Unless anyone wishes to rethink their position of co-operating."

Seconds ticked by. The room remained silent. Then a burly man near the back of the group spoke up. "No need to send the girl. I'm a diver. I'll go."

"Excellent." Liz beamed. "See what happens when we work together? Do I have a second volunteer?"

One of the other men spoke now. "I'll go with him."

"Now we're talking," Liz said. "What are your names?"

"Philip," the man who'd spoken up first replied. "My dive partner here is Ozzie."

"Guess his parents were Black Sabbath fans," Liz commented. She turned to Jerry. "Get them suited up."

"Sure." Jerry nodded.

"And be quick. I want that money back on dry land as soon as possible." Liz swatted at a mosquito that had settled on her arm. "Then we can get out of this hell."

FIFTY-SEVEN

WITH PHILIP and Ozzie suited up and ready to go, Frank accompanied them to the water's edge.

The rest of the group watched the action from the control tent via a live feed transmitted by small HD wireless cameras mounted to the diver's face masks. Once Liz had sliced through the ties securing Alex's wrists, he was able to bring up the feed on a large overhead screen mounted above a white plastic table that held his laptop, two widescreen monitors, and a couple of external hard drives.

"How are they able to relay video like this?" Decker asked, watching the feed as the divers entered the water and descended below the surface.

"The cameras transmit real time video via a super-efficient wireless signal. It's pretty awesome technology. Still experimental."

"We'll be able to see their progress?" asked Liz. She leaned forward, fascinated by the feed.

"If they are looking at it, we'll see it." Alex typed furiously on the laptop. "We have audio too."

"We can communicate with them?"

"Yes." Alex nodded. "There's a transducer built into the

divers' masks. It converts their voices into ultrasound signals. A receiver does the same thing in reverse, converting our replies back into sound that the divers can hear. They can communicate between each other using the same system too. It's a lifesaver in dark or silty environments where hand signals won't work."

"That's incredible," Decker said.

"Where do you think the bag will be?" This was Jerry.

Alex shrugged. "If it was heavy enough to sink, it should be pretty much right below wherever your man went in."

"It's heavy all right," Liz said. "Tell the divers to look for a navy-blue backpack with gold zippers."

Alex leaned forward and spoke into a microphone sitting on a desk mounted tripod, relaying the message.

There was a moment of crackle, then a voice came back in return. "Roger that."

Frank had returned and rejoined his companions, who stood a few feet distant from their captives, guns lowered now, but still a threat.

He scratched his chin. "It shouldn't be too hard to find. It'll probably be on the back of Louie's corpse."

"That's true," Liz agreed. "Should be a pretty easy recovery."

"We're approaching the bottom now." Alex looked up at the larger screen above him. "Thirty feet to go and descending."

Water swirled around the divers' cameras. The image on the screen dimmed, blackness creeping in at the edges of the picture.

"Are we losing the transmission?" Liz asked.

"No," Alex replied. "The further down they are, the less sunlight filters from above. We have to rely on LED lights mounted to each side of the divers' masks. It's the only way to see in the caves."

"Caves?"

"Yes. This spring is an entrance to the Floridan Aquifer. It's a vast flooded system of subterranean caverns. It took millions of years to carve out. Most of Florida's drinking water comes from the aquifer."

"Enough already," Liz said. "We don't need a high school science lecture. All I care about is getting our money back."

"Shouldn't be too much longer," Alex replied, subdued. "We're on the bottom."

All eyes were on the screen now, and the split images relayed by the two divers' individual cameras.

The bottom was a sandy plateau, interspersed by an occasional boulder. It was also dotted with man-made objects that had found their way below at one time or another. A rusted bicycle. Beer cans. A single shoe.

"How did that get in there?" Nancy asked, fascinated by the video feed despite her fear.

"Who knows?" Alex said.

"Some of these waterholes are pretty popular party spots for teenagers," Emily added. "Someone probably threw it in."

"Or whatever is down there ate the owner." Alex zoomed in on a still image taken from the feed. "There's no foot in it, so probably not."

"Cut it out," Liz snapped. "We're not here to determine how trash got down there. Can we get back to the job at hand?"

"You're the boss," Alex said. He instructed the divers to start a sweep.

On the screen, more of the bottom came into view, a gritty flat plain with no vegetation. There was more trash everywhere the divers turned, mostly the remains of soda and beer cans, a half-burned log, and a diver's mask with a crack splitting the glass.

"That's unsettling," Bill said.

"The quicker we get those guys back on dry land, the better," Emily said, biting her lower lip with her teeth.

"I don't see Louie," Frank said. "Or the money. It should be pretty easy to spot him, right?"

"Yes. It should be." Alex asked the divers to take another turn around, just to make sure. When they were done, it became clear. Louie and the money were nowhere to be found.

Liz cursed. She paced back and forth. "Where is he?"

"Maybe he was never down there," Frank said. "Just because we found the gun and a few bills on the shore doesn't mean he actually went into the water. He might have escaped whatever attacked him and fled."

"I don't think so." Alex leaned forward and spoke into the microphone again. The divers shifted position and closed in on a jagged black hole in the cavern's sidewall.

"What are you doing?" Liz asked.

"I saw something when the divers were making their sweep." Alex craned his neck up again to watch the overhead screen.

The hole in the cavern wall lit up as the divers trained their lights on it to reveal a tight cave leading off into gloom. And at the entrance, a pale white object caught between two boulders.

Nancy turned away, not wanting to look.

Emily gasped. "Is that a—"

"A hand." Decker completed her question. "Yes, it is. Looks like it's been severed at the wrist."

"Oh my God." Emily had gone white. She looked like she about to keel over. "Daniel?"

"Your missing boss?" Frank asked.

"Yes."

"It's not him." Frank stared at the screen. "It's Louie."

"How can you tell?" There was measurable relief on Emily's face. She knew her friend was dead, of course, but the hand was a graphic reminder of his fate.

"Between the thumb and forefinger." Frank pointed up toward the grisly find. "A tattoo of five dots. It's called a quincunx."

"What's that?" Emily asked.

"It represents doing time. Four dots in a square symbolizing cell walls, and a fifth dot in the middle."

"To represent the prisoner," Emily said.

"Correct." Frank sighed. "Louie carried that tat. It's him all right. Or at least, a bit of him."

227

"Which begs the question," Liz continued. "Where did the rest of him go?"

"Wherever it is, the money's probably in the same place." Frank grimaced. "Looks like we're dead in the water... Pardon the pun."

FIFTY-EIGHT

"WE'RE NOT DONE YET." Liz was still pacing. She turned to face the group, a resolute expression on her face. "Tell the divers to go into the cave."

"I don't think that's a good idea," Alex said. "The caves are dangerous at the best of times. Even experienced divers have died in them. With a dangerous creature possibly down there somewhere—"

"I'm not asking." Liz patted her gun. "I'm ordering."

"Alex is right," Decker said. He'd been at the scene of a triple fatality as a sheriff in Louisiana. A trio of cavers became disoriented and went too far into a flooded cavern system and didn't have enough air to get back. They died alone and surrounded by watery darkness. It took three weeks to locate them and get the bodies back to the surface. "It's not worth risking two lives over a sack of money."

"I'm in charge here. I'll decide what's worth risking," Liz said. She raised the shotgun. "Now, do as I say. Instruct the divers to go into that cave. I want to find Louie."

Alex hesitated.

"Don't make me prove my resolve." Liz turned the gun on Emily.

"You'd better do as she says," Frank said. "She isn't joking, trust me."

"Okay, okay. Just don't hurt Emily. I'll do what you want," Alex said, the words tumbling out. He spoke into the mic. "Deep Dive One, Deep Dive Two, proceed forward into the cave and follow through to Satan's Alley. We're still on mission."

"Roger that," came the reply. "Proceeding to Satan's Alley."

Philip, the lead diver, pushed through into the tight space, his camera picking up close, claustrophobic walls and a tunnel that ran forward into darkness beyond his lights. The second video feed showed Ozzie following behind. They wriggled along, reeling out a thin nylon guideline as they went.

"What's Satan's Alley?" Decker asked, his eyes on the screen.

"It's a narrow tunnel that runs deeper into the system. There are jagged outcrops to snag on your wetsuit. Wicked twists and turns. No room to turn around if something goes wrong," Alex said. "If you have a death wish, Satan's Alley is a good place to scratch that itch."

"You're going to send the divers in there?" Nancy asked, concerned.

"Depends. Hopefully we find what we're looking for before it comes to that. We've only been in there once, and that was with an ROV."

"ROV?" Nancy asked.

"Remote operated vehicle. That's what we've been doing out here—testing a state-of-the-art submersible named LISA."

"If you have an ROV," Decker asked, "why are we risking the lives of those divers?"

"Because we don't actually have the ROV anymore. It was damaged during a test dive. It's stuck somewhere down in the caves on the other side of Satan's Alley."

"Damaged isn't really the right word," Emily said. "More like attacked by the same creature that took Daniel." She looked at Liz. "And probably killed your friend."

"It's irrelevant," Liz said. "I'd have sent those divers down anyway. There's nothing a machine can do that humans can't do better."

"I'd disagree with that rather sweeping and generalized statement," Alex said. "But hey, you're the one with the gun."

"Yes, I am. And don't forget it. Besides, you'll cooperate better if your colleagues' lives are on the line." Liz nodded toward the screen. "Speaking of which, how long until they get to this Satan's Alley?"

"Not long." Alex studied a map of the caves on his laptop and the two dots that represented the divers moving slowly through the maze. "They're closing in on it now."

"How are you doing that?" Decker asked. "Tracking them?"

"We have transmitters in their wetsuits. All very high-tech stuff. Cutting edge. I can watch their progress in real time," Alex said, indicating the map on his monitor. "See. Looks like they've arrived."

As if on cue, the lead diver spoke up, his static filled voice filling the tent. "Control, we're at the entrance to Satan's Alley. Still no sign of further human remains or the bag."

On the view screen, two nearly identical viewpoints showed a tight cavern with walls that looked like they were made of rocky swiss cheese and a narrow slit that dropped off into oblivion. Satan's Alley.

"Instruct them to keep going," Liz said.

Alex shook his head but didn't put up a fight. He ordered the divers to press on.

Emily looked worried. "We haven't sent divers this deep into the caves before. Just the ROV."

"Nothing I can do about it." Alex glared at their captors. "It's out of my hands."

Minutes passed. The mood in the control tent grew tense and nervous. The divers moved with precision, careful not to snag their equipment or suits on the jagged walls of Satan's Alley.

Decker wondered if the tunnel would simply go on forever, a hellish shaft leading directly to Hades, but soon enough the cave walls widened again. The divers had made it through the worst part of the shaft. Still there was no sign of Louie or the money. Just sandy, boulder strewn ground. And then, without warning, the floor dropped away into a dark, wide chasm.

The divers surveyed this new terrain and then kicked off, descending into the unknown. For a while the cameras picked up only disturbed water swirling in the twin beams of the LED lights, but then the chasm floor came into view, and with it, something else.

Decker drew a sharp breath.

Emily grinned despite the guns pointed their way. "Will you look at that?"

Alex was smiling too, unable to contain himself. When he spoke, his voice was heavy with excitement. "We've found LISA."

FIFTY-NINE

LISA WAS RESTING with her nose buried in the sand. Three feet long and two feet wide, the sub was smaller than Decker had imagined. An oblong box painted a bright yellow with a multitude of devices attached and two LED floodlights resembling a pair of staring eyes, it didn't look any more high-tech than the ROVs he'd seen on documentary TV shows. But it was, he suspected, worlds apart from those machines, in both capability and technology.

"Can we get her working?" Emily asked.

"Beats me." Alex hunched over his laptop, enlarging the video and studying the rover on his own, smaller screen. "I don't see any damage from this angle."

"The front is buried in sand," Emily said.

"Right you are." Alex nodded. He spoke into the mic, instructing the divers to extract the ROV from the bottom.

The viewpoint on the monitor changed as the divers swam to the front of the craft and cleared away the sand, lifting the unit free.

And then they saw the problem.

The front of the ROV looked like it had been caught in a shredder. The protective cowling that covered the delicate

233

electronics and provided aerodynamic flow was peppered with a series of deep gouges that had sliced through the metal.

"Those are bite marks," Alex said. "From the creature that attacked it."

"And look at the size." Emily was transfixed. "The bite radius is huge."

"Can it be fixed?" Decker asked, hopeful that if the ROV was repaired they could recall the divers.

"I'm not sure." Alex was still studying the rover, looking at stills captured from the video feed. "It doesn't look like there's damage to the internal mechanisms, but the battery wiring harness is severed for sure. That's why we lost contact. Good news is that if we reconnect it, the battery should still have juice. Since it was completely disconnected, it wouldn't be running any onboard systems, ergo no power drain."

"Great." Decker felt a surge of relief. "Let's do it."

Alex shook his head. "Not that easy. We'll need a new wiring harness. We have one here, but it's in the equipment store. The only way to fix LISA is to take that new harness down and install it. Even then, we won't know for sure if there's worse damage until we try to bring her online."

"Then we should recall the divers and send them back down with the spare parts," Decker said. "It's worth chancing."

"Hey." Liz waved her gun. "I'll remind you that I'm in charge here. I don't care about fixing that sub. I want to find that money. We already have people in the water. We keep going."

"The sub may be your best bet of finding that money," Alex said. "I know you think that you have more control over us if you use the divers, but that's not a logical line of thought."

"Alex, careful," Emily warned.

Alex ignored her. "The divers have limited range. There's only so far that they can go before they won't have enough in their tanks to get back, and we're fast approaching that limit. They'll also need to decompress before surfacing."

"How long before they reach the point of no return?" Liz asked.

"They've been down for thirty-four minutes," Alex said. "Accounting for the air in their tanks and the trek back to the surface, another five. Ten tops."

"Then what are you waiting for?" Liz replied. "Keep going."

Alex gritted his teeth and gave the command.

The sub disappeared from view to be replaced once again by the cavern's sandy bed, and a wall of rock that marked the far edge of the space. Three separate caves meandered off in different directions. The divers paused at the intersection, unsure where to go next.

"This is as far as we've ever been," Alex said. "Everything past here is completely unexplored."

"So what?" Liz said. "We search them all."

"Each cave could run for miles and connect up to other caverns with even more branches. It's not feasible." Alex leaned back in his chair.

"Then they split up," Liz said. "Take a cave each."

"No." Alex folded his arms. "This is dangerous enough as it is. Splitting up is a death sentence. You can wave your gun all you like, but you'll never find that money if the divers are dead."

"Fine." A scowl crossed Liz's face. "Tell them to take the left-hand cave. But they'd better find something before they have to turn back. If not, I'm sending two more people down as soon as they're back on dry land."

A nervous silence hung over the captives.

Emily stepped closer to Alex. "Just do as she says. The quicker we get these people their money, the quicker they'll leave us alone."

"I'm not so sure about that," Alex said, then relayed Liz's instructions to the divers.

On the monitor, the twin views from the two divers' cameras changed again as they entered the cave, going single file now. From the lead diver's perspective, the screen showed nothing but bare shaft walls and shifting silt that rose up and wafted around them, disturbed by their passage. The other half of the screen showed a rear view of the front diver from the other man's perspective.

"Wait," Emily said. "There's something on Philip's feed. What is that?"

The diver had seen it too. He approached through the murky water until he was right on top of a bulky object resting on the cave floor and stopped, treading water in the swift current.

At first Decker could not make out what it was either, but as the billowing sediment cleared, he realized what he was looking at. A human torso, arms and legs severed, and minus the head. And on its back, still strapped tight, a backpack.

SIXTY

"THAT'S IT." Liz let out a whoop of joy. "We've got the money."

Decker felt a rush of relief. So far, they hadn't encountered anything out of the ordinary, and certainly no man-eating denizens of the deep. "We should wrap this up and get the divers back here."

But Philip was way ahead of him, cutting at the straps with a diving knife until the backpack floated free of its macabre anchor.

That done, the divers back-paddled, inching their way out of the cave in reverse until they were in the larger cavern again and could turn around with ease.

They kicked upward toward Satan's Alley. The drifting cloud of sediment that had escaped with them into the larger cave cleared as they rose higher, and soon the water was crystal clear again.

Satan's Alley loomed ahead.

Philip reached the entrance and pushed inside, dragging the newly recovered backpack with one hand while pulling his way into the shaft with the other.

The video feed bobbed around as the diver moved his head,

237

the beams from his twin LED lanterns dancing across the confined walls.

And something else.

Philip let out a terrified yelp as the light picked out a skulking form in the tunnel ahead.

Cold yellow eyes observed him from behind a slender, tooth-filled snout.

Philip tried to back up, but found his way blocked by Ozzie at the rear.

Alex grabbed at the mic, thumbed the push-to-talk switch, and screamed into it. "Deep Dive Two, reverse! Now. Get back into the cavern. I repeat, get back into the cavern. Clear the way."

There was a garbled, static-laden reply that Decker couldn't make out.

The twin views on the screen descended into chaos, jerking this way and that so fast that the relayed images were nothing but a blur of frantic, stuttering motion.

A high-pitched scream tore through the speakers, filling the tent. Philip's remote feed flickered once, twice, then cut to black.

Decker held his breath.

No one spoke, their eyes fixed on the monitor.

"Control, this is Deep Dive Two." Ozzie's ragged, terrified voice broke the silence. "There's something down here. I don't know where it went."

He twisted his head from side to side, causing his own video feed to spin wildly.

"Deep Dive Two, this is Control." Alex was shaking, but he did a good job of keeping the fear from his voice. "Do you see Deep Dive One?"

"No. He's gone." The video feed was stabilizing now as the diver regained his composure. "It all happened so fast. Oh God. I don't want to be here anymore."

"Get him out of there," Emily said.

"Is the tunnel free?" Alex asked. "Is Satan's Alley accessible?"

"I don't know." The view shifted as Ozzie looked toward the cave. "I think so."

"Good." Alex leaned close to the mic. "Get out of there, right now. We're aborting."

"Roger." The diver turned and approached the tunnel.

"What are you doing?" Liz lunged forward, twisted Alex around in his chair. "Tell him to get my backpack."

"You heard what he said," Alex countered. "Deep Dive One is gone, along with your money."

"Then order him to find it. I don't want that man back here without my bag." She took a swipe at the mic. "If you won't do it, I will."

"No." Emily shrieked, racing forward despite her bound hands. "You'll kill him."

Liz whirled around and brought her gun up. Frank stepped between them, scooped Emily in his arms and dragged her backwards, despite her furious attempts to break free.

"I wouldn't do that if I were you, missy, or you'll end up with a chest full of lead."

The speaker crackled to life. "Control!"

The abrupt interruption seemed to defuse the situation. All heads turned to look back at the screen and the remaining camera feed.

"I'm at the entrance to Satan's Alley. No sign of the creature. I'm going to proceed into…" Ozzie's voice trailed off. He turned and glanced backward, the video feed following his gaze.

A speeding blur cut through the water.

"Oh, sweet Jesus," Ozzie screamed. He lifted his arms to shield his face, blocking the camera's view of the approaching beast.

The video feed jolted from side to side.

Then it was descending toward the bottom, the camera panning across the sides and roof of the cavern in lazy arcs. And above, sliding in and out of shot, Ozzie's headless corpse transformed the water into a gushing, crimson nightmare.

SIXTY-ONE

EMILY WAS SOBBING.

Alex was frozen in mute horror, one hand still poised to retake the mic.

"Those poor men," Nancy said through her own tears. She glared at Liz. "You sent them down there to die."

"I sent them down there to get my money," Liz responded.

"They had families." Emily gulped. "People who loved them. Philip had a daughter. You could try to show a little emotion."

"What the hell was that thing?" Jerry was still watching the headless corpse tumble in and out of view on the big screen.

"An alligator," Liz replied. "It was an alligator, that's all. There's probably hundreds of them living in these caves."

"It wasn't an alligator," Frank said. "We all saw it. Besides, gators don't live in caves."

"How would you know?" Jerry replied. "You're some kind of wildlife expert now?"

"He's right," Alex said, finally managing to regain some composure. "Whatever did this isn't an alligator, or at least not a modern one. We think it's a relic, a creature that somehow survived extinction."

"I got a good look at the beast when it took Daniel." Emily

sniffed. "It's bipedal, which is unheard of in modern crocodylians. My best guess is an animal similar to Carnifex, a prehistoric relative of modern crocodiles. It lived lived millions of years ago. Paleontologists nicknamed it *the butcher*."

"Apt title," Decker said. "But how could it have survived undetected for so long?"

"I don't know," Emily admitted. "Maybe it adapted to life in the caves and swam out to the ocean to hunt. Water levels have been dropping in the aquifer due to humans pulling out drinking water. It might have gotten trapped and resorted to coming onto land for food. It's a wild theory, but I have nothing else."

"Could there be more of those things out there?" Frank asked.

"Maybe. Then again, it might be a dying species. The last of its kind."

"Or there could be hundreds, even thousands of those monsters," Bill chimed in.

"Highly unlikely," Alex said. "We would have noticed them before now if there was a large population. Emily's probably right. It's a dying species. A relic."

"Enough," Liz said, eyes blazing. "This is irrelevant. All I care about is my money, and now we know where it is."

"You're not seriously suggesting we send someone else down there?" Emily looked shocked. "You saw what just happened."

"Yes, I did. We fed the damned thing, which means it isn't hungry now. It's probably lost interest and swam off already."

"You can't be sure of that," Decker said. "You put someone else in the water, it's a death sentence. Your money's gone."

"It's gone when I say it is." Liz turned to Jerry. "How many wetsuits did you say there were?"

"Three."

"Who does that third suit belong to?" Liz examined the group. She nodded toward the crane operator. "What about him?"

"Carlos? He's ground support. No dive training," Emily replied. "The suit's a spare. There were two divers on the team, and they're both dead thanks to you."

"Shit." Frank said. "We're screwed."

"I don't think so." Liz smirked. "We have a whole bunch of expendable people here. I just need to pick one. The only question is, who?"

"Send me." Decker stepped forward. "I have some scuba experience."

"See?" Liz glanced at Frank. "It worked out after all. We have our man."

"No!" Nancy cried, stricken. "You can't do this."

"I have no choice," Decker said. "If I don't go, these people will send some innocent person to their death. I learned to dive in the NYPD."

"Not cave diving."

"Your girlfriend's right," Emily said. "It's much too risky. Cave diving's dangerous even for qualified, highly trained professionals."

"I'm aware of that," Decker replied. "I don't want to go, but what other option is there?"

Liz turned to Jerry. "Go get the wet suit. I want this guy in the water as soon as possible." She glanced up at the overhead monitor. "And for the love of God, will someone turn off that freaking video feed."

SIXTY-TWO

DECKER STOOD on the sandy shore near the waterhole, kitted out in the last of the three wetsuits. A bulky air tank hung on each side of his body in the cave diving configuration, rather than the more common back mounted tanks. The zip tie securing his wrists was gone. In his hand he held a guide reel, although he figured he could probably follow the lines already strung by the previous divers all the way to the cavern where the backpack had been found, then lost again.

"We'll be able to see you on screen in the control tent," Alex said. "Just like the others."

"And we can communicate too," Emily said. "Get down there, get that bag, and get yourself back here as quick as you can. The less time you're under, the less decompression time you'll need. Speaking of which, there are air tanks strung on a nylon rope at intervals under the water. These are your stopping points to decompress. You'll need to use those tanks, not the bottles you're carrying. The oxygen mix is different."

"How will I know how long to stay under to decompress?" Decker asked. Cave diving was different than open water, and there had been no time to get up to speed or plan the dive in the usual manner.

"Don't worry about any of that. I'll work it out and let you know once you get back. Just focus on the job at hand." Emily tried to flash a reassuring smile but failed.

"Will do," Decker said. He didn't want to be in the water one moment longer than necessary.

"Good luck down there," Emily said. She turned away, possibly because her eyes were moistening and she didn't want him to see.

"I wish you weren't doing this," Nancy said. "I'm so scared."

"Hey. We've been through worse." Decker gave her a brief hug. "This isn't my first monster."

"Stop." Nancy sniffed. "You need to take this seriously."

"I am."

"And come back to me. I can't lose you. Not now."

"I know."

"Okay." Liz stepped up and gave Decker a shove toward the shoreline. "Cut the dramatics."

"All right." Decker held his arms up. "I'm going."

"And behave yourself." Liz tapped her gun. "Don't even think about trying any heroics. Don't forget, we'll be watching. That camera better stay on, and you'd better stay in the water." She nodded toward Nancy. "Try anything I don't like, and she's the first one that I shoot."

"I get it." Decker clenched his teeth and ignored his seething anger.

"Good." Liz looked around the group of captives, now down to five. Emily, Alex, Bill, Nancy, and the crane operator, Carlos. "These people's lives are in your hands."

"I need something to protect myself with," Decker said. "Or I'll be helpless down there."

"Jerry." Liz motioned to her associate. "Give the man a knife."

"You sure about that?" Jerry replied.

"Yeah. I'm sure." Liz moved close to Nancy and pressed the gun into her neck. "He won't do anything stupid."

Jerry hesitated, then held out a six-inch dive knife in a rubber sheath.

Decker took it and slid the knife out to reveal a sharp blade with a hollow-ground edge on one side and a serrated edge on the other. Satisfied, he slipped it back and strapped the sheath and knife to his thigh. He stepped into the water and waded in up to his knees, then turned back and met Nancy's gaze. "I love you."

"Love you too." Her voice trembled when she spoke. "Be careful."

Decker nodded. He secured the regulator mouthpiece between his teeth, activated his dive lights, and turned his back on the assembled group. As he slid beneath the surface and dropped into the depths toward the underworld realm of the aquifer, he wondered if he would ever see her again.

SIXTY-THREE

DECKER FOLLOWED the line strung with decompression tanks down as far it went, the fragile link to the surface providing a measure of comfort in the empty expanse of the waterhole. When the line ran out, he paused to get his bearings, then kicked off toward the bottom.

The caves were easy enough to find — a dense black opening against the lighter walls of the natural spring's basin. Decker approached and paused, steeling himself for the journey ahead. A metal sign affixed to the rock near the entrance, warning of the dangers ahead and bearing an image of the Grim Reaper, did little to ease his nerves.

"You okay down there?" Alex's voice arrived via the ultrasound receiver in Decker's mask.

"Yes," Decker replied. "Just taking a breather to get in the right headspace."

"You might want to get moving." Alex sounded harried. "A certain gun-toting friend is getting rather antsy."

"I'm going. She'll get her money." Decker positioned himself and gripped the cave entrance. The rock felt cold and sharp under his gloved hands. He pushed forward, the beams from his

LED lights cutting through the inky blackness, playing off the shaft's walls.

He was halfway in, twisting around an inconveniently positioned boulder, when the lights picked up something else. A bulky form moving toward him, bearing down fast. Startled, Decker lost his grip on the cave walls.

His head smacked an overhead rock.

Decker grunted, clenching his teeth to avoid losing the regulator. Pain drilled down from the back of head to behind his eyes. His vision blurred. He ignored his throbbing head, forced himself to focus, and scrambled backward.

Clear of the confined space, hanging in open water now, he reached up and gingerly felt his scalp. A shock of fresh pain jolted through him when he touched the area where his skull had cracked against the cave roof. He blinked to clear his vision. A concussion down here, under these circumstances, would not be ideal.

He glanced back toward the cave's entrance, unsure if he should stand his ground or swim for the surface. The thought of Liz, shotgun in hand, threatening Nancy, made up his mind.

"Decker." Alex's voice rang in his ear. "What's happening down there?"

"I don't know." Decker tugged at the knife attached to his leg and freed it from its sheath. "There was movement in the cave. Something came at me."

There was no answer from above. Decker imagined Alex arguing with Liz, him saying it was too dangerous to continue, her adamant they retrieve the money regardless of the risk. He was not going to receive any help from the surface.

There was nothing they could do anyway, because the beast was approaching the mouth of the shaft, moving quickly. Decker gripped the knife, ready for whatever was about to come.

A flurry of displaced sediment gulped out of the cave's entrance ahead of the creature.

Decker lifted the knife, ready to defend himself. But instead of a prehistoric swimming carnivore, he was surprised to see the terrified face of Deep Dive One emerge through the muck.

"Holy crap!" Alex exclaimed; his voice so loud Decker winced. "I can't believe it. Philip's alive."

"Me either." Decker lowered the knife. "Can you talk to him?"

"No. We don't have communications," Alex said. "The attack must have damaged his comms."

As if to prove the point, the diver waved frantically at Decker, thumbing upward toward the surface with one hand. The other hand, Decker now noticed, was a torn and bloody mess, seeping crimson blood into the water. His wetsuit was shredded, and one of his two side tanks was gone.

"I don't think we're out of the woods yet," Decker said. "He's motioning for us to surface."

"I'm not sure that's a good idea."

"And I'm not sure we have much choice," Decker countered. "This guy is clearly scared witless, and he's badly injured."

"No. You don't understand," Alex said. "*You* should be fine, but if Philip comes up without decompressing, he'll be in for a hell of a time, and it will likely kill him."

Decker couldn't tell if the diver's comms equipment was still capable of receiving an inbound signal, and if he'd heard any of this back and forth, but regardless, Philip was striking for the surface. And he was ascending much too fast, swimming past the first decompression stage and the life-saving oxygen bottle hanging there.

Decker thought about chasing him to force the panicked diver to slow down and purge the deadly gasses that had built up during his time underwater from his bloodstream. But he never got the chance.

Something else was emerging into the spring now. Something much more deadly.

Decker drew in a sharp breath.

"Get out of there!" Alex had seen the beast too and was

screaming, frantic, in Decker's ear. "You don't stand a chance in the water."

"I know that." Decker brought the knife up again, a paltry defense against what he now saw was a twelve-foot long beast with a sleek, scale-clad body, muscular frame, and a pointed, deadly snout full of teeth like steak knives.

But the beast wasn't interested in him.

It was following the blood trail Philip was leaving in his wake. It reminded Decker of documentaries he'd seen on TV and the way a shark homed in on stricken prey with single-minded resolve.

Decker brandished the knife and kicked toward the creature, unwilling to be a passive spectator in another man's death.

But the beast was moving faster now, cutting through the water with an ease Decker could not match. It closed in on the fleeing diver, then leveled out and turned to the left, coming around in a wide arc.

Decker knew he wouldn't reach the diver in time. Even if he could, he was clearly outmatched, armed with only a six-inch knife. All he could do was watch as the stricken man made one last, terrified scramble upward to safety.

Not fast enough.

The beast shot forward with a flick of its tail, slicing through the water. It scooped the diver up and snapped its jaws closed. The water roiled and turned an angry red, hiding the man's dying moments from view.

Decker glanced toward the surface, which now seemed an impossibly long way off. When he looked back, the beast was on the move again.

And now, it was coming for him.

Decker's urge was to turn and swim, but there was nowhere to go. He was exposed and vulnerable in the open water. Even if he could reach the caves, the beast would just follow.

And then his back contacted something hard.

It was one of the bottles hanging from the decompression

line. Decker gripped the line and positioned the flimsy shield between himself and the beast.

His heart was thudding against his ribs so fast that Decker feared it might simply give out. Thoughts of Nancy filled his mind, a minor comfort as he faced certain death. And then the creature was upon him. It barreled into the line, mouth agape. The pressure of water surging ahead of the beast sent Decker tumbling away. He steeled himself for the beast's jaws to snap closed and finish him, but they didn't.

The creature was enmeshed in the decompression line; the thin nylon rope snagged in its mouth and wrapped around its lower jaw like a lasso. The creature thrashed one way and the other. Blazing, angry eyes watched Decker. And in its mouth, Decker noticed, the oxygen bottle he'd been using as a shield. Then, before Decker could react, the beast snapped its jaws shut in an effort to free itself and the water exploded in a wash of violence that sent him crashing into the rocks.

SIXTY-FOUR

THE VIDEO FEED in the control tent cut off a millisecond after the oxygen tank ruptured and sent Decker tumbling backwards through the water.

"John!" Nancy let out a shocked scream and bolted from the tent, her face a mask of fear and grief.

"Stop her." Liz wheeled around and snapped at Jerry. "Bring that woman back here. Now."

Jerry hesitated, caught in a moment of surprise, but then he turned and gave chase.

Liz was not done. She barked a second order at Frank. "I want you to go get one of those trucks parked over on the other side of the water. There's no point in staying here anymore."

"We're leaving?" Frank raised an eyebrow. "What about the money?"

"Forget the money. It's gone. All three divers are dead. There's no way to get it back now." Liz scowled. "Christ, this has turned into a complete disaster."

"Suits me," Frank said, glancing at the remaining hostages. "Are you going to be okay dealing with these people alone?"

"I think I can handle myself. The cop's got a cartridge full of buckshot in his shoulder, and he's the only one I'm worried about. Besides, they're all tied up except the geek. You just worry about fetching the truck." Liz slapped at another mosquito that was lazily sucking blood from her arm. "And make it quick. I'm getting bitten to death out here."

"Sure thing."

"And by the time you get back, the situation will be resolved permanently."

"What does that mean?" Frank asked.

"It means I don't want to leave any witnesses behind to identify us," Liz said. "You got a problem with that?"

Frank shook his head, gave the hostages a last, lingering look, then exited the tent.

SIXTY-FIVE

NANCY RACED TOWARD THE WATER, stumbling to stay upright because of the way her hands were lashed behind her back.

To her rear, closing fast, Jerry was in pursuit. But she didn't care. John was dead. After all they had been through — the carnage back in Wolf Haven, being forced to sell the diner for a fraction of what it was worth, getting drummed out of town — it had come to this. The only man she had ever truly cared for, gone. And for what? A pathetic bag full of money? It didn't make any sense. She reached the shoreline and fell to her knees, sobs wracking her body.

Jerry came to a skidding halt a few away, puffing and panting and kicking up sand. "Jesus, lady, why'd you take off like that?"

"Why do you think?" Nancy replied through her misery.

"Come on now." Jerry reached down, took her arm and dragged her to her feet. "Let's get you back to the tent."

"Get the hell away from me." Nancy twisted free of his grip and lurched backward. Her foot caught on a tree root, and she almost fell. When she regained her balance, she expected Jerry to be bearing down on her again.

But he wasn't.

Instead, he was looking the other way, his face a picture of slack-jawed terror.

Nancy followed his gaze, and what she saw sent a chill of primaeval fear up her spine.

Erupting out of the water, like something from a nightmare, the creature that had attacked Decker. It shot from the spring, propelled forward by muscular legs, head tilted to one side and mouth agape.

Jerry mumbled something incoherent as he stared up into the face of the beast.

"Run," she screamed, backing away, not willing to take her eyes from the hellish sight.

But Jerry did not run. He appeared to be frozen in place, a victim of his own overwhelming fear. His hands fell to his sides. He let the gun drop, useless, to the ground.

The beast thundered ashore with a guttural roar and took a swipe at Jerry, scooping him up in its mouth. His final agonized scream, warbling and shrill, was cut short as the jaws snapped closed, cleaving him in two.

SIXTY-SIX

LIZ WATCHED Frank depart and then turned her attention back to the captives huddled before her. She observed them with cool indifference, then, making up her mind, raised the shotgun and leveled it at Bill.

"You don't have to do this." Emily said, a frantic urgency in her voice.

"She's right," Bill said, his own tone calm despite the weapon. "You pull that trigger, it's murder. And not just any murder. You'll be a cop killer. That'll earn you a trip to the electric chair."

"They'll have to catch me first," Liz said. Her confidence in evading capture was buoyed by the knowledge that no one except the gathered hostages even knew she was in Florida. Besides, she had a foolproof plan to ensure success. "Regardless, there won't be any evidence of a crime to charge me with, thanks to our friend in the water. Seems to me, all I need to do is drop your bodies in the spring and let whatever is down there eat the evidence. You did come up here to investigate an animal attack after all. Nobody will bother to look much past that, even if they do manage to find what's left of you."

"That's horrible." Emily recoiled. "You're as much a monster as that creature in the aquifer."

"She's worse," Alex said. "The creature is just following instinct."

"Enough, all of you." Liz was growing tired of the back and forth. "Any more chatter and I won't bother to shoot you before you go into the water. See how you like being eaten alive while you drown."

"Like those divers you sent to their deaths?" Emily said.

"If you're trying to nudge my conscience, don't bother. I don't have one." Liz peered down the barrel of the gun, setting her sights squarely on the cop's forehead.

Her finger flexed on the trigger.

Jerry's tortured scream ripped the air like a knife.

Liz faltered and turned her head toward the sound.

When she looked back, Carlos, the crane operator, hurtled toward her. He was fast, but she was faster. Liz turned the gun from the cop and fired. Carlos bore the brunt of the blast point blank. He flew backward, his chest a bloody mess, and landed on his back several feet away.

But now there was another threat.

Bill, taking advantage of the distraction Carlos posed, was also lunging forward. And this time she couldn't get a shot off. Bill crashed into her, sending both of them sprawling to the ground. The breath excited her body with a whoosh as Bill's lowered head slammed into her chest. The shotgun was jolted from her grip and clattered away.

She pushed at Bill, tried to dislodge him, but he was already scrambling up of his own volition.

She rolled and made a dive for the discarded gun. Then, as her fingers closed around the stock, just as she thought she would be able to bring it to bear and fell her attacker, Bill's booted foot caught her hard under the chin.

Her head snapped back.

A second kick connected with her torso, spinning her sideways.

The gun clattered away a second time, but by then, unconsciousness was already closing in.

SIXTY-SEVEN

DECKER WAS SLOWLY DRIFTING DOWNWARD toward the bottom of the waterhole when he regained his senses. His head hurt, probably from the crack it had taken when he was blown into the rocks by the exploding tank. He twisted in the water, momentarily disoriented, but eventually found which way was up. And then he remembered the reason for his current situation. He looked around, frantic, expecting to find the beast closing in for a kill. The diving knife was still in his hand, his fingers clutched around the hilt so tight they ached. How he hadn't dropped it was anyone's guess. Now he raised it in defense, knowing it would do little against his much larger adversary.

But the beast was nowhere to be seen.

And then he glanced up, saw the rippling, disturbed water at the surface. Had the beast, appetite sated, retreated back into the caves? Or had it gone up to the surface?

Terror clutched at his chest.

Nancy was up there.

Then he realized something else. Alex's voice, which had been in his ear the entire dive, was absent. There were only two reasons for that. His communications gear had been damaged when the oxygen tank ruptured, or the beast had attacked the camp and there was nobody left to reply.

The second scenario made his spine tingle with dread.

"Hello?" He tapped the mask, adjusted it, even though he had no idea if his meddling was fixing anything. "Hey. Anyone hear me up there?"

No response.

He didn't even get static for his efforts, just complete silence.

There was only one way to find out what was happening on the surface. Decker slipped the knife back into its sheath and kicked upward, at the same time offering up a silent prayer that Nancy was safe.

SIXTY-EIGHT

FRANK WAS within fifteen feet of the parked trucks when he heard Jerry's scream. He turned in time to see the beast lunge from the water in a blur of speed and snatch the stricken man in its jaws. And then he saw Nancy, her hands still bound, fleeing from the creature much too slowly.

"Shit." Frank put on a spurt of speed, sprinted to the truck and yanked the door open.

He searched the cab. Checked the ignition. Pulled the visor down. No keys.

He slammed the door and ran to the next truck.

Same.

"Dammit." He could hotwire it, but that would take precious seconds that Frank didn't have.

There was one truck left.

He skidded to a halt and pulled open the door, and to his relief, he saw a set of keys sitting on the dash.

Frank hopped in and scooped up the keys. He started the truck and slammed it into first, wincing as the gears grated, then sank his foot on the accelerator.

The truck spun its wheels, kicking up sand.

Frank eased off the gas, tried again. More sand flew up behind the vehicle.

He cursed, slammed the steering wheel with his palms. Then, just when he thought the pickup was hopelessly stuck, the vehicle lurched forward.

Frank let out a yelp of joy. He ignored second gear and went straight to third, then fourth.

The truck tore around the small pool of water.

Up ahead, the beast had finished with Jerry and turned its attention to Nancy. She stumbled along, hands bound behind her back, struggling to stay on her feet. The creature sniffed the air, gave another roar, and took off after her.

It was not a fair race.

Frank wavered. Liz was waiting in the tent. It would only take a second to swoop in, pick her up, and make their escape in the truck while the beast was busy. Yet that would mean leaving Nancy to die. He'd done some shitty things in his life and hurt a lot of people one way or another, but Frank wasn't sure he was ready to completely abandon his morality just yet. He glanced toward the tent. No sign of Liz. Most likely she was finishing off the rest of the hostages and there was nothing he could do about that, but at least he could help the woman. He swore under his breath and pushed the accelerator pedal hard to the floor, ignored the sickening way the truck lurched and the back end fishtailed on the soft ground. Two more steps and the beast would have her in its mouth.

But the truck was speeding along now, a two-ton battering ram. Frank closed the distance between the truck and the beast, his front end ploughing into the creature just as it lowered its head to snatch Nancy up.

The truck's bull bar hit like a sledgehammer, sweeping the beast off its feet. And then he was under it, the truck careening wildly forward as the animal cartwheeled over the roof.

The breath caught in Frank's throat. An image of the creature crashing down on the truck, crushing him, raced through his mind.

But when he glanced at the rearview mirror, he saw the beast catapult all the way over and slam into the earth behind the vehicle. It slid along, kicking up a mound of sand, and came to rest several feet distant.

Frank uttered a satisfied grunt and turned his attention forward again — just in time to see the pine tree a second before the pickup smacked into it.

SIXTY-NINE

BY THE TIME Bill finished fighting with Liz, Alex had already freed Emily and was rushing to help, a pair of scissors held high like a dagger, just in case Liz got up. He cut the zip ties securing Bill's wrists and then turned his attention to the crane operator.

"I don't think he's breathing." Alex gasped.

Bill knelt down, placed a finger against the man's neck, and felt for a pulse. He shook his head. "He's gone."

Emily had scooped up the shotgun and now hovered over the prone and unconscious Liz, aiming the weapon toward the robber with shaking hands.

"Do something. Like CPR or mouth to mouth," she screamed, her voice teetering on the edge of hysteria. "You can't let him die like this."

"I don't think CPR will help," Bill replied, looking down at the man's ruined, bloody chest. "He's gone."

"This is awful." Emily leaned forward and pushed the gun to Liz's head. "I should just pull the trigger and do to her what she did to Carlos."

"That won't fix anything," Bill said. "All it will do is burden you with guilt for the rest of your life."

"I know." Emily pulled the gun away.

263

"Good girl." Bill stood and took the gun from her.

A squeal of tires stopped him from saying anything else. Moments later a thumping crash shook the tent.

"What in blazes is going on out there?" Bill moved toward the tent flap.

"Whatever it is doesn't sound good," Alex said.

Emily had pulled herself under control. "Your friend is out there."

"Nancy!" Bill reached out and pulled the tent flap back. The first thing he noticed was the pickup truck, front end buried in a pine tree. There was no sign of a driver, but Bill guessed it must be the third robber. The one named Frank.

Nancy was on the other side of the clearing, running for the trees. He was about to call out to her, but then he caught a movement in the periphery of his vision.

They were not alone.

A mighty beast, bigger than anything Bill had ever seen, was hauling itself up from the dirt. Bleeding and dazed, the creature took a teetering step, then another, becoming surer footed with each stride. It shook its head from side to side and let out a rumbling and throaty bellow.

"We need to get out of here," Bill said, beating a hasty retreat back into the tent. "Right now."

"What's out there?" Alex asked.

"Trust me, you don't want to know." Bill pumped the gun's slide and loaded a shell into firing position. He nodded toward Liz. "Pick her up."

"Are you kidding?" Alex said.

"We're not leaving her behind," Bill replied. "Now hurry."

"She doesn't deserve this," Emily said, but nonetheless she helped Alex haul the limp woman up.

Liz groaned and opened her eyes.

"She's waking up." Emily was caught in a moment of hesitation.

"Let go of me," Liz hissed. She kicked at Emily and elbowed

Alex, who doubled over, the wind knocked from him. Then, breaking free, Liz fled toward the exit.

"Not that way," Bill shouted after her, but she ignored him.

The front of the tent crumpled and tore apart. Guide ropes snapped. A pole crashed down, barely missing Bill.

Liz skidded to a halt.

She froze, staring up at the injured and angry beast.

"Go," Bill screeched, pushing Alex and Emily toward the rear of the tent even as the roof tore open.

A roar split the air.

Bill pulled the canvas up and waited while the others scrambled out. He was about to follow them, but something made him turn and look toward Liz.

The beast towered above her.

Then she found the will to run. She turned to escape, and for a moment her eyes met Bill's in a silent plea for help. But there was nothing he could do. Before the urge to flee had even traveled from her head to her legs, the beast swung its head down in a quick, fluid movement, and snatched her up.

Bill turned and slipped under the canvas, Liz's dying shrieks ringing in his ears. Then he sprinted for the woods, just as the tent came tumbling down.

SEVENTY

DECKER HAULED himself from the water and struggled out of the twin tanks that now weighed him down. He ripped the mask from his face and discarded it, along with the cumbersome flippers.

To his left a pickup truck was nose first into a tree, the driver slumped over the wheel. Decker could not make out who it was, but he noted with some relief that the occupant was male.

Not Nancy. Thank God.

On the other side of the clearing he spotted the beast. It was tangled in what remained of the control tent. A ball of fear knotted his gut. Was Nancy inside when the creature attacked? He scanned the area, looking for something, anything, with which to take on the beast. And then his eyes fell upon the track crane sitting idle near the woods on the spring's opposite shore, a heavy-duty sling hanging from a hook on the boom.

"John."

The voice startled him, drawing his attention. "Nancy?"

"Over here." She was standing near the trees, her hands still tied behind her back. "Quickly."

But her cries had drawn more attention than she bargained

for. The beast stopped its assault on the shredded tent and focused its attention on Nancy instead. It cocked its head, as if processing this development, then took off toward Nancy in a lumbering, awkward gait.

"No!" Decker motioned for her to run. "No, no, no."

Nancy realized the danger she was in. She ducked back between the trees and was soon lost amid the dense foliage.

"Hey! Over here." Decker waved his arms, hoping to draw the creature from its pursuit of Nancy. He took off running, heading toward the crane.

The beast paused, then changed direction.

Decker arrived at the crane, threw open the cab door, and climbed aboard. He slid behind the wheel. There were no keys in the ignition. He scrabbled around, searching desperately in the vain hope that the keys would be in some less than obvious place, but he came up short. The most likely explanation was that they were in the now destroyed control tent.

The creature was closing in fast.

The crane looked pretty banged up and old. If he was lucky, it wouldn't have an electronic ignition. Decker drew his diving knife and rammed it down into the plastic cover surrounding the steering column and twisted. There was a sharp crack, and the cover loosened. He pried it off and discarded it, then reached under the column for the ignition wiring harness. As he suspected, the crane's age predated modern security measures to prevent exactly what Decker planned to do. He used the knife to strip back wires, careful to avoid an electric shock.

Moments later, the crane rumbled to life.

And just in time.

The beast was closing in. It glared at Decker with angry yellow eyes, closing the gap between them at a lick. Too soon for Decker to get the crane moving. Then, as he braced for impact, the beast swerved sideways and took off in a new direction.

Decker was relieved. But the relief was short lived, as he saw

Nancy near the woods, drawing the beast's attention. She must have seen Decker struggling to start the crane and decided to buy him some time. It was stupid and dangerous.

Decker slammed the crane into gear and trundled forward, the unwieldy vehicle hard to control in his inexperienced hands.

Nancy was running now, keeping close to the trees, leading the beast back toward Decker. She drew level with the crane and sprinted behind it.

The creature roared in frustration and lowered its head, attempting to avoid the bulky metal vehicle in its path.

Decker steered left to stay between the beast and Nancy. The crane began a wide turn. Sluggish. Painfully slow. The boom was still raised in the air. Decker had no idea how to lower it, but a cluster of levers seemed like his best option. He tried them, one by one, noting how the boom turned left, then right. Finally, he found the lever that controlled the vertical axis. He pulled it toward himself, gratified when the boom inched down in response.

The sling hit the ground, chains clanking.

The beast made a faltering attempt to sidestep the lowering boom, but its forward momentum made avoidance impossible. It slammed into the crane, lifting the front of the vehicle a foot in the air, tracks churning air, before the whole rig crashed back down.

The creature retreated and shook its head, dazed. Then it roared forward again in a fresh attempt to reach Nancy, who was fleeing back toward the woods. And Decker could not get the crane to respond fast enough to cut it off.

But he didn't need to.

From the left, a pickup truck came barreling into the fray, screeching around the beast and causing it to recoil before changing course once more.

It was all Decker needed.

The creature was heading directly for the sling, now pooled

across the ground under the horizontal boom. Decker took a deep breath, anticipated the creature's arrival, and pushed the boom lever forward.

At first nothing happened.

But then at the exact moment the beast was stepping over the floored sling, the boom juddered, jolted, and rose back into the air.

The chains went taut.

The double rubber straps that had held the submersible now rose, snagging the creature's feet as they did so. It stumbled and thrashed as the chains and sling ensnared it, lifting it from the ground.

The truck came to a halt and the door flew open. One of the robbers, the man named Frank, exited with his shotgun held high. There was a deafening blast then another in quick succession.

Others were emerging from the woods to aid in the struggle. Decker saw the scientists, Emily and Alex, following along behind Bill, who also brandished a shotgun.

The beast screeched in anger as it was fired upon.

"The water." Frank was shouting over the melee. "Get it back to the water."

But Decker was way ahead of him, turning the frustratingly slow vehicle and thrashing cargo in the direction of the spring.

The crane trundled forward.

Decker waited until the boom was over the water and the caterpillar tracks were biting into the sand at the edge of the waterhole before he pushed the cab door open and jumped.

He hit the ground hard and rolled, tumbling away from the now driverless crane.

When he looked up, the vehicle was ploughing into the water. The wounded beast struggled against the chains and straps that entangled it, but that only trapped it further. Then, with the crane submerged up to the top of its tracks, the vehicle pitched off the shallow ledge at the edge of the pool and into the depths. Front heavy thanks to the boom and the struggling creature it held, the crane toppled and crashed into the water. The creature howled with fury, thrashed in the water to stay afloat, but then the crane's weight tugged at the boom and dragged it down, out of sight.

SEVENTY-ONE

A MERCIFUL SILENCE descended on the clearing. Decker laid his head back on the sand, hurting too much to get up.

"John!" Nancy rushed over to him, came to a skidding halt next to his prone form and dropped to her knees.

"I'm fine." Decker pushed himself onto his elbows.

"I thought you were dead."

"Not quite yet." Decker hauled himself up despite his protesting muscles and helped Nancy to her feet. He unsheathed the diving knife, slipped it between her wrists and sliced the zip tie that bound her wrists. She wrapped her arms around him and showered his face with kisses.

Further away, near the smashed but somehow still operational truck, Bill had disarmed Frank and was pushing him along in front. Emily and Alex were walking behind, arms around each other.

"Do you think it's over?" Nancy asked. "Is it dead?"

"There's a five-ton crane on top of the damned thing, not to mention the shotgun blasts it took. I'd say there's a good chance it's a goner."

"Good." Nancy rubbed her chaffed wrists. "I think I need a spa day after this. Can we get back to our vacation now?"

"Sounds fine to me." Decker took her hand in his. "Or, we could make it a honeymoon."

"You're seriously asking me to marry you right now?" Nancy asked. "Five minutes after a monster tried to eat me?"

"We're both alive. We love each other. Can you think of a better time?" Decker asked. "What do you say?"

"I'd say…" Nancy looked up into Decker's face. Her brow furrowed. Seconds ticked by. "I'd say I need time to think about it. I've been married before, John, and I'm not sure I'm ready for that commitment again just yet."

"Oh." Decker felt a thud of disappointment. "If that's what you want."

"It is, right now," Nancy replied. She reached up and touched his cheek. "I love you so much, but after all that's happened… I need time. Will you give me that?"

Decker nodded, unsure what to make of her reticence. He took her hand and, after casting one last look toward the now still water, led her toward the rest of the survivors.

SEVENTY-TWO

TWO DAYS LATER

DECKER STOOD on the hotel balcony and gazed out over the beach and rolling ocean beyond. Behind him, in the hotel room, Nancy was getting ready for dinner. He still didn't understand why she had turned down his marriage proposal. Maybe she didn't think he meant it, or maybe she just didn't want to marry him. Either way, it hurt. But he loved her, and if she wanted time, he would honor that.

He strolled back into the room. The sound of a shower running reached his ears. He crossed to the mini fridge, opened it, pulled out a beer and popped the cap. He was about to take a swig when there was a knock at the door. When he answered, a familiar, if unexpected, face was on the other side.

"Adam Hunt." Decker stepped into the hallway and pulled the door closed. "I was wondering when you were going to show up."

"You haven't answered my calls. Texts."

"I know."

"Want to invite me in?" Hunt glanced toward the door. "Better not to discuss business out here in the open."

"No." Decker positioned himself between Hunt and the door.

"Fair enough." Hunt shrugged. "I saw the report on your little adventure in the woods."

"There's a report?"

"There's always a report." Hunt smiled. "We keep close tabs on our operatives."

"I'm not your operative." Decker sipped his beer. "Not even close."

"But you should be." Hunt glanced around, checking that the corridor was empty. "You have an answer for me?"

"Maybe." Decker had been considering saying no to Hunt. His life with Nancy seemed more important. But now, after she turned his marriage proposal down, he wasn't so sure. "Can I ask you something?"

"Shoot."

"Are you the good guys?"

"Good guys?" Hunt chuckled. "There's no such thing. But if you want to know if our motives are pure, then yes, we're the good guys. So, about that answer…"

Decker studied Hunt's face and saw no sign of deceit. He shrugged. "Fine. I'm in."

"Wonderful."

"For now. But I can't promise anything long-term."

"We'll discuss all that later." Hunt took a business card out of his pocket and held it out.

Decker took the card. On the front, embossed in black lettering, the acronym CUSP, and underneath, *Classified Universal Special Projects*. Below this was a motto in italics, *Verum Conquisitor*.

"That's Latin," Hunt said, as Decker read the card. "It means *truth seeker*."

"And you gave me this, why?"

"Turn it over."

Decker flipped the card and saw an address scrawled on the back. "What is this?"

"The executive airport. It's not far from here. A short cab ride. Be there at 7 AM. There will be a private jet waiting."

"Am I going somewhere?"

"You ever visited to Europe?"

"Nope."

"Well, that's about to change." Hunt flashed a grin and turned to leave. "See you tomorrow morning, my friend."

"Wait." Decker had a million questions, not the least of which was his destination. "I didn't pack for a trip to Europe. And while we're at it, where in Europe? Which country?"

"The Emerald Isle." Hunt was already at the elevator. "And don't fret the packing. We've taken care of that."

"How? When?" Decker called out.

But Hunt had stepped into the elevator already. The ding of the closing door was his only reply.

Decker lingered in the hallway, unsure what to make of the sudden turn of events. When he reentered the room, Nancy was out of the shower, drying her hair with a towel.

"Who was that?" she asked.

"Adam Hunt." Decker put his beer down. He wasn't thirsty anymore.

"What did he want?" Nancy wrapped the towel around herself and sat on the bed.

"To send me to Ireland." Decker went back to the balcony and stepped out. Had he made the right decision? He wasn't sure. He turned Hunt's card over in his hand, read the Latin inscription again. Whatever his future had in store it wouldn't be dull. Of that, he had no doubt.

ABOUT THE AUTHOR

Anthony M. Strong is a British-born writer living and working in the United States. He is the author of the popular John Decker series of supernatural adventure thrillers.

Anthony has worked as a graphic designer, newspaper writer, artist, and actor. When he was a young boy, he dreamed of becoming an Egyptologist and spent hours reading about pyramids and tombs. Until he discovered dinosaurs and decided to be a paleontologist instead. Neither career panned out, but he was left with a fascination for monsters and archaeology that serve him well in the John Decker books.

Anthony has traveled extensively across Europe and the United States, and weaves his love of travel into his novels, setting them both close to home and in far-off places.

Anthony currently resides most of the year on Florida's Space Coast where he can watch rockets launch from his balcony, and part of the year on an island in Maine, with his wife Sonya, and two furry bosses, Izzie and Hayden.

Connect with Anthony, find out about new releases, and get free books at www.anthonymstrong.com

Made in the USA
Las Vegas, NV
29 April 2024

89256251R00157